PUFFIN CLASSICS
Shyamchi Aai

Shyamchi Aai

SANE GURUJI

TRANSLATED FROM THE MARATHI BY SHANTA GOKHALE

Introduction by JERRY PINTO

PUFFIN BOOKS
An imprint of Penguin Random House

PUFFIN BOOKS

USA | Canada | UK | Ireland | Australia
New Zealand | India | South Africa | China | Singapore

Puffin Books is part of the Penguin Random House group of companies whose
addresses can be found at global.penguinrandomhouse.com

Published by Penguin Random House India Pvt. Ltd
4th Floor, Capital Tower 1, MG Road,
Gurugram 122 002, Haryana, India

Penguin
Random House
India

First published in Puffin Books by Penguin Random House India 2021

ISBN 9780143447702

Typeset in Minion Pro by Manipal Technologies Limited, Manipal

Printed at Manipal Technologies Limited, India

www.penguin.co.in

MIX
Paper | Supporting
responsible forestry
FSC® C043100

This is a legitimate digitally printed version of the book and therefore might not
have certain extra finishing on the cover.

Contents

Introduction

Hi!

I like you very much already.

You're reading. That's a good sign.

Because books are seeds you plant in your head. They grow into huge trees, and if you read enough books, eventually, you have a forest through which you can walk. And the trees will bear fruit, fruit you have never seen before, because they will be ideas you have thought up yourself.

And ideas? Real ideas? Original ideas? They are the most important thing you can have.

Sane Guruji's *Shyamchi Aai* is a great seed to plant. You are a lucky young person because you're reading it in a good translation. I read a bad translation and I wanted to give up by about page 25. I wasn't reading Marathi then. I could but I wasn't going to read it in Marathi when it had been translated into English. (I was a lazy bounder. There. I've said it.) This is a big mistake. If you can read Marathi, put this book down and go read the Marathi original. But if you can't, never mind. The number of languages you can read in will always be smaller than the number of languages you can't read in and so we have translation. But good translation is a rare thing and this is a great translation.

How do I know?

I read it through in one night. *And I discovered an entirely new book.*

Okay, you can argue that I am another person now and therefore this is a new book. (This is a good reason to reread books. Because when you change, the book you're reading changes.) But it is also because a new translation is a new book and a good translation makes a world of difference.

So, where was I?

Right. I was reading some other translation of *Shyamchi Aai* and got quite tired. But someone had told me that it was an important book, a classic and I was the kind of young twit who liked to go about reading the classics. Someone else told me that I would understand a lot about how we think about women and how we think about mothers if I read this book. I had just seen *Mother India*—where a mother picks up a gun and . . . Nah, if you haven't seen it, I won't spoil it for you.

This time I discovered that *Shyamchi Aai* begins with a most interesting conversation about the nature of memory and how we think about ourselves. This is an odd thing for young men to be discussing, but here's the thing: *Shyamchi Aai* is a novel of ideas. Each night, the young men sit and talk. They listen as Shyam tells them an episode from his life.

Each of these conversations is a seed and this means that you don't just get one idea, you get a whole granary of them. Shyam says: 'We are proud of our religion but our deeds turn our words into a joke.' He warns us that words can hurt. And on a much more homely level, his mother recommends that we ask before taking flowers from other people's gardens for our pooja!

You may not agree with many of these ideas. Sure. That's part of the delight of a novel of ideas. But I'd say you should write your own conversation. Talk back to Shyam, discuss it with him. Tell him why he's wrong. And as you're writing, another little bit of magic will happen. *Your ideas will become clearer to yourself.* You think this is odd?

Think about the idea of an idea. It's just a little energy, some neurons in your head firing and carrying electrical messages about your busy busy brain. Some of this is memory, some of this is invention, some of this is desire. You sit up and you think: Oh my goodness, oh my gosh, if this were a comic book, someone should draw a light bulb above my head.

Someone asks you: What are you thinking about?

You say: I was thinking . . .

And as you begin to tell that person, the idea loses shape. You want to say: No, listen wait, let me also tell you the colour of this and the feeling and the way it was in my head, so wonderful and alive . . .

Yes, turning the idea into words is a difficult thing.

So you love books?

Would you copy out a book? Shyam does. He does it for the love of God because he wants to learn a prayer and he hasn't got a copy of the prayer. So he borrows the book from a neighbour, a boastful chap, and writes out the book. But then Shyam's home, Sane Guruji tells us, is full of books that have been copied out.

How much do you love books? Would you love them enough to copy one out and try to make sure there are no ink stains and no mistakes? Then there is this lovely moment where Shyam's mother looks at his work and tells him to ask the cloth merchant for a label that depicts the deity so that he can stick it on the cover.

I almost wept at that. Because I was thinking of a story I had read about children in rural India who copied out story books from the small village library so they could own them and read them when they wanted. We are a nation of book hunger. Many, many children, like Shyam, still want to read but can't. You and your friends could do something about that, no? Oh and please don't think of sending some village library your used Enid Blytons and Geronimo Stiltons. How would you like it if you walked into a library and all of it was in Norwegian? You'd walk right out again. The village libraries of India, the rural and tribal and zilla parishad schools of your country need books, but they must be in the home language of the children.

Sorry. You see what Shyam's mother is doing to me. I'm fizzing with ideas.

For instance, there's a time when Shyam does not want to do something for his mother because it is women's work. What do you think is women's work?

Cooking? Well, then why are so many of the master chefs men?

Stitching? Well, then why are so many of the designers men?

Answer: Because if you're going to get money for it, then it's men's work. And if you're not going to get paid for it, it's women's work.

Shyam's mother says there is only good work and bad work; work doesn't have, shouldn't have gender labels on it.

Oops. Sorry. There I go again.

There's a lovely story about the children trying to rescue a fledgling and killing it out of love. I thought of Beth in Louisa Alcott's *Little Women*, sitting with the small cold body of Pip, her canary, in her hands and weeping because she had forgotten to feed him and he had died of starvation and thirst. Here the children overfeed the little bird and it dies too. You can kill something with love too.

You see what I mean? Ideas are buzzing around in my head after I read this book.

Did you pick up this book on your own? You are a brilliant *bashibazouk*.

Did someone give it to you? You're a lucky lollapalooza.

However you got it, get on with it.

Happy reading!

And may there be many ideas in your forest!

Jerry Pinto
November 2020
Mahim, Mumbai

The Beginning

It is generally believed that individuals become great because of their parents. Parents are responsible for how they turn out. The foundation for their future is laid when they are young. The seed from which the tree grows is sown when the child is still in the cradle or playing around its mother.

When I say great I do not mean men and women whose names dance on people's tongues. I mean people who are akin to trees that grow on Himalayan peaks or valleys. I mean people who tower towards the sky but remain unknown to the world, people who are like beautiful, divinely scented flowers, growing in some remote corner of a jungle or pearls of rare lustre lying on the ocean bed, news of which has not reached the world. Perhaps there are diamonds of greater brilliance than the stars buried deep in the womb of the earth, diamonds that no human has set eyes upon. There could be whole galaxies of stars that even the most powerful telescope has not revealed to the human eye.

To me, being known around the world is not what makes human beings great. They become great when they consciously shed their flaws one by one and evolve into better human beings. Their parents have inculcated in them the urge to keep growing as human beings. Only parents can give them this divine gift. It is they who, consciously or unconsciously, encourage their children to grow tall as human beings, for if they don't, they will remain stunted.

A child's education begins before it is even born. Preparations for its education are afoot before it even comes to life in the mother's womb. The values that parents live by, the emotions that fill their hearts, the deeds—good or bad—that they perform, these are the books of knowledge that are already being written for the child. It is not only parents who teach the child. Knowledge comes from the outside world too, from animate and inanimate nature. But again, it is the parents who teach the child what it must learn from the world. Parents are thus unquestionably the chief source of a child's education, and, between the two, the mother in particular. After all, the child takes life in her womb. When it emerges, it remains in many ways a part of her. Its earliest years are spent close to her. It laughs in her company and cries in her company. It is fed by her, plays around her and is lulled to sleep by her. A child's every activity is connected with her. That is what makes the mother a child's first and most important teacher.

Shyam was fortunate to have had a wonderful mother. Not a day went by when he did not thank her silently for this, sometimes shedding tears of gratitude. The boys in the ashram often asked him to tell them about his life. They often shared stories about their lives with one another, but Shyam would never tell them about his. Once in a while a story would bring tears to his eyes because it reminded him of a similar incident from his own life. His friends would say to him then, 'Shyam, you have heard us tell our stories. Why don't you ever tell us yours?'

On one such occasion, when the boys had been pestering him, he said in a voice heavy with emotion, 'I find it very painful to remember my past because, along with the good, I remember the bad. Along with virtuous deeds, I remember my sinful deeds. I have been trying hard to bury my faults in as deep a pit as I can dig so the demons don't return to establish their hold over me. My struggle, my aim, my dream is to live a blameless and transparent life. Why do you want to compel me to face my past?' *When will my life shine forth like a star / That question alone troubles my heart.*

'Fine. Then tell us only about the good things that have happened to you. You are fond of saying that a person becomes good by thinking good thoughts,' piped up little Govinda.

'But if we remember only the good, we might come to believe egoistically that we have always been blameless,' Bhika pointed out.

3

Shyam grew serious and said, 'Just as a person feels ashamed to speak of his downfall, he feels embarrassed to speak of his rise from good to better. My constant prayer to God is that I never let a single word of self-praise pass my lips.'

Narayan laughed lightly and said, 'You might end up priding yourself on not being proud. Saying you are not praising yourself is also self-praise!'

Shyam said, 'True. You can't be too careful in this world. There are temptations at every step. Cliffs that you can fall off. All one can do is watch one's step, keep trying, fight honestly and not delude oneself. I agree. Pride can take subtle forms. We must beware of it at all times.'

Shyam's dear friend Ram said, 'Are we strangers to each other? Have we not come close enough even now to feel we are one? Nothing is private in our ashram. Whatever there is belongs to all of us alike. Then why do you hide your rich experience from us? How can telling us about yourself be called pride or boasting? Tell us how you came to have this sweet temper, this naturalness, this tenderness, this love, this affectionate smile, this selflessness, this willingness to do any kind of work without the least sense of shame? We nurse the sick and so do you, but you become a mother to the patients. Why can we not be the same? You only have to smile to win a person over. We cannot win a person over even after hours of talking to him. Tell us where you found this magic. Tell us who instilled this fragrance in your life, so like the elusive musk? Shyam, a popular legend in our Varhad region says, a large mansion was once being built for a rich merchant. One day a musk seller from Nepal was passing by. The merchant asked him how much the musk cost. The musk seller said contemptuously, "You southern people are too impoverished to buy it." His words angered the merchant. He said, "Weigh your entire stock of musk. I'll mix it with the mortar for my walls. Go north and announce that the people of the south build their walls with musk." They say that the mansion still smells of musk. Tell us who poured musk in the mortar when the walls of your life were being built. Our lives are devoid of fragrance, form and colour. Who gave yours fragrance and colour? Tell us.'

Shyam could not remain silent any longer. He said seriously, his throat choking with emotion, 'Friends, if I have any of the qualities you speak of, they are gifts from my mother. Whatever good there is in me belongs to her. Aai has been my guru. Aai has been my wish-fulfilling tree. I possess nothing that she hasn't given me. She has gifted me her capacity to love, to speak with the warmth of affection. She has taught me to love not only human beings but animals, butterflies and coconut and toddy palms. She was the one who taught me to pour my heart and soul into every piece of work I did, however irksome I found it, without a word of complaint. She taught me how to savour bran as I would fresh bread; to live with self-esteem and dignity even in the direst of circumstances. I haven't been able to follow even a small fraction of what she taught me. The seed she sowed in me is still germinating. Who knows when it will put out shoots. My mother is the fragrance and colour in my life. I am nothing. She is my all. My dear, dear mother.'

Shyam was choking with emotion as he spoke. Tears fell unrestrained from his eyes. His lips, his hands, his fingers trembled. Everybody fell silent for a while. When the high tide of emotions had ebbed a little, Shyam said, 'My friends, I can say nothing about myself. But I will tell you about my mother and the kind of person she was. I will tell you stories that I remember about her, one story every night. Will you be happy with that?'

'We will, we will,' came a chorus of voices.

Ram said, 'It's like asking God for one eye and receiving two.'

Govinda said, 'It's like getting to drink lemon syrup every night. It's like taking a dip in the holy river every night.'

First Night

The Savitri Fast

The evening prayers in the ashram were over. The residents sat in a circle, their eyes fixed on Shyam. It was a rare sight to see such a community of brothers. The spring that flows through a desert seems clearer and holier than any other. A single ray of light in the dark is a sign of hope. In today's world, a world that says 'what do I care?', such bonds of love fill us with hope. The love that binds the residents of the ashram together would be difficult to find anywhere else. The ashram is like a sacred, life-giving stream that cleanses the stagnant life of the village.

That night the village was still. The sky was still. Cowbells tinkled sweetly in the distance. The only thing that was not still was the wind which circumambulated the world, humming its eternal prayer.

Shyam began.

My mother's family wasn't wealthy, but they had enough to eat and drink and were happy. They lived in the same village as my father. Aai's father was a very religious man. He practised all orthodox rituals strictly. My mother was the eldest of the siblings. Her parents loved her very much. Some people in her family called her Avadi, others called her Bayo. Avadi! The loved one! How right the name was. She was everyone's favourite. And Bayo! That too was a fitting name. She was indeed Bayo, mother to the world. It was indescribably sweet to hear the family's old retainers call her by that name even after she had become an adult. Filled with love, the name went straight to the heart.

My mother had two brothers and a sister. Her mother was a very disciplined and industrious woman. The utensils in her kitchen shone like mirrors.

Aai was still a young girl when she got married. My father's family was wealthy. In the eyes of the village, they were the local nobility. Or perhaps it was they who regarded themselves as such. They loaded my mother with gold and pearls. She wore all the traditional married women's ornaments every day, necklaces and chokers, heavy chains and armlets, cummerbunds and bangles of varying thickness. Her new home overflowed with people. It was a veritable Gokul*. Her new family renamed her Yashoda. She lacked for nothing as she grew to early womanhood.

---

* *Gokul was the village in Mathura district where Lord Krishna grew up. His childhood, spent in the company of cowherds and cowmaids was so happy that for devotees of Krishna, the very word 'gokul' means a blissful place.*

She had the best clothes and the best food. Of course, she had to do a lot of housework, which is how it is in joint families. But when you are surrounded by happiness and appreciation, work doesn't feel like drudgery. Instead, it brings you great satisfaction and joy.

'Friends! When my grandfather grew too old to manage the affairs of the family and its lands, the responsibility fell on my father's shoulders. He was barely seventeen or eighteen at the time. Suddenly he had to run the household and manage the family affairs. We used to call our father Bhau. The village called him Bhaurao. The surrounding villages knew us as Khots.'

'What's that?' asked Bhika.

'A Khot is a man who collects taxes from the people and sends them to the government. He isn't paid for the work. He is an unsalaried middleman,' Shyam replied.

'You mean he earns nothing from the work?'

'Of course he does. He gets almost one-fourth of the total farm revenue he collects. The Khot assesses the value of the harvest in every village. He may even decide the harvest is good when it isn't. If villagers don't pay up, the government sends help to confiscate their land. If the revenue doesn't arrive on time, the Khot has to pay from his pocket.'

'We have *malgujars* in Varhad and Nagpur. This sounds like the same thing,' said Bhika.

Govinda was getting impatient. 'Stop babbling, Bhika. Please continue, Shyam.'

Shyam returned to his story.

We were the Khots of a village called Vadavali. We owned a large orchard there. Water flowed through it in abundant quantities. We had built trenches to channelize it from a great distance. It fell into the orchard like a cascade. We grew bananas, betel nuts and pineapples. We had jackfruit trees that bore all three varieties of the fruit, *kapa*, *barka* and semi-kapa. I'll show you these varieties when you come to the Konkan. The orchard was supposedly our wealth, our fortune. But my friends, it was actually our sin. Sin smiles for a brief while and weeps for life. It stands erect for some time and then turns to dust. Sin enjoys temporary honours, but its status is transient. Virtue, on the other hand, is like Venus. It shines with a serene, steady light through eternity.

The Khot had the power to put anybody he chose to work. If he called you, you had to go or invite his rage upon your head. Peasant women worked hard, planting brinjals, chillies, corn, yams and sweet potatoes, and training creepers of pumpkin and watermelon. But the fruit belonged to the Khot. Truly, there is no worse sin than living off another's labour. No crime is less forgivable than slave-driving people to work night and day, tiring them out with toil, heaping them with scorn and luxuriating oneself on soft beds and pillows. Where do you think the ornaments that dripped off my mother's neck and arms came from? That nose ring of lustrous pearls—was its gleam not like the teardrops that fell from the eyes of peasant women's children? Were the thick bangles on my mother's wrists not forged from their lost smiles? But God had plans to make my mother aware of this. He was determined to shake her awake.

My father wasn't an evil man. He was only carrying on his ancestors' legacy. He was proud of the extraordinary authority he enjoyed as a Khot. When his orders were not followed, he had it in his power to say things like, 'These *kunbat*s have become too arrogant'. To call a Kunbi caste man kunbat and a Mahar caste man *mharda* was daily practice. My father didn't realize that uttering those pejorative words only proved how arrogant he himself was and how blinded by power.

My father had only just started running the family business. He had very little experience. In his newly found power, he would occasionally say things that would hurt people. He also carried the burden of his ancestors' sins. Sin, like merit, never dies. Nothing is wasted in the world. The seed you sow will sprout as sure as anything. What you plant will burgeon and bear fruit.

Once Bhau had gone to Vadavali, arriving there around eight in the morning. The family had been urging him not to go because it was the night of the new moon. But he had insisted on going, saying, 'Whether it is new moon or Saturday, what is to happen will happen. Every day is a sacred day. Each day comes from God's house.' After spending the day in Vadavali, he was all set to return home at twilight when an old woman said to him in the local dialect, 'Bhauda, twilight is the devil's hour. And there will be a new moon tonight too. Don't go today. By the time you reach the stream, it will be pitch-dark. Stay the night. Leave at cockcrow.' Bhau would not have it. 'What's wrong with the night, old woman? The road is still there to walk on. I'll walk fast and be home by cow-milking time.'

The old woman was saying don't go. The sins of Bhau's forefathers were saying don't stay. Bhau left. A servant went with him. The villagers saw him off. One fellow grinned. A few exchanged significant looks. Soon darkness gathered. Tears glittered in God's eyes and the eyes of saints. A brook flowed through a deep valley a few miles away from Vadavali. There was no way to cross it during the rains. It was surrounded by a dense forest where tigers roamed. People were afraid to walk there even in daylight. But Bhau wasn't afraid. He didn't know fear. He wasn't afraid of anything, not ghosts or spirits, or animals or insects.

Bhau was approaching this valley when suddenly he heard a whistle. Bhau was alarmed. Out of the bushes sprang a group of Mangs*, their bodies smeared with red

---

* *A caste once treated as 'untouchable'. Even today they are expected to live outside the village boundaries like other castes previously considered 'untouchable'. Mangs are found in four states in India under similar sounding names—Maharashtra, Gujarat, Madhya Pradesh and Karnataka.*

earth. Bhau felt a hard knock on his back and he collapsed to the ground. The servant ran away. The knives in the Mangs' hands gleamed. One man sat on Bhau's chest, all set to slice his neck. Crickets chirruped in the thorn bush. A snake went slithering by. The Mang paid no attention to them. Just then an old woman cried out, 'Run. They've killed the Brahman. They've killed the Khot. Run! Oh, run!' The Mangs were startled. Bhau pleaded piteously with them. 'Please don't kill me. What harm have I done you? Let me go. Here's a ring. Here's a pair of toe rings. Here's a hundred rupees. Take them all and let me go.'

The old woman's cry seemed to have reached some people's ears. Footsteps could be heard approaching. The Mangs gathered up the ring, toe rings and money and fled. They weren't born murderers. It wasn't in their blood to murder. Their poverty had driven them to it. You could even say love and compassion had driven them to it. They murdered for the love of their children, to ease their gnawing hunger pangs. Some people say that strife and cut-throat competition are natural to the world. But perhaps love lies at the root of both. The only problem is that it is a narrow love. Love, not war, fellow feeling, not hatred or jealousy, are the ultimate truths of life. But enough of that. To return to Bhau's story, the servant who had run away, had gone straight to Palgad, our village, where he fearfully narrated the whole story to the family. All the menfolk in the family and the village made straight for the police station where they filed a complaint.

There was crying and wailing in the house. Throats were dry, eyes were wet. The lights in the house shone, but the faces within were dark. Nobody ate or drank. Their only thoughts were of death. We were not born yet. Aai, my mother, had acquired wisdom as she grew. Perhaps women become wise early. She sat at God's feet. He is the final succour. She held her hands out to Him in supplication. She said to Him, 'Lord Narayana, you have always looked after me. Mother Jagadambe, I am your daughter. Please don't let the axe fall on my marriage. What must I do to appease you? Dear God, have pity on me. You are an ocean of compassion. Keep my husband safe. Let me fill my eyes with his living image again. I want nothing else. I don't want these ornaments, these rich clothes, this wealth. My husband is my only ornament. Bring him back to me. With your blessings we will live together till the end of our days.' Aai pleaded. Aai wept.

Although Aai called upon God and pleaded with Him, of what use were mere prayers? Every wish must be earned with sacrifice. With a fast. That night, my mother made a pledge to keep Savitri's fast. Friends, there are many women and men in the history of Bharat who shine like gems, to whom we can turn for courage in difficult times. Ram, Harishchandra, Sita, Savitri. Whether Savitri appears in history books or not, she is immortal. She will always remain a source of strength for women. She will give them the courage to fight against death. If a woman is pure and selfless in her desires, she is bound to find the strength to fight death.

My mother's marriage was saved. Bhau returned home. Aai's pledge to keep the Savitri fast began that year. She would start the fast two days before full moon in the month of Jyeshtha. Once you have made a pledge to fast, you cannot give it up. The fast involves worshipping the banyan tree. It is believed that one's marriage lasts a lifetime when one prays to the everlasting, immortal banyan tree that soars skywards. Every woman who prays to the banyan tree imagines that she is praying for the growth of her family. She prays that, like the tree, her family too should offer shade to the world, be a support to others. She hopes that, like the tree that seems to soar upwards to touch God's feet, her family too should desire to rise, grow and put out a myriad aerial roots like the tree, making it stronger by the day.

Aai would grow solemn as the days for the Savitri fast approached. I will now tell you a story about what happened on one of these occasions. What I have said so far was only the preface to the real story. I must have been about eight or nine at the time. The fast was due to begin. My mother was down with malaria. She had been suffering with it on and off for many days. In one of the rituals attached to the Savitri fast, you have to circumambulate the banyan tree 108 times. Aai's condition would not have allowed her to do that. Even a few steps would have made her faint.

Aai called out to me.

'What do you want, Aai?' I asked. 'Do you want me to massage your legs?'

'No, son,' she said. 'I don't want my legs massaged. Nothing stops the pain. You must be fed up of massaging them every day. I wish you didn't have to. But I'm helpless.' I wept on hearing her pitiful words. 'Shyam,' she continued. 'I know you are tired after the day's work. But you'll have to do one more job from tomorrow for the next three days. Will you do it?'

'What job, Aai? Have I ever said no to anything you wanted me to do?'

'No, never,' said Aai. 'Shyam, the Savitri fast starts tomorrow. I can't go around the tree 108 times. I'll pass out. I will make it somehow to the seat under the tree if you hold my hand. I will pray to the tree and go around it three times holding your hand. But you will have to complete the remaining rounds, dear.'

Aai took my hand in hers as she said this. She looked at me with eyes filled with love and pity.

'Aai, how will my rounds help?'

'They will, my dear. God has eyes to see. He isn't dead. He knows and understands everything. Aren't you and I one? Aren't we the same flesh and blood? That makes you a part of me. Every sacred round you take of the tree will be as good as mine. I am ill and weak. God sees that.'

'But the women will laugh at me. I won't go to the tree. My friends will see me on their way to school. "Look at that woman," they will tease me. I'll feel ashamed. I won't go. I'll have to miss school too. The teacher will scold me. I won't go.'

Aai's wan face grew sad. 'Shyam, what shame is there in helping your mother? This is God's work. Those who laugh at you for doing it will prove their own foolishness. People shouldn't feel ashamed to do God's work. They should feel ashamed to sin. Shyam, the other day you ate a piece of coconut I had kept near the hearth, on the sly. I saw you. I said nothing because young boys do that kind of thing. You didn't feel ashamed when you did it. But now you are ashamed to do God's work. Of what use is reading books like *Bhakti Vijay** and *Pandav Pratap*? Your favourite Lord Krishna would graze cows and clean up the leftovers in Dharma's house. But you are ashamed to work, to perform holy rituals. If you won't do it, I will. I will faint doing it, but that doesn't worry me. If I die I'll escape from all this. I will go to God. But Shyam, I live only for you, my children.' Aai dabbed at her eyes with her sari.

---

* *This book of compositions on Sant Dnyaneshwar's life was written by Mahipatibuwa Taharabadkar (1715–1790), an artist, poet and saint. He went on to write many other biographies of saints.*

Aai's words sank deep into me. My heart melted. It overflowed. It felt blest. 'Don't be ashamed of doing God's work. Be ashamed of sinning.' Noble words! They still ring in my ears. How important they are today! We are ashamed of doing right, but proud of doing wrong. That has become our culture. It is a sad thing.

I touched Aai's feet and said, 'Aai, I will do as you say. I don't care what people think. Pundalik became a great man because he served his father and mother and drew God to his side. I will serve you and ensure you and God love me. I don't mind if my teacher beats me. Are you angry with me, Aai? Are you disappointed?'

'Of course not, my pet. Can I ever be angry with you? I am incapable of being angry with you, Shyam. You know that, don't you?'

'Friends. Whenever I happened to be at home and it was time for the Savitri fast, I would always accompany my mother when she walked around the banyan tree. I will never forget Aai's words: "Feel ashamed of sinning. Don't feel ashamed of doing good work."'

Second Night

Akka's Wedding

Dinner was over. The residents of the ashram were fond of going for a walk between dinner and prayers. There was a river nearby called Bahula and a small Mahadev temple on its banks. Beside it grew a massive and ancient *peepal* tree. A stone seat had been built around it where villagers often sat and chatted.

That evening Govinda and Shyam had climbed up a hillock and were sitting at the top. Govinda had brought his flute along and was playing a sweet melody. Shyam was listening intently, his poetic spirit stirred. Suddenly Govinda stopped playing. Glancing at Shyam he noticed that his eyes were closed and his face glowed with a sweet and tender smile.

'Aren't we going back to the ashram? It will soon be prayer time,' Govinda said.

Shyam opened his eyes. 'Govinda, what a sublime thing the flute is. When Lord Krishna played it, stones and rocks turned soft and animals' hearts melted.

'When I was a boy,' Shyam continued, 'and we had holidays during the rainy season, I would accompany the village cowherds to the forest. While the cattle grazed, they played their flutes. My uncle used to make lovely flutes. Simple bamboo pipes, but how magical was their sound! Nowadays people buy foreign-made brass flutes, which sound shrill and cost two whole rupees a piece. How can poor villagers afford them? But they do very well with their bamboo flutes. They are easy to play, beautiful to look at and sweet to hear. Please continue playing, Govinda. Play that tune again.'

'No, I mustn't. There's the bell for prayers. We must go.'

'I suppose we must. But tell me, did I ramble a lot last night when I talked about my mother? I must finish early today.'

'Your story didn't last longer than ten or twelve minutes. Please don't hold back. Even your digressions don't strike us as a waste of time. They are full of thoughts and ideas that we can learn from.'

Soon they were at the ashram. The terrace had been prepared for prayers. The residents of the ashram were all there and some villagers as well. As soon as they were done with the prayers, the residents grew eager to hear Shyam's story. He began.

Aai loved us all equally, but I think she loved our sister a little more. My sister, whom we called Akka, is just like my mother. She is an embodiment of compassion and forgiveness, hard work and endurance. Her husband's family ill-treated her, but she never breathed a word about it at home. She never slapped her children. If they upset her beyond bearing, she went away from them for a while till she calmed down.

Today's story is about Akka's wedding. My parents had been looking for a match for her for a long time, but were unable to find one. Our family had a big name, but we were actually like a mansion with hollow beams. Some people in the family wanted us to continue living in the old style, with the same pomp and show. This meant that our debts grew. Akka was introduced to many families. Those who liked her expected to be paid a dowry. The dowry is like a boulder on a girl's back. It doesn't allow her to grow as she deserves to. She is consumed with anxiety about her dowry. 'The girl's getting old. We must marry her off. God knows where the wretched girl's future husband is hiding.' Girls hear their families say such things day in and day out. Life becomes unbearable for them because the young men in our country are not strong enough to speak up.

Twenty years ago in Bengal, a girl called Snehalata burnt herself to death because of dowry. Young men protested for a few days following that incident. They organized meetings. They made resolutions not to accept dowries. But then everything cooled down. It was back to demanding dowries. We want our education to be paid for. We want a gold ring. We want a bicycle. We want a wristwatch. Exchanging human beings for money is wrong. And yet we sell our sons and daughters. What can be more sinful than that? We speak with pride of our religion, but our deeds turn our words into a joke. Young men's hearts, which should be liberal, are actually dead. Men are worth nothing unless they show the courage to rise against evil. How can young men who cannot shed customs and traditions that make life unbearable for their sisters, claim to love freedom? Can they? But enough of that. I must not get carried away by emotion.

'Everything you say is like music to our ears,' said Govinda. 'Remember the story you once told us about the famous actor Ganpatrao? You said he was acting once in *Hamlet*, but whenever he stepped on the stage he would start speaking lines from *Sant Tukaram*. The audience said, "Please continue". Anything Ganpatrao said was music to their ears. That's how it is between you and us. Whether you tell us a story or read us a sermon, both give us equal joy.'

'So tell us, how did Akka get married?' asked Ram.

'Good. Ram has brought us back to the point. So listen,' Shyam said.

After a long and hard search, a match was finally found for Akka. The wedding was to take place in Ratnagiri. We had to travel there from Palgad. I was about six or seven then. I don't remember the incident that Aai narrated later. I remember other things like the surging sea and the bullock carts. Some seventy-five of us, family and friends from the village were travelling. A few helpers also went with us. The bullock carts halted at the Harnai harbour. Sea journeys were difficult in those days. There was no jetty at Harnai. Ferryboats would stand out at sea in waist-deep water. Sailors would carry people on their shoulders to the ferries, which would then transport them to the boat. Harnai was a difficult harbour, but a beautiful place. It used to be called Suvarnadurg or golden fort in the old days.

The Harnai shore is lined with thick coconut groves. The palm fronds dance to the beat of the heaving sea. You can hear its thunder miles away. A lighthouse with a revolving red light stands on a tall hill nearby, warning boats wordlessly of embedded rocks. It is like our saints who also stand tall above us and guide us silently. In life's journey, saints are like lighthouses. A village neighbour who was with us instantly recited a line from a hymn composed by a saint: *In the light of a saint's grace / A devotee is sinless.* Our Warkari pilgrims can recite many more hymns and verses than any of us educated people can. We know our English poets by heart. But we do not know Dnyaneshwar and Tukaram.

How beautiful the red light of the lighthouse looked. On a night when the moon is out, it dances in a hundred images on the surging waves of the sea. It is as though a fond father has captured myriad pictures of his beautiful silver son.

A little boy asked, 'Why is the sea the moon's father?'

Namdeo answered, 'Because the moon was one of the fourteen jewels churned up from the sea aeons ago.'

Shyam was in his own reverie.

The hundred moons are like glittering ornaments scattered over the sea. Or they are the moon's way of playing with the waves. It is a fascinating sight. The wind blows, the palms sway, the waves surge, the lighthouse blinks, the moon rides the sky and, down below, a boat fills up with people. The boatmen shout. Somebody's luggage has been left behind or has got exchanged or is missing. Someone is seasick and throws up on someone else who then loses his temper. All the chaos, confusion, apathy and insensitivity of life in Hindustan is suddenly on show.

We climbed into the ferry. The oarsmen began to row. Slap, slap went the water as the oars dipped into it and lifted. Spray flew with the wind, wetting our faces. The oarsmen cried, 'Go to it, boys, go,' while the crowd in the boat pushed and pulled. My mother and aunt sat in a corner nursing their babies. My aunt was ill. She did not have enough milk for her baby. She had to supplement it with cow's milk. But nothing can replace mother's milk, not only because it has a unique taste, but also because it comes with all the love in a mother's heart. The baby grows plump on the milk and the love of its mother. In that giving and taking, both giver and taker feel blessed.

We could hear the faint tinkle of bells from the bullock carts on the other shore. We could see the dim shape of a ship in the distance, making its way to the harbour. The red light on its mast was now clearly visible. And yet it would take us another half an hour at least to reach the harbour and for our ferry to meet the boat there.

Just then I heard my aunt shout at her baby whom she was trying to nurse.

'Stop biting. There's nothing there for you.' The baby began to cry and would not stop. The boat was crowded. There was no place to move. When a baby starts crying in the middle of a crowd, the mother wants to die. Mothers want their babies to laugh and play. They want people to hold them and kiss them and praise them. Then they are in heaven. A cranky child puts them to shame. Who will want to pick him up? People turn away from him. A crying baby is in need of soothing. But in this world you have friends only if you are happy. If you are unhappy, poor and helpless, you are alone. The one who needs sympathy is the one who does not get it.

The sound of a crying child is irritating. People say, 'What's the matter with him, for God's sake?' or 'He's at it again.' When such remarks fall on a mother's ears, she wants the earth to swallow her up along with the baby. That is how my aunt felt in that crowded ferry as her baby continued to wail. My mother who was sitting next to her, handed over her own baby to a servant and said, 'Let me take him. I'll nurse him.' She put my aunt's baby to her breast and let him have his fill. The baby began to laugh and play instantly. Throughout the wedding, my mother fed my aunt's baby before she fed her own. Aai did this with all the love in her heart. She felt deeply gratified that she could do it.

When Aai told us this story, she would invariably end by saying, 'Shyam, one should always give what one has to whoever is in need. No bliss in the world can be compared to the joy of stopping another's tears, bringing a smile to his lips and making him happy. There is no merit in caressing your own baby. Caressing another's requires a generous heart. That is where real merit lies.'

Third Night

Mute Flowers

'Barku, have you had your bhakri? Let's go to the ashram.'
Shiva was at the door.

'Aai, give me my bhakri quickly. They'll start soon.'
Barku tried to rush his mother.

'What are these stories you want to hear every night?
Stop pestering me. Starve. Eat when you come back.'

Barku took her at her word. An empty stomach did not
bother him when Shyam was going to fill his heart with
a story. Barku and Shiva walked fast. On the way, Shiva
stubbed his toe. But did he care? As they approached the
ashram they heard a bhajan. By the time they reached,
the last verse had been sung.

Shyam began to speak.

My story today is about flowers. I used to love flowers
as a child. To me, nothing in the world was purer and
more beautiful than them. Flowers on the earth and stars

27

in the sky, both affected me deeply. My father too loved flowers. He would bring heaps of them home for his puja. Our fields were full of several varieties like hibiscus, rose, trumpet flower and *rastura*. My father was a great devotee of Ganapati. He would offer twenty-one blades of *durva* grass to the deity every day. The grass had to be bright green, plump and long bladed, never stunted or wilted. He would walk any distance to collect the best. 'We offer nothing more than durva grass to God. Should we not get the freshest we can find?' he would say.

I inherited my craze for flowers from Bhau. But I learnt to love them from Aai. Every morning I would rise early to collect them. There were many *bakul* trees in our village. Bakul flowers are pretty, like tiny pearls, sweetly scented and full of honey. I used to carry home baskets full of them. When I returned from school at ten o'clock for lunch, I would string them together for Bhau to garland the idols in the village temple.

Gulbakshi flowers bloomed in the evening. So as soon as school ended, I would run to the neighbours' gardens to pick them. I was sure that our neighbours did not love flowers as much as I did and equally sure they did not offer them to their family gods. More likely they used them to adorn their own oily hair. I think differently now. I think we should pick only as many flowers as we need for our puja. We should leave the rest on the bush, where they are at their loveliest. To do that is also to make an offering to God. Tender and beautiful, flowers are themselves images of God.

The gulbakshi flower is very pretty. It has a long, thin, tender stalk. The bud sits at the end of it like a bead. When it blooms, it displays rainbow colours—deep yellow, lemon, red, white and crimson. Aai would sit in the tulsi garden and weave them into garlands. She did not need a needle and thread for that. She would braid their stalks together in a variety of patterns to form garlands that looked like thick bangles.

The neighbourhood boys went together every weekday evening to collect flowers. We would throw down our satchels and slates at home and run. But Sundays were different. You could go any time of the afternoon. Those who came late got the fewest flowers. On one particular Sunday, I got none at all. So, on the following Sunday, I decided to go as early as I could and collect all the flowers there were, although most were still tight buds. The buds would only start blooming after four in the afternoon and be fully open when the sun went down.

When I set off, the sun was still bright. It must have been around three in the afternoon. I took a piece of cloth with me to wrap the flowers in. I visited Dhondopant teacher's and Govindshastri's gardens next door and picked all the buds there were. Back home, I filled a basin with water and put the buds in it. In the evening Aai asked me if I wasn't going to collect flowers that day. 'If you go late like last Sunday, you won't get a single one,' she said. 'Then you'll sit crying. I don't mind if there aren't enough flowers for garlands. Just get a few for the evening aarti.'

'I've already collected them,' I said. 'There are more than enough for a garland.'

'Will you get them then? I'll sit here by the tulsi. I don't want the stalks to lie around in the house.'

I went to fetch the basin of flowers. Not a single bud had bloomed. I was mortified. But I put them in a basket and carried them out to Aai anyway.

'What's this? Why are they dripping water?' she asked. 'Don't tell me you picked buds. Really, Shyam. You should let flowers bloom on the plants. Why did you have to be so greedy?'

Even as Aai was scolding me, Banya, Bapu, Babi and the other boys next door came over. Babi said to Aai, 'Your Shyam picked all our flowers. He hasn't left a single one for us.'

Bapu said to me, 'When did you slink off like a thief to pick them?'

'Why like a thief? Don't I come to your gardens every day to collect flowers?'

'But we go together, don't we?' said Banya.

'When I came late last Sunday, you didn't leave a single flower for me.'

'Didn't I offer you some from my basket? But you went off in a huff. Why didn't you wait for me? Now watch out, you said and left. So this is the revenge you planned,' Babi fumed.

Aai was listening quietly. Then she said, 'Banya, Bapu, here, take some of these flowers. Shyam won't do it again. Will you, Shyam?'

'And you'll come with us every evening, won't you? Don't sit sulking,' said Banya. 'Why don't you come with us now? We'll play hide-and-seek or some other game.'

Aai said, 'It's a little late. Why not play tomorrow?'

My playmates left. I was feeling crushed. Aai said, 'Shyam, you shouldn't pick flowers from other people's gardens without asking them, should you? If you get there early, call out to them. But more importantly, never pick flowers when they are buds. Buds are mute. What did you gain by being impatient? Nothing. Flowers bloom only on plants. Put them in water for as long as you like, they will not bloom. A baby grows on its mother's milk. You grow healthy on home-cooked food, not on things you eat in restaurants, however rich that food may be. Plants are mothers to their flowers. They nourish them and help them blossom. Our gods don't mind if we offer them a few flowers less. If Banya and Bapu offer their gods more, it makes no difference to God. God is unhappy if you think He wants all the flowers. Even one flower is enough for Him, but let us offer Him one that has had a chance to bloom.'

My friends, only a mother can think this way about flowers. She nourishes her children, helps them grow and only then sends them out into the world to serve people. Plants too are happy if they have had a chance to help their flowers bloom before they are offered to God. Nothing is of any use before it has become its complete self. Work half-done is also useless. Whatever task we undertake, we must do it with all our hearts and concentration and take it to completion. It does not matter if it takes time. It is better to give it all the time it requires than to do it shoddily. Otherwise, don't do it.

Aai always said to me, 'Shyam, never pick buds. Give them a chance to open. Let them blossom.'

Fourth Night

Yashwant, a Blessed Soul

'It was Saturday and Ekadashi,' Shyam began his story.

'Can we wait for Barku? Yesterday he came without eating his bhakri,' Shiva said.

'Oh, there he is. Come, Barku. Come and sit here.' Govinda made place for Barku beside him.

Shyam continued.

It was the monsoon season. Oh, the Konkan rain! You know what that is like. It simply never stops pouring. Wherever you look you see rivers of rainwater gurgling down the slopes. We shivered with cold on the way to school. We protected our heads and backs with long hoods woven from coconut fronds. You didn't see many umbrellas around in those days. The frond hoods were called *irli*. They were beautifully made. That Saturday, only my elder brother Dada and I were going to school. Our younger brother Yashwant was ill in bed.

While we were at school, his illness took a sudden turn for the worse. His joints had been swollen for a couple of days, but he had recovered from that. Now some other illness had attacked him. It began with a stomach ache in the morning. Gradually the pain increased. Then his stomach began to swell. He could neither pee nor excrete. There was no doctor in the village and no enema can in the shops. All you could do was trust home remedies.

Our servant Govinda came to school to fetch us home. Yashwant had been calling for us—Dada one minute, Anna the next. By the time we reached home, a crowd of neighbours had gathered. Pitambarbhai and Kusha Appa, the Ayurvedic doctors from the village had also come. My brother was writhing in pain. His stomach was becoming more and more distended and he was so intensely thirsty that he would fling himself at the water when it was fetched and had to be held down.

He must have been around six years old then. Aai had scolded him the day before. She had spread channa dal out in the courtyard to dry. A goat had barged in and eaten some, scattering the rest. Yashwant had driven it away and was tidying the channa when Aji saw him and said, 'Little thief. Eating dal, are you? And tidying it up so nobody suspects. You're a fine one, aren't you?'

'Aji, don't say that. I wasn't eating it,' Yashwant said tearfully.

Aai was down with an attack of rheumatism. She could barely walk and was very weak. She was lying down in the house. When Yashwant went in to sit with her, she too scolded him. 'Why were you eating dal? Haven't I told you not to touch things?'

'Aai, I swear on God I didn't eat the dal. Why is everyone scolding me?' Yashwant went out and sat under the mango tree weeping. The day after that he took ill. They say heaven is the only place where you get justice. Was Yashwant so hurt that he had chosen to go to heaven to prove he had done no wrong?

It was clear to everyone that Yashwant was not going to survive. By nine o'clock, he was in a terrible state. He called out to Aai in a weak voice, 'I want to be with you, please.'

Aai said, 'You are right here beside me, my little one.' Weak and ill herself, Aai got up and placed Yashwant's head on her lap. Her eyes were wet with tears.

'Put my head down, Aai. Your joints must be hurting,' Yashwant said in a hollow, distant voice.

Aai's heart broke. 'My joints are fine, little one. I am feeling really well. A mother's illness vanishes when her child is ill. She finds strength to fight for his recovery. Don't worry about me. My only worry is my bones might hurt your head.'

Yashwant held Aai's hand.

'It is enough that you are sitting by me. That's all I want.'

Every word Yashwant uttered was like a stab in our hearts. Suddenly Aai remembered the previous day's scolding. Her eyes filled with tears. Her heart filled with pain. She bent over the face of the dying child and showered it with kisses, blessing it with her tears. Yashwant opened his eyes and looked at her with love and devotion. A little while later, he left us.

Aai always said, 'Yashwant was a blessed soul. That is why he went to God on Ekadashi day.' Bhau always said that when blessed souls die, they become stars. We believed him. We would look up at the sky, point to a star and say that it was Yashwant.

Today neither Yashwant nor Aai are with us. But the love we saw between them on the night of his death lives on in our memories. I feel blessed to have had a mother and a brother like that. I am nothing compared to them. Just a worm. If there is any goodness and love in me at all, it is because I had a brother like Yashwant and a mother like Aai. I must have done something extraordinarily good in my last birth to deserve them. Only merit that you have earned can bring such gifts. I don't claim to have earned any merit. In my case, the gift came entirely through God's grace.

Fifth Night

Mathuri

Shyam was feeling a little unwell. Ram said, 'Why don't you rest today? You don't have to tell us a story.'

'To remember Aai is the best medicine I can think of to cure any illness,' Shyam said. 'A devotee forgets his pain when he takes God's name. That's what happens to me when I speak of Aai. I've just remembered something very beautiful about her. Sit down all of you.'

And so Shyam began his story.

Friends, a man may be poor, really down and out, but he is rich if he has spiritual wealth. Many of the world's worst problems are caused by poverty of people's hearts and minds. I don't care if outsiders take away all of India's material wealth as long as they do not take away our inner wealth.

In the Konkan, every house has a large mortar that is half-buried in the courtyard. It is used to pound and husk paddy that comes from our fields. We used to employ local women to do this work. They were called *kandpin*. Every household had its own ancestral kandpin. Generations of a kandpin's family pound paddy for the same household, making it a traditional entitlement. We had three regular kandpin: Mathuri, Gajri and Lakshmi. Mathuri's son Shivram used to work in the house. He was about ten or twelve years old.

In the summer months, Mathuri used to bring us ripe karvandas and alus. Ripe black karvandas are the poor man's grapes. Alus are also a sweet fruit—brown with large pips. There was an alu tree in Mathuri's garden which bore particularly sweet fruit.

One day, Mathuri didn't come to our house. 'Gajri, why hasn't Mathuri come today? And who is this?' Aai asked.

'Mathuri has a fever,' Gajri answered. 'She has sent Chandri in her place.' Mathuri had made sure our work was not held up.

When Shivram came, he told Aai that Chandri would fill in for his mother till she was well enough to come herself. He went off to do his work, the women turned back to their pounding and Aai set off for the well with the washing. We finished our lunch around 12.30 p.m. Shivram asked if he could go home.

'Have you given the cattle water?' Aai asked. 'And raked away the dung? We don't want them walking around or sitting in it, do we? And don't forget to leave them some grass.'

'I've done all that,' Shivram assured her. 'May I go now?'

'Wait,' Aai said. She went to the kitchen and came out with hot rice and a slice of lemon pickle on a banana leaf in one hand, and a tumbler of buttermilk in the other. 'This is for your mother, Shivram. I hope she gets well soon.' Shivram left with the banana leaf parcel of rice and the tumbler of buttermilk.

Dusk had fallen. We were back from school and were reciting our tables. 'Gajri,' Aai called out. 'Can you clean the brass lamp with the paddy husks please?' The lamp was lit every night before our idols. It was scrubbed with husk once a week when the paddy was pounded. Rice husk makes brass shine. Gajri scrubbed the lamp while Aai measured the pounded rice. She gave the pounders fine bran and broken rice and saw them off.

Shivram, who had returned for his evening chores, had watered the plants and milked the buffaloes. Aai used to milk the cows herself. When Shivram was ready to go home, Aai, who had asked me to fetch some lemongrass, dug up a piece of ginger root from the tulsi planter and gave both to Shivram. 'Boil this lemongrass and ginger together in water with a few coriander seeds and a peepal leaf. Ask your mother to drink the brew while it's still hot. Then cover her with a blanket. That will make her sweat and she'll be free of the fever. Wait, let me get you some sugar candy.' Aai went indoors and came out with two pieces of sugar candy before sending him away.

At home, Mathuri asked Shivram, 'Who gave you all these things?'

He answered, 'Shyam's Aai.'

Mathuri said, 'She's a saint. She cares for the whole world.'

Mathuri drank the lemongrass brew at night, but she neither sweated nor did her temperature come down. When Shivram returned to work the following day, Aai asked, 'How is your mother, Shivram?'

'She has a terrible headache. It's like having a hammer in there. She's sitting with her hands pressed to her forehead. She didn't sleep a wink last night.'

'Oh dear. All right,' Aai said. 'When you go back at noon, I'll give you some dried ginger and herbs. Make a paste with them and put it on her forehead. She'll feel better.'

After that the two got busy with their chores. He swept the cowshed and made dung pats. She chopped vegetables. When Shivram was done, he went home with rice and lemon pickle like the day before and the dried ginger and herbs that Aai gave him.

A few days later, although still weak, Mathuri felt well enough to return to work. Aai said, 'You've grown so thin, Mathuri. Are you sure you can manage the pounding?'

'I'm sure I'll manage with breaks,' Mathuri replied. 'Enough of the lying around and not earning my food,' she added. 'I can walk now. I'll be fine in a few days. Your love gives us strength, Aai. If we have that, we lack nothing.'

'It is all God's grace,' Aai said. 'We can do nothing without that. But listen. The children are having their food. Have a few mouthfuls of rice with them. It will give you strength to pound. And have a good full lunch here today, do you hear?'

Mathuri ate with us that day, her face glowing with gratitude.

Mathuri is old now. When I go home, I always visit her. Her face is a mesh of wrinkles. But you can still see her generous spirit and the love in her heart through them. When I touch her feet, she says, 'No, Shyam, don't do that.' Then she remembers my mother. 'Shyam, if your mother had been alive, she wouldn't have let you wander around single, like an ascetic. She would have found you a girl to marry. She's gone, poor soul. How full of love she was for everybody.'

That was the kind of loving and compassionate mother I was fortunate enough to have.

Sixth Night

The Tears of the Virtuous

'From the time I was a boy, I have been used to taking a bath twice a day,' Shyam began.

We children would be out playing every evening. We played tap 'n sit, catching cook, hop 'n catch, hide-and-seek and Lakshumbai-give-me-buttermilk. Then I would take a bath. Aai would have a basin of hot water ready for me and help scrub my back. Taking a bath twice a day is an excellent habit. You feel clean and light when you've washed away the day's dirt. We pray before we sleep to cleanse our minds. We should take a bath to cleanse our bodies. When both mind and body are clean, you sleep more soundly and peacefully.

One evening I came home after playing, took off my shirt, put a slick of oil on my *shendi** and squatted on the

---

* *It is a practice among certain upper caste Hindu men to shave their heads completely, leaving only one tuft hanging at the back. This tuft is called shendi in Marathi.*

bathing stone for my bath. The large flat stone was placed such that the bathwater would run off it straight into the *tondli* creeper. The evening bath didn't require a lot of water. Aai scrubbed me down and went indoors. Within a few minutes, I had poured mugfuls of water over myself and was done. Then began my usual yelling. 'Aai, wipe me quickly. I've finished my bath. I'm cold.' In those days, we didn't use towels. The men used their own squeezed out dhotis and an old length of cloth was set aside for the children. Aai often used the pleats of her sari to wipe me after my evening bath.

Aai came out, wiped me dry and said, 'Now go in and fetch the flowers for our puja.'

I said, 'My feet are wet. They'll get dirty. First dry them.'

'What's wrong with wet feet, Shyam? What am I supposed to wipe them with?'

'Spread out the pleats of your sari on the stone. I'll stand on them, dry my feet and jump on to the verandah. I hate mud on my feet. Go on. Spread your sari on the stone.'

'You're so stubborn, Shyam! Where do you get these fancy notions from?' Aai spread her sari on the stone. I stood on it and dried my feet thoroughly. Then I jumped. Did I spare a thought for Aai's wet sari? Did I wonder if she would have time to change it? No. But these questions had not occurred to her either. Her son wanted dry feet. If her sari was going to get wet in the process, so be it. There was nothing she would not give, endure or forgo for her son.

I went indoors and collected the flowers. Aai came with our small oil lamp. 'You are so careful not to get your feet dirty, Shyam,' she said. 'Take care not to soil your mind either. Ask God to keep it pure.'

Friends, those were simple words but so true. We take such pains to clean our bodies. We use sandalwood soap, no less. We employ dhobis to launder our clothes. Shoeshine boys polish our footwear. We do everything we can to keep our outward appearance clean. But how careful are we to keep our minds clean? We paint our temples, but don't really care about God. Do we ever shed tears over our soiled minds? Only the virtuous weep over them. We don't see many others do it. We see tears shed over lack of clothes or food, over failure in an examination or somebody's death. Rivers of tears flow for these sorrows, but not a tear is shed when the mind is corrupted. Mirabai* says she watered the plant of devotion in her heart with her tears. I often hum the line: *The creeper of love can only grow with tears.*

---

* *Mirabai was a great saint and devotee of Krishna. She was born in Rajasthan in the sixteenth century. She composed many devotional songs that are sung across India even today.*

Seventh Night

Leaf Plate

In many homes in the Konkan, meals are eaten off leaf plates. It makes work easier. The plates are thrown away after a meal is done. They are simple, clean and beautiful. Brass plates call for frequent tinning. Who knows what that puts in your stomach along with food!

My father loved eating off leaf plates. He would leave for the fields early in the morning, finish his rounds and return home by ten with flowers for his puja, fresh leaves for our plates and vegetables for lunch, either given to him by a peasant or picked by him. He would take his bath and do his puja. Meanwhile, we returned from school and made plates and bowls from the fresh, bright green leaves.

At first, my leaf plates used to look terrible, and my bowls even worse. There's a saying in the Konkan: A son-in-law who can make leaf bowls before he can make leaf plates must be a clever man indeed. Our whole family sat together to make plates. Aji would be in charge. She would decide how many plates each person was to make and distributed the leaves accordingly. The leaves could come from any tree—banyan, palash, white frangipani—as long as they were large. Funeral meals were always served on moha leaf plates. Women often took oaths to eat off mango or jackfruit leaf plates during Chaturmas, the four months of penance and fasting that fall between July and October. Leaf plates have a religious significance in the Konkan.

One day Aai said, 'Shyam, you had better learn how to make your own leaf plate or you won't get lunch.'

'I can't make them and I won't make them,' I answered angrily.

My sister had come home from her in-laws' village. She said, 'Come. Let me teach you. It's not difficult, you know.'

'I don't want you to teach me,' I answered my loving sister rather rudely.

My sister used to make beautiful plates. So did my father. He was famous in the village for them. But there was another man who was a legendary leaf plate maker. His name was Rambhatji. Give him any leaves and he would tack them together into a perfect round plate. He would never discard a leaf that was torn or misshapen. Every leaf had its place in his plates. There was a custom in the village that seems to be vanishing now. When a family celebrated a wedding or a thread ceremony, the villagers would gather in their house to help them make leaf plates and bowls amidst friendly chatter and laughter.

There was no reason why I couldn't learn how to make them, except that I was stubborn. I didn't make one that day and Aai didn't set my place for lunch. Her rule was that we ate off the plates we made. Since I hadn't made one, there was no plate for me.

My sister began to mediate on my behalf.

'Shyam, you'll make a plate tomorrow, won't you? I'll teach you how. Aai, serve Shyam his lunch. He'll make his own plate tomorrow. Won't you, Shyam?' But my cheeks were puffed up. 'I will not make a plate. Don't give me lunch. I don't care. I'll starve.'

I marched off to the verandah. But I was ravenous. Surely someone would come out and coax me to have lunch. Finally, it was Akka who came. She had no ego.

'Shyam, please come and have lunch. I won't be around to coax you when I've gone back to my in-laws tomorrow. Make a small *thikola* and eat off that.' We called a small plate made with three leaves a thikola. A four-leaf plate was a *chouful*. Sometimes we children even ate off a single large palash leaf. A full adult plate was a perfect round one, made with several leaves. It was called *gheredar patrawal*. My father liked eating off a generously proportioned round plate. He would say there was no shortage of leaves in the forest, so why scrimp?

Akka's words melted my heart. She had come home for just two days and even during that short time I had behaved badly with her. I felt very guilty. My eyes filled with tears. She gave me a fresh leaf. 'Use this for support,' she said. I picked up a bamboo tack and tried to pin two leaves together on the supporting leaf. But the tack was blunt and wouldn't go through. 'Here's a better one,' Akka said, giving me another tack from the bundle. I made big, careless stitches and carried the thikole to the kitchen.

'Here's my plate. Serve me,' I said to Aai.

'Have you washed your hands and feet?' she asked.

'Long ago,' I said. 'I'm not a dirty boy.'

'You're not dirty. But you're sniffling. Go blow your nose while I serve your lunch.'

I came back with a clean nose and sat down to eat.

'Now eat your fill. Why throw tantrums? Look at Vasu. He's younger than you, but what lovely plates he turns out.'

I was devouring my food angrily. I hadn't made my plate carefully. A tack came off and got stuck in my throat. I panicked. Luckily it came out. 'See, I almost swallowed that tack,' I said angrily. 'I've told you I can't make plates, but you insist I must.'

'Why don't tacks go into our throats? You did a shoddy job and you were punished for that. You will have to eat off your own plate till you learn to make a good one,' Aai said.

I knew I could no longer escape learning to make good plates. The next day I watched Akka closely to see how she made them, how she crimped the edges of the leaves before tacking them together. You should learn to do things from people who do them well. Why should you be ashamed of that? Whatever you do you should do as well as you can. That should be your motto whether the task at hand is making leaf plates or dung pats, writing books or weaving shawls. Bhau lived by this motto. When he hung clothes on the line, they fell perfectly, edge to edge, corner to corner. The man who hung up clothes for the Gondhalekars was another one. You had to stand and stare when he was doing it. When Bhau watered our vegetable patch, the water fell in a thin, steady stream. This happened because he concentrated all his attention on the job. We should try and make everything we do look neat and beautiful.

My mother taught me to put my mind to everything I did. The leaf plate you have made could be set for anybody, she said. If it is badly made, a tack could get stuck in the poor soul's throat. When you are making a plate, say to yourself, 'I want the person who eats off this plate to enjoy his food. I must make sure he doesn't have to eat tacks. I must make sure half his food doesn't leak out of the gaps in the plate.' That's how I learnt to make good leaf plates.

One day, a plate I had made was set before my father. He looked at it and said, 'Chandre, is this one of yours?'

Akka said, 'No. Shyam made that one.'

Bhau said, 'When did he learn to make them so well?'

'I threatened not to serve him lunch one day. I told him he would have to eat off his own plates till he learnt to make good ones. That forced him to learn,' Aai said.

I said to Aai, 'Why are you talking about old things? I make them well now, don't I, Bhau?'

'Not just well. Beautifully. But what about bowls?'

'I've made one of those too. I found one of Akka's sitting on the parapet of the well. I tried copying it. I'll show you mine when we've finished dinner.'

I was thrilled when Bhau praised my plate. After dinner, I showed off my bowl to him. 'It's quite good,' he said. 'But you've made a mistake here. The opposite corners must be pinched to exactly the same angle.' He showed me how. I took the improved bowl to show Aai.

'Now why will anyone scold you?' she said. 'You throw such tantrums saying you can't do this and you can't do that. Anyone who has arms and legs is capable of doing everything. Only, you must want to. Chandre, give Shyam a dried apricot. That's his gift for learning a skill.'

Akka gave me an apricot from the jar in the cupboard. How sweet it tasted. Even the nectar that the gods churned out of the ocean couldn't have tasted sweeter. Sweetness doesn't belong entirely to the thing itself. It also comes from the work you have done to earn it. True happiness lies in doing work well.

Eighth Night

A Prayer for Forgiveness

It was a night of crisp bright moonlight. The ashramites were sitting on the terrace of the temple. The river in the distance looked like flowing silver. The river knows no rest. She only knows how to flow and keep flowing. This is her prayer and it never stops. As she flows she hums, or gurgles with laughter, or turns playful or solemn or even angry. The river is a beautiful and profound mystery.

Shyam stood looking at the river. He was driven mad by the beauty of his surroundings. Sometimes, watching a sunset would put him in a trance and make him compose verses spontaneously.

Had he gone into a trance again? Ram said, 'Shyam. Everybody is here. They are waiting to start their prayers.'

'So sorry. I was lost in myself,' Shyam said as he took the place reserved for him. When the prayers had come to an end, he began to tell his story.

Friends! Our culture, our sanskruti, is about how we live. Every caste and community has its own culture, its own way of doing things. Put all these cultures together and you have our national culture. Culture pervades our every custom. We must learn to recognize its unique quality, its particular fragrance, so to say. We must examine our customs all the time and discard those that are no longer relevant. But we must never allow those that are a vital part of our culture to die. The customs we follow in our country and in our diverse communities are an education in themselves.

Our family had a long-standing custom. Before we started our midday meal, which was the main meal of the day, each one of us had to recite a shloka. Bhau scolded us if we didn't. He had taught us many shlokas, hymns and morning songs and also some lovely poems by the old Pandit poets, Vamanpandit and Moropant. He would wake us up at daybreak. When we sat up, wrapped in quilts, he would teach us new verses. We didn't have blankets in those days. We slept on and under quilts or just mother's old saris folded four times over. Bhau used to teach us morning hymns in praise of Ganga, Ganapati and other deities. He didn't like us to learn by rote. He would explain the meanings of the shlokas first before we memorized them. 'Who was Soumitra?' he would ask. If we couldn't answer, he would ask, 'Who was Laxman's mother?' We would say, 'Sumitra'. 'So who would Soumitra be?' We would guess, 'Her son Laxman.' He would say, 'Good'. Then he would go on to ask who Radheya was, who Soubhadra was and so on. He had his own technique of teaching. As a result, we learnt the meanings of hundreds of Sanskrit words.

Bhau taught us in the mornings and Aai in the evenings.

We were addicted to learning verses by heart. If we recited something that we had learnt by ourselves, we got a pat on the back from Bhau. That encouraged us. Children would recite verses even at weddings and thread ceremonies. Whoever recited well was applauded. That encouraged the village children further to memorize shlokas and poems. It was lovely to hear such sublime thoughts and beautiful words at mealtimes. It was like having a sage as our dinner guest.

Our family was always invited to dinners in the village. Before the meal began, Bhau would signal to us to begin reciting shlokas. Although I knew many verses and could recite them perfectly, I was very shy to do so in public. I am still not comfortable with people. My voice wasn't the best in the world and I suffered from stage fright. Even as a little boy I was fearful of what people would say. I'd feel very hurt if somebody laughed or said something critical while I was reciting a shloka. But if Bhau was sitting beside me, I would have no choice but to recite.

One day there was a religious ceremony at the house of a very good family friend, Ganguappa Oak. Bhau was away and somebody had to represent the family. I used to be very shy of going to people's homes for meals. But we couldn't not go. It would have been very rude not to. The responsibility fell on me. We got a message in the afternoon to say lunch was ready. I went. The courtyard was decorated with lovely rangoli. Glossy banana leaves had been laid out for lunch. I sat down in an inconspicuous place. The air was redolent with the scent of incense sticks. It was summer, so the brass water-pots were wrapped in wet cloths and the water was scented with khus. Inquiries were made after those who had not come. Children were sent off to the homes of families that had promised to come but had not turned up. Finally the gathering was complete. Guests sprinkled water around their banana leaves, intoned 'Har Har Mahadev' and began to eat.

I ate in silence. Boys began reciting shlokas one after another. This was considered a polite thing for guests to do. If a woman helping with the serving noticed that her son had sat down for lunch, she would urge him to recite a shloka. Soon I was being reminded of how many shlokas I knew and was pressed to do my duty. I didn't have the courage to recite a shloka publicly. Govindbhat, who was sitting next to me, said, 'Don't be so coy.' I kept mum, busily polishing the coin I had received as dakshina. I ignored what people were saying.

A boy down the row rose before the rest of us had finished eating. That was an impolite thing to do and many people shouted at him for it. When everyone had finished eating, the lunch sitting rose as one. I didn't eat the supari that was offered at the end of the meal. Bhau said children should not eat betel nuts or betel leaves. I came home. It was a Saturday and there was no school in the afternoon. 'So what did you have for lunch?' Aai inquired. 'What vegetables had they made?' I described the lunch to her in detail. Her next question was, 'Did you recite a shloka?' How was I going to answer that one? With a lie, followed by another to support the first? Take one wrong step, then a second to gloss over the first. One sin leads to another, each worse than the last. I lied to Aai. 'Yes, I did.'

'Which one? Did people like it?'

Another lie. 'I recited *Eyes, bright as diamonds*.' That was one of my father's favourites. It is really lovely. This is how it goes.

> *Eyes, bright as diamonds, spreading radiance,*
> *Sindoor on the forehead, a durva grass spray.*
> *Look at Ganesha's image, poet Vasudev says,*
> *Your spirit will soar, your worries fly away, your worries*
>   *fly away.*

As I was telling Aai all these lies, the neighbourhood children trooped in. Like all children, they enjoyed teasing and taunting, carrying tales and getting their friends a beating. Bandya, Banya, Vasu chorused, 'Yashoda aunty, Shyam didn't recite a shloka today. Everybody was pressing him to, but he refused.'

Vasu said, 'I recited one that Shyam had taught me.'

Govinda said, 'I recited *Here comes the chariot* and Narsu Anna gave me a pat on the back.'

Aai said, 'Shyam, did you lie to me? You said you recited a shloka.'

'When did you do that?' Vasu asked.

Banya said, 'Must have been in his mind. That's why we didn't hear it.'

Bandya said, 'I hope God heard it.'

The boys went away laughing. Children are the village judges. They will not let anybody get away with wrongdoing. They are like newspapers that expose people's bad deeds in the public square.

'Shyam, you were wrong not to recite a shloka. But to lie to me was worse. Go touch God's feet and say you will never tell lies again.'

I didn't move. I was like a statue.

Aai said, 'Go on. Go touch God's feet. Otherwise I'll have to tell your father about it when he comes home. Do you want him to scold you and beat you?'

I still didn't budge. I didn't believe Aai would remember to tell Bhau. I thought she'd forget and her anger would vanish by the next day.

Aai said, 'So be it. I'll say nothing more now.'

Bhau returned late at night. He woke us up the next morning and began to teach us shlokas. We recited them after him. Then he said, 'Shyam, what did you recite yesterday?'

Aai was making buttermilk. I could see her shadow dancing on the wall. She had to churn the cream standing because the pot was tall and the churner long. When Bhau asked me the question, she stopped churning and said, 'He didn't recite anything yesterday. He told me he had. But the next-door boys said he hadn't. I told him to touch God's feet and promise never to tell lies again. But he wouldn't budge.'

Bhau got angry.

'Is that true? Get up. Up. Go stand by that wall. Now tell me, did you recite a shloka yesterday?' I was scared of Bhau's temper. I began to cry and said, 'No, I didn't.'

'Why did you lie then? Haven't we told you dozens of times not to tell lies?' Bhau's anger and voice had risen. I was trembling with fear. 'I won't lie again.'

'When your mother told you to ask God to forgive you, why didn't you listen to her? Don't you know you're supposed to do what your parents tell you to do? You have grown too smart for your boots.'

I was sure Bhau was going to beat me. I went to Aai crying, and put my head on her feet. My hot tears bathed them. 'Aai, I did wrong. Please forgive me.' Aai was overcome by emotion and couldn't speak. She was the embodiment of love. She couldn't bear to see me dissolving like a clod of earth soaked in water. But she reined in her emotions and said, 'Now go and touch God's feet. Pray to him to keep you from lying.'

I stood before God. Still sniffling, I prostrated myself before Him and prayed hard. Then I went and stood by the wall.

Bhau's rage had mellowed by then.

'Come here,' he said.

I went to him. He held me close and stroked my back. 'Go now. You have school, don't you?'

'No, it's Sunday today.'

'Then go sleep a little more if you want to. Or would you like to come to the fields with me? We'll bring back leaves for plates.'

'I'll come with you,' I said.

Bhau was a very clever man. He had turned the mood in the house right around. The grey clouds of anger had vanished, their place now taken by the radiant sunshine of love. The two of us, father and son, went to the fields as though nothing unpleasant had happened between us. Although my mother was the personification of love, there were times when she became very tough. But this was also an expression of her love. That is how she raised me and my siblings, sometimes with tender love, sometimes with tough love. Sometimes she would pat us lovingly, sometimes beat us angrily. In both ways, she was shaping me. She was turning the ugly and lazy slob that I was into something beautiful. A child requires both warmth and cold, day and night to help him grow and develop. If the sun is out for all twenty-four hours of the day, it will burn up and destroy nature, including human beings. Hence the poem:

> A child grows with mother's love
> Also with its reverse.
> The sun nurtures trees and flowers
> The moon is equal nurse.
> Thus do things grow and thrive
> In this our universe.

Ninth Night

Our Mori Cow

'Is Barku here? I scolded him in the afternoon because I caught him beating a cow. Someone go get him from his house,' said Shyam.

'He's sitting outside and listening. He feels too ashamed to come in,' Shiva said.

Shyam rose and went outside. He took Barku's hand. Barku felt embarrassed. He struggled to free his hand. Shyam said, 'Barku, I'm very fond of you. That's why I scolded you. Are you angry with me for that? I'm like your elder brother. Come now. I'm going to tell you a story about our *mori* cow. Do you know what mori means? It means a brown cow with white spots.'

Touched by his warm words, Barku allowed Shyam to lead him into the prayer hall, where the others were waiting for the evening's story. Shyam began.

We had a mori cow. I can still see her vividly. People said she was the finest cow in the village. She was tall and powerful, but her expression was solemn and tranquil. Our pail held five seers* of milk when full. When she was ready for milking, she would give enough milk to fill it to the brim. We took great care of her.

Aai would go to the cowshed early in the morning to feed her grass. Later she would bring to her the water in which our rice had been washed. The water off washed rice was said to be nutritious and cooling for cows. Aai would also give her a portion of the food she had cooked for us.

Our mori cow loved Aai very much. Love begets love. You give love, you get love. The cow would lick Aai's hand when she stroked her. When Aai scratched her dewlap, she would raise her head higher and higher for more. When she heard Aai call her, she would moo in answer. She had to be milked by Aai. She would not allow anybody else to milk her. If someone else came anywhere near her at milking time, she would sniff at the person suspiciously. Cows recognize people by their smell. If the person sat by her side and actually dared to try milking her, she would kick both the person and the pail.

---

* *This was a measure of weight used in India and many other parts of Asia until the late 1950s. Parts of Asia continue to use it even today. The seer indicated different weights in different parts of our country. The standard seer known as 'Government seer' was equal to 1.25 kg. As a measurement of fluids, one seer was equal to roughly 1 litre. So the milk pail used by Shyam's family held 5 litres of milk when full. India adopted the metric system of measurement in October 1958.*

The cow was the joy and pride of our home. She was the very embodiment of all that was loving, warm and beautiful in the house. But unfortunately, one year, there was an outbreak in the village of the terrible foot-and-mouth disease. This disease kills cattle in large numbers. Sores appear on their feet, which get infected by maggots. The poor animals stamp their feet furiously to ease the pain. But nothing relieves the pain or cures the disease. Soon after they catch it, they die.

Sadly, our mori cow contracted the disease. We treated her with every home remedy we could think of, but to no avail. She would not touch grass during her illness. She did not eat a single blade. She just lay in the shed, getting weaker by the day, her head drooping. We prayed and prayed for her, but it was no use. Finally she left us. The day she died, Aai did not eat a morsel of food. How can I describe her sorrow? Only a person who has loved feels the absence of the loved one. What do others care?

In the years to come, Aai would often say to Bhau, 'When our mori cow died, your family's fortunes turned.'

Tenth Night

Cottage

Vacchi was pestering her brother one evening. 'Take me with you, Bhau. You go to the ashram every evening to listen to stories. Aai, tell him to take me.'

'You'll fall asleep there. I'm not going to take you.'

'Why not?' their mother asked. 'Everybody should have a chance to hear good stories. Even I would like to come. But by the time I finish my chores, it's too late to join you.'

'Bhimi from next door goes,' Vacchi said. 'So does Hanshi. Harni's brother takes her. Aren't you my brother?' Vacchi was trying hard to melt her brother's heart.

'All right, come then. But don't you dare say you're sleepy and make me rush home.' Bhau took Vacchi with him to the ashram. Children and older people from the village, who came to hear Shyam's nightly tales, had already gathered. By the time Bhau and Vacchi arrived, Shyam had begun his story.

Finally, my father's brothers drove him out of the ancestral home. Sibling rivalry. There's a lot of that in our country. It's been going on since the time of the Kauravas and Pandavas. There is no real freedom in a home where brother does not love brother. This was the home where my father had grown from boy to man. This is where, for thirty years, he had tried his best to manage the family's affairs, where he had given his brothers and their families milk and butter while he made do with tamarind water, where he had got his brothers and sisters married and fulfilled their every need and want. It was from this home that he was driven out. Aai too had to face insults. We were too young then to remember anything. But Aai often told us about that cruel separation with tears in her eyes.

Little as I was, I still remember one day vividly. The Maghi Ganapati Chaturthi festival was being celebrated in the village at the time. The Ganapati festival, which is generally celebrated, falls in the month of Bhadrapad. But the one in Magh was a local festival, celebrated to fulfil a pledge that a wealthy family from the neighbouring town of Mahad had made. That year a famous *keertankar* named Abhyankar Guruji was delivering the sermons in the temple. The whole village would gather to listen to him whenever he gave a sermon. On this particular evening, we were not allowed to go and were sent to bed early instead. Aai woke us up around 9 or 10 p.m. My parents were about to leave their home. Aai's eyes were brimming with tears. This was the home where she had milked our mori cow each morning, where she had served generous meals to the servants, where she had once been weighed down with gold ornaments. This was the home she was now leaving forever. She had chosen to leave at night because daylight would have revealed our shame. My younger brother, the one who came after Yashwant, sat on her hip. Bhau walked in front, Aai and I walked behind him. We were silent. We were going to my mother's family home, which was also in the village. Our grandparents were not home. They were away in Pune, staying with Aai's elder brother. But they would soon return. The village was alive with festivity while we were in mourning, exiled. In God's vast world, people live contrasting lives at one and the same time.

Soon we got used to our new home, but Aai's face continued to look sad. Some time later, Aji, my grandmother, came back. Although Aji was good-hearted and affectionate, she was rather strong-willed. Keenly aware of our circumstances, Aai tried her best to adjust to Aji's wishes. It humiliated her to have to live with her husband in her parents' house. She believed death was preferable to such a fate. She was a proud woman. One day, our grandparents were at the temple listening to readings from the sacred books. Bhau was in the verandah, working on his daily accounts. Aai went out to him and said, 'I can't bear living here any longer.

If you want me to live, please build us an independent house. It kills me to eat and drink here.'

Bhau said, 'Come on. We grow the rice we eat. We only live here. It is no joke to build a house. You say these things without understanding the problems I have to deal with.'

Aai lost her temper and said, 'You have no self-respect.'

Bhau said quietly, in a sad voice, 'Yes, I have no self-respect. Men aren't human beings at all. When a man is down, the whole world insults him. Why shouldn't his wife? Go ahead then. Join the rest. Insult me.'

Aai wept at hearing that.

'I didn't mean to insult you. Please don't take it that way. But truly, I cannot bear to continue living here.'

'Do you think I'm happy living here? But you know our circumstances. I can't even pay the interest on my debts, let alone the money I have borrowed. What do I build a house with? We don't want to build a cowshed for ourselves. That would be just as humiliating.' Bhau was trying his best to placate Aai.

'I don't mind living in a cowshed as long as it is ours and we are independent. Build a simple village hut. I will feel no shame in living there. But I don't want to live with my parents. When my brothers marry, their wives will also have things to say to us. It is better to leave before we are insulted. I'd rather live in a thatched hut than in a large tiled house. It won't cost much to build a hut like that, will it? Here, take these gold bangles. If they don't fetch enough, add my nose ring to them. Ornaments hold no value for me. I don't visit people. Our independence is our true ornament. I don't want gold without independence.'

So Aai took off her bangles and nose ring and set them down before Bhau. He was taken aback. 'I had no idea you were so unhappy here. I'll build a home for us immediately,' he said.

Aai always said we should be ready to sacrifice anything for independence. Independence makes us more beautiful than any ornament can.

Soon after, Bhau began building our hut on the small plot of land that had fallen to our lot. The walls were built with what we call *mapay* in the Konkan. These are unfired bricks, larger than the regular ones. The roof of the hut was thatched. The floor was merely levelled. The ritual of our entry into the new home was planned for an auspicious day. Aai was both sad and happy. Sad, because her brothers-in-law were living in a large, well-appointed house next door while we were living in a thatched hut. Happy, because she believed that whatever happened, we owned the place. She would say, 'I am the mistress here. Nobody in the world can order me out.'

We performed a puja for peace in the new home. The first thing we did was instal our gods in their place. Then we brought the rest of our belongings in. Aai made ghatlay to celebrate the day, with flour, jaggery and coconut. The day was very busy. Bhau kept telling people, 'This is only a temporary home. We'll soon build a proper house.' But Aai would say to us, 'I don't see your father building a big house. I'll have one when I go to live with God. Till then, this is my heaven. Here I have independence. I am not under obligation to anybody. The bhakri and salt that we eat in our own home is sweeter than any basundi-puri we may have in a home that doesn't belong to us.'

That night we sat out in the yard. The stars glittered above us. The moon had set a long time ago. Aai looked fulfilled. The hut itself was small, but the front and backyards were large. The front yard was our real home. 'Do you like our new home, Shyam?' Aai asked.

'I like it very much,' I replied. 'It's like a peasant's house. Like Mathuri's. She'll like it a lot.' Do you think Aai was saddened by what I said? After all, Mathuri used to pound our rice for us. But no. She was not a bit sad. She said, 'True. Mathuri is poor. But her heart is not. Let us also try to become large-hearted while we live in this little house.'

Just then a star shot across the sky. Aai suddenly became grave. My younger brother said, 'What a large star that was.'

Aai continued to look grave. 'Shyam, do you think that star was telling us that your mother's star too will fall soon? Is this vast dome calling out to me? Was that star a messenger?'

'Not at all, Aai,' I said. 'The star came down to see our independent home. Perhaps it found it more attractive than heaven. Doesn't your favourite book *Hari Vijay** tell us that the gods would descend to eat the grains of rice that fell into the Yamuna after Krishna had washed his hands in it? That's what attracted the star. Because love dwells in our home. And there is you.'

Aai stroked my back and said, 'Shyam, who taught you to say such wise things? You speak so sweetly and beautifully. You are right. Stars are sure to find this simple, lovely home attractive. Why only stars? Anybody who sees it would.'

_____

This is a devotional work based on stories of Shri Krishna's life, composed in a simple devotional style by Shridhar Brahmanand Nazarekar (1658–1729). The title means 'victory to Hari'. He composed the work in 1702. He wrote his next book Ram Vijay *in 1703 and* Pandava Pratap (*the deeds of the Pandavas*) *in 1712. Not only were these books popular, but they were revered as sacred texts.*

Eleventh Night

Universal Compassion

'Ram, please turn that lamp away a bit. It's getting in my eyes,' Shyam said.

It was drizzling and a cold breeze was blowing, prompting them to move indoors. Otherwise they always held their prayers and storytelling sessions outside, under the stars. Shyam found direct lamplight disturbing. Before Ram could turn the lamp away, Bhika said, 'But we see the expressions on your face better when the light is turned towards you. We listen to you, but we also need to see you. Your expressions add meaning to your words. If the voice by itself had been enough, plays would have been staged in the dark.'

'I'm not acting in a play here. I am speaking from the heart,' Shyam said.

'I didn't say you were acting. I only said watching your face as you speak makes a greater impact. When Swami Rama Tirtha, who went around the world preaching his philosophy of practical Vedanta, visited Japan, he spoke in English. The Japanese who did not know English also went to hear him. The expressions on Swami Ram Tirtha's face must have conveyed to them what he was saying,' Namdeo said.

'Let the lamp be then,' Shyam said. 'What makes you happy, makes me happy.'

And so Shyam began his story for the evening.

One day we were playing in the long front yard where our tulsi plant grew. A wild tree stood at the end of it. Suddenly we heard a soft thud. My younger brother and I looked around for the source. Something had surely fallen. We looked everywhere! Finally we noticed a tiny baby bird under the wild tree. Its chest was pumping hard. It had fallen from a great height and was in really bad shape. It was so tiny it wasn't even fully fledged nor had its eyes opened completely. Its little chest was heaving up and down like an ironsmith's bellows. The slightest touch and it would stretch its neck and go *chi chi chi*. We decided to carry the little thing indoors. We laid it gently on a piece of cloth and took it in. I got hold of some cotton wool and put the baby bird on it. We too were young. We looked after the bird the way our little brains told us to. We fed it grains of broken rice. We put water in a tiny spouted can and poured it drop by drop into its beak. We didn't stop to ask ourselves whether the bird was old enough to eat and drink or whether we were hastening its death by feeding it.

Love and compassion alone are not enough to make life beautiful and rewarding. Along with love you need two more things: knowledge and strength. The one who possesses all three lives a fulfilled life. Take a mother who loves her child very much. If she has no knowledge of how to look after the child when it is ill, she will lovingly feed him precisely what she should not and the child might even die of her love. Now take a mother who has both love and knowledge, but is weak. How can she show her love or use her knowledge? That is why we must make sure we grow in heart and mind and body. When our hearts are filled with love, our minds with knowledge and our bodies with strength, we have what we need to live a useful life.

We loved the little bird; but without knowledge, we kept stuffing its beak with flour and grain, followed by water to chase them down. The poor creature must have felt tortured by our attentions. In the end, it lay its head down. We assured it, 'Don't worry. We aren't going to lock you up in a cage. As soon as you're well, we'll let you go back to your tree where your poor mother must be waiting for you. For her sake, please don't die, little bird.'

The little bird didn't seem to hear us.

I called out to Aai. 'Aai, look at our bird. It won't lift its head. What shall we feed it?'

Aai hurried out of the kitchen and picked up the bird tenderly.

'Shyam, this baby isn't going to live. Let it die peacefully. Don't keep touching it. That must be painful. The poor thing has fallen from a great height.' She put the baby bird back on the cotton wool bed and returned to her chores. We sat staring at the bird. Soon its beak fell open.

It had died.

It died alone, without its parents, brothers and sisters around it. We felt terrible. We had to give it a proper burial. We went to Aai. 'Where can we bury the little bird? What's the best place?'

'Bury it by the *shevanti* or mogra bushes. It will make their flowers brighter and even more fragrant. The bird won't forget your love. The scent it will put in the flowers will be its return gift to you.'

'This is just like the story of Sonsakhli,' I said. 'Her stepmother killed her, buried her and planted a pomegranate tree on the spot. But Sonsakhli came in a pomegranate to meet her father. Isn't that right?'

'Yes. But bury the bird soon. You shouldn't keep the dead for longer than you need to.'

'Give us something nice to wrap it in,' we said. Aai gave us a piece torn from an old silk blouse of hers. We wrapped the bird in it and dug a small pit between the shevanti and mogra bushes. Our eyes streamed with tears as we scattered flowers in the pit and laid the little body on them. We did not have the heart to cover it with earth. But in the end, we closed our eyes and did it anyway. Then we put a pretty stone on top so the cat wouldn't come and dig up the bird. We returned indoors and sat in a corner crying.

'Why are you sitting in a corner like that?' Aai asked.

'We are in mourning for the bird,' I said.

Aai laughed. 'You don't need to do that.'

'Why not?' I asked. 'Don't we sit apart to mourn someone from the family who has died?'

'That's because that person might have died of a disease. That's why people who have been caring for him should stay away from others for a few days. The disease could have been infectious. When you sit apart in mourning, you are taking care that the germs don't spread. That poor bird didn't die of a disease, did it? It fell from a tree and died.'

'Who told you all this?' I asked.

'I overheard a visitor. He was sitting on the verandah with your father. I was convinced by his explanation. Now go wash your hands and feet. That's good enough. And don't feel so downcast. You did the best you could for the bird. You gave it love. God will love you for that. If you fall ill and your mother isn't around to take care of you, God will make sure a good friend turns up to take her place. Give something to one of God's creatures—insect, bird or animal—and you get a hundredfold in return. If you sow one grain, you reap a whole ear of corn, don't you, Shyam? I hope you brothers will grow up to love one another the way you loved the baby bird. It is no use loving animals and birds if you don't love your brothers. I hope you will grow up to care for one another. You have only one sister. Don't ever abandon her. Give her all the love you can.'

Aai's voice had grown heavy with tears. Perhaps she was thinking of how Bhau's brothers had treated him. Or was she thinking of her own brothers who had never once invited her over for a change of air when she was ill? Whatever the source of her sadness, she had spoken the truth. People will feed sugar to ants and use the same hands to twist people's necks. They will shower love on cats and parrots but not on their neighbours and brothers. Don't we see this happening every day around us?

Twelfth Night

Shyam Learns to Swim

In the Konkan, wells fill up to the brim during the monsoon. The water stands so high you can scoop it up with your hands. It is a great time for swimming. Children are taught how to swim in this season. The dried husk of a coconut or a piece of light wood is tied to the learner's back and he is pushed into the well. Expert swimmers wait for him in the water. They are so skilled that even when the water is so deep you can't see the bottom, they can dive down to the bottom and come up with a fistful of mud. They do somersaults in the water or hold hands and spin around or lie on their backs, feet-to-feet and raise their necks to imitate boats. All my uncles were expert swimmers. My father could swim too. Only I couldn't. I would watch the fun from the outside but was too scared to go in. Even tiny tots from the neighbourhood leapt in, but not me. If I heard someone say let's push Shyam in, I'd take to my heels.

Aai would often say to me, 'Why don't you learn to swim, Shyam? Why are you so scared? Do you think people will let you drown? Go tomorrow. It's a Sunday. Varavdekar's Balu will teach you. Or go with your uncles. Wells are a part of our lives. We don't have water taps like they do in Mumbai and Pune. You should know how to swim. Even Kusumtai's daughters, Veni and Ambi, know. Go tomorrow. Balu has a lot of husks. Tie them all on your back. You can even get them to tie a dhoti round your waist and hold it while you're learning. Do anything, but go.'

I said nothing. Sunday dawned. I had planned to hide. I knew Aai was determined to force me to learn swimming. I went up to the loft and hid. Around eight o'clock, Vasu, Bhaskar, Banya and Bapu came by. Banya said, 'Aunty, Shyam's coming today, isn't he? I've got these husks for him.'

'Of course he's coming. But where is he? I thought he had gone over to your place. Has he gone out somewhere?'

Aai began to look for me. I was listening to all this from my hiding place.

'He didn't come to our place. He must be hiding somewhere. Shall we look for him in the loft, aunty?' they asked.

'Yes, why don't you do that? He loves hiding like a mouse or a bandicoot. The other day I found him hiding under the cot. Careful when you go up there. The mat might suddenly fold up under your feet. Be careful.'

The boys began climbing up to the loft. I knew they would soon find me. I made myself as small as I could. But just as the frog in the story can't bloat up to become a bull, a bull can't contract to become a frog. I wished I could have been like Sant Dnyaneshwar whose great deeds are praised in *Bhakti Vijay*. He turned into a fly to drink from the pond. All I could do was squeeze myself into the space behind the grain bin.

One boy said, 'He isn't here. There's no place to hide in all this clutter.'

Another said, 'Let's go. It's getting late.'

Just then Bhaskar said, 'There he is! Behind the bin. Isn't that Shyam?' The others peered at me.

'Come on, Shyam. The game's up,' the boys chorused.

Aai called from below, 'So he's there, is he? I thought as much. Take him with you.'

The boys tried to drag me out. But they were friends after all. They weren't giving it all they had. And I had dug my heels in.

'Aunty, he isn't budging,' they called out.

Aai lost her temper.

'See if I don't make him budge. Let me get hold of him.' She came to the loft with a twig. She took hold of my hand and pulled it. She was dragging me forward and I was pulling her back. So she began using the twig on my back. 'Pull him from the front,' she said. 'I'll drive him from behind with this twig. Let's see how he still refuses to go.'

The boys kept pulling and she kept whacking me on the back with the twig. I howled, 'Don't hit me, Aai. I'm dying.'

'Oh no, you're not. Now get up and walk. I won't let you get away this time. Dunk him in the water a few times, boys. Let it get into his nose and mouth. Will you still not stand up, wretch? Aren't you ashamed to hide? Even the girls have come to watch.' And Aai laid harder into me.

'Don't, please don't. I'll go,' I pleaded.

'Get going then. And don't you dare run away. I won't let you into the house if you do.'

Venu was out there. She said, 'Jumping into the water is such fun, Shyam. The other day, uncle jumped with me on his shoulders. It was terrific.'

Banya said, 'Let go of his hands. He's coming with us now. Shyam, there's really no need to be scared. Once you've jumped in, you'll see how easy it is. You won't come out even if we want you to. Don't cry. Please.'

The other boys had already gathered around the Deodhars' well. 'Ah, Shyam, there you are. Come. I'll tie husks on your back,' Balu Varavdekar said. Balu tied husks on my back. A few expert swimmers were already in the well. I was trembling from head to foot. 'Now jump,' Balu said.

I walked to the edge of the well, peered in, stepped back, peered in again and, once again, stepped back. I would hold my nose preparing to leap, then let go of it. This went on for a long time. Venu's brother said to her, 'Why don't you jump in? Shyam will jump after you.'

Venu hitched up her long skirt and jumped. Suddenly somebody pushed me in after her. 'I'm dead!' I let out a scream.

I hit the water, came up and threw my arms around another swimmer's neck. He wouldn't let me cling to him. 'Lie flat on your stomach. Stretch out. Now start moving your arms,' he said.

My swimming lessons had begun. Balu jumped in, slipped his hand under my stomach and began to teach me.

'Don't be scared,' he said. 'Fear tires you out. And don't stretch out to touch the edge. Hold it only when you're near enough.'

'Now go up and jump in again,' Banya said.

I climbed up the steps. I held my nose, went back and forth a few times before I finally jumped.

'Bravo, Shyam. You'll learn fast now. Once you've lost your fear of water, everything becomes easy,' Balu said and gave me a few more lessons.

'Now,' said the boys, 'One more jump and we're through for the day.'

I went up and jumped in. I swam around a little without Balu's support. I wasn't afraid of drowning because I had husks on my back. I was no longer afraid of water. We left, and the boys came to see me home. Banya said, 'Aunty, Shyam jumped in by himself in the end. He wasn't a bit scared. With husks on his back, he even swam a little. Balu uncle said Shyam will learn to swim well.'

'You can't lose your fear unless you leap in and let the water get into your nose and eyes, Shyam. Now go wipe your head dry,' Aai said.

The boys left. I wiped myself dry and wore a fresh *langoti*. I was still sulking though. After dinner I was sitting on the verandah when I heard Aai call me in a sweet voice. 'What?' I said as I went in.

'There's some dahi in that clay pot. That's for you to lick clean. You like doing that, don't you?'

'I don't want it,' I said, close to tears. 'You beat me black and blue and now you offer me dahi. Look at the welts you've made. I spent so long in the well, but they are still there. I won't have dahi until the welts go away. Don't think I'm going to forget them so soon.'

Aai's eyes welled up. She couldn't swallow her rice. She left her dinner unfinished. I felt bad for having hurt her with what I'd said. Aai fetched some oil in a katori and applied it on the welts. I didn't say a word. She said tearfully, 'Shyam, would you like the world to call you a scaredy-cat? I don't want my Shyam to be called names. That's why I beat you. Would you like people to say to your mother, what scaredy-cats your children are? Wouldn't that be an insult to her? I would never tolerate my children being insulted, and my children shouldn't tolerate their mother being insulted. That is how a mother and her children should be. Don't be angry with me, Shyam. I want you to grow into a courageous man. Now eat that dahi and go play outside. Don't doze off. Sleeping after swimming can give you a cold.'

Shyam looked at his audience, seated around him. 'My mother wanted her children to be brave, not fearful.'

Thirteenth Night

Self-Respect

'Alms are not meant for the man who has the means to make a living. Only a priest is entitled to them because he has no income. He devotes his life to the study of the Vedas. Priests in some countries and religions are paid by the government. Our priests are paid by the people.' Shyam began his story.

We have a pre-wedding ritual called *vangnishchay** during which both the bride's and groom's sides give alms to priests. Their family priests walk around their respective wedding tents, distributing alms. The alms have to be equal on both sides. If the groom's side gives four annas to each priest, the bride's side must do the same. All he does is

---

* *The engagement ceremony performed the day before a wedding in Maharashtra. The engagement ceremony is conducted by a priest after the couple pray to the family's patron deity. This is followed by a feast for guests.*

put out his hand to receive alms. When a family attends a wedding, children become familiar with such customs. Parents explain what is happening and why. Then they say, 'We aren't supposed to stretch our hands out for alms.'

These days I find people have no self-respect. The guiding principle seems to be to take whatever comes free. I have noticed that Japanese agents* travelling by train give away cigarettes for free. I have seen even well-to-do people accepting and smoking them. These people go to free medical clinics for treatment. They apply for scholarships meant for the poor. Slavery gives birth to mean minds.

There was a wedding in our village once. I was with a group of children. The point of sitting together was to play pranks. You could place the beard of a coconut on somebody's cap, or put pebbles in somebody's pocket or pinch someone without his knowing who did it. When alms were distributed, some boys held out their hands. I followed suit without thinking. Not that I thought I was doing anything wrong. When you are young, you love to have money clinking in your hands. I came home excitedly with the two annas I was given. I ran to Aai to give her

---

* Sometimes Sane Guruji interprets something he has observed in a way that supports the point he is making. It is possible that he saw a Japanese or Chinese man offering free cigarettes on a train and assumed he was an agent for Japanese or Chinese goods. There is no record of any Japanese or Chinese goods being sold in India at the time that he was writing.

the money as though I had earned it with my own labour. Priests study for twelve years to learn the intricacies of rituals. Alms are their right and reward. People like us should work and earn money. That brings us respect.

Aai said, 'Where did you get this money?' I said, 'During the vangnishchay.' Aai's face fell. She looked deeply embarrassed. Did she think I had held my hand out for money because we had become poor? Or that the family priest offered me the money out of pity? Normally, if a boy from a well-to-do family held his hand out, the family priest would say, 'Don't be silly. Aren't you from the Dongre family?' Why had the priest not said that to her son? Surely it was because he pitied me. There is nothing more humiliating than being the object of somebody's pity. Aai's mind was whirring with many such thoughts. But she did not say a word to me. She just stared into space.

'Aai, why don't you take the money? I didn't steal it,' I pleaded.

Aai said, 'Shyam, we may be poor, but we work for our living. We are not priests. They have no means. They have no lands. They only do religious work. Alms are their only income.'

'Pandurang bhatji is so rich. Why should he accept alms? He lends money on interest. He has fields. What kind of a priest is he then?'

'The wrong kind,' Aai said. 'In the old days, if a priest had surplus alms, he gave them away to the poor. King Nala in *Pandav Pratap* gave a lot of wealth to a priest, who gave it away on his way home. Rishis taught their disciples free of charge. So don't ever hold your hand out for alms again. We are supposed to give to the world, not take from it.'

'Aai gave the two annas away to Balu, a poor servant. Friends, the more we take from the world, the more we grow accustomed to bowing and scraping and the more pathetic and dependent we become. We look abjectly to others for support. It is a sin to demean ourselves. But it is also a sin to think too highly of ourselves. We must not become dependent on others. European children are taught to be independent from a young age. They consider it below their dignity to live off their parents' money. I've heard a story about President Hoover's son. True or false, this is how it goes.

When Hoover became president of America, the wealthiest country in the world, his thirteen-year-old son was working on a construction site as a mason's assistant. The boy is said to have fallen off the building and died. Sorrowful though Hoover was, he said, 'My son died teaching the country the importance of independence and the dignity of labour.'

Independence is the foundation of education in the West. It allows you to hold your head up. Dependence forces you to hang your head. Never accept anything unless you have worked for it and never give anything unless someone has worked for it. Supporting a man who does not work is an insult to God; an insult to the limbs and brains given to us. In Russia, people are taught the virtues of independence, self-respect and labour.

An American psychologist visited Russia recently to study the condition of the people in view of the great transformation that had taken place in their lives. He had carried gifts like fountain pens, chocolates and pocketknives for Russian workers. When he visited their homes and offered them the gifts, not a single hand came forward to accept them. 'Please take them,' the American said. 'They are given with love.'

The workers said, 'We only take the rewards of our labour. Even a gift given with love might inject laziness, dependence or a sense of obligation in us. We are very careful not to allow these weaknesses to enter our system.'

The American psychologist was stunned. This kind of thinking was revolutionary. In Russia, where lakhs of labourers would have been only too happy to receive gifts not so long ago, not a single hand had come forward to receive his gifts. This was true independence. This was humanity at its shining best. This was devotion to labour.

Work ennobles our spirit. To take something for nothing lowers it. The day Indian society understands this will go down as a golden day. This is the education we must give at home and at school. Real dharma lies in encouraging people to work. The man who begs out of laziness and the man who luxuriates in bed because he is wealthy are both leeches. Both live off other people's labour. Both are parasites feeding off society. The labourer who toils under the sun, the sweeper who cleans our roads, the scavenger who takes away our night soil, the skinner who skins animal carcasses, the cobbler who makes our shoes, they are all purer and more worthy than those who live off others. Produce something—ideas, food, a clean environment. Create joy, beauty, anything that benefits humanity. Only then do you earn the right to live. Only a nation that is built on social welfare and social growth, where socially beneficial work is worshipped, will attain glory. The rest will be reduced to beggary.

'My mother taught me the value of independence and self-respect. "To be helpless and abject is death to a human being," she said. She taught me not to take from others but to give instead.'

Fourteenth Night

Shrikhand Vadis

My mother was an expert at making shrikhand vadis. Her syrup never crystallized and the vadis always turned out soft but snappy. The women in the neighbourhood often asked her to make some for them. Aai was always happy to do so. Being of use to others was her greatest joy.

Once, Parvatibai's daughter Venu had come home on a visit. Aai and Parvatibai were good friends. Whenever Venu dropped in to see us, Aai would ask her to sing. Once Venu came over when Aai had scolded me. Venu had wiped away my tears that day. She was like an elder sister to me.

One day, Parvatibai said to Aai, 'Venu is going back to her in-laws day after tomorrow. I want to send shrikhand vadis with her. Could you come over and make them for me tomorrow evening? They are for her in-laws, so I want them to be perfect.'

'Of course I'll come,' Aai said. 'But why is Venu going back so soon? I thought she'd stay till Sankranti. She is such a lovely person to have around. She has sung so often for me.'

'Her in-laws have written, asking us to send her back,' Parvatibai said. 'I'm happy she came at all, even if it was for only a few days. You know Krishni. She's been married two years, but her in-laws haven't let her come home even for a day. Her mother weeps over it. Venu is better off. So you'll come tomorrow, won't you? I'll send Venu to fetch you.'

Aai put kumkum on her forehead and Parvatibai left. Aai wasn't feeling too well the following day. She managed somehow to clear up after lunch and lay down. 'Are you not well, Aai?' I asked.

'I have a terrible body ache. Can you massage it for me please?' When I touched her forehead I realized she had fever. She also had a severe headache.

I was out playing while Aai rested when Venu came over. 'I've come to fetch you, aunty,' she said in her sweet voice. 'My mother is waiting for you.'

'Oh dear, I dozed off, did I?' Aai said upon hearing Venu's voice. 'I hadn't forgotten, mind you! I was about to come over. Let's go.'

Aai went to Venu's house and made vadis, chatting all the while. When I came home from playing, Aai wasn't there. I looked everywhere. Then I went over to Venu's place. Venu said, 'Are you looking for your mother, Shyam? Come. She's making vadis for me. I'm going to my in-laws tomorrow.'

'Who will console me when Aai scolds me now?' I asked. 'Who will take my side?'

Venu saw that I was saddened by her departure. She said, 'Come, I'll powder the saffron and you can peel the cardamoms.'

Aai noticed me and said, 'Why are you here, Shyam?' I guessed from her tone what she suspected.

'Not for the vadis!' I answered quickly. 'Venutai, do you think I'm greedy? You gave me something to eat the other day. But I hadn't asked for it, had I?'

'Of course you hadn't, Shyam. You're a good boy. Aunty, please don't scold him.'

Aai looked hurt. 'Venu, don't you think I love him? I scold him for his own good. I don't want people to criticize him! Of course he's a good boy. But I want him to be better. Parvatibai, the syrup is done. See, the drop I put in the water has come together.'

The hung curd was mixed into the syrup and poured into a plate. Aai used a banana leaf to pat it down so she wouldn't burn her hands. When the mix had cooled a little, she cut it into diamonds. 'Parvatibai, remove the vadis from the plate after a while. I'll take your leave now, shall I?' she said.

'Can you wait a bit and see the vadis through to the end, please?' Venu said. Aai couldn't refuse her. After some time, she used a spatula to lift the vadis off the plate. They looked perfect. Parvatibai stored them in a jar. Venu put one vadi

91

before God as an offering and gave one to me. Parvatibai said, 'Shyam, eat the scrapings off the plate. They're all yours.' I attacked the plate like a warrior and devoured the scrapings. Parvatibai gave Aai a few vadis and put kumkum on her forehead. Aai left, but I stayed back.

Venu said, 'Shyam, the button on your shirt is loose. Take off your shirt. I'll fix it for you.' I gave her my shirt. She pulled out her *fanere*. Fanere is the word we use in the Konkan for the pouch women use to keep their needle and thread in. Venutai fixed my button and darned a little tear she had noticed in the shirt. I put my shirt back on. Venutai said, 'Come, let's pick gulbakshi flowers for you to take home.'

We picked the flowers and carried them home. Venutai came with me. 'Aunty,' she called out. But there was no answer. *Could Aai have gone to the well or the cowshed?* we wondered. We went in and found her in bed. 'What is the matter, aunty?' Venu asked. 'Aren't you feeling well? Do you think you sat too long at the stove?'

Venu touched Aai's forehead and felt a stab of heat. 'Aunty, you have very high fever.'

'She hasn't been well since the afternoon,' I said. 'She was resting and I was massaging her legs.'

'Oh dear. I didn't know that. Was that why you were lying down when I came to call you? And you didn't say a word about it. You shouldn't have come and sat by the stove when you were unwell.'

Aai brushed off Venutai's concerns. 'Venu, the fever had come down by then. It was nothing more than a little body ache. Nothing more. Shyam, will you light the lamp please? Dusk has fallen.' I lit the lamp, held it first before God and then the tulsi plant. When I came back, Venu was nearly in tears. 'Aunty, your fever went up again because of the vadis. Making them wasn't more important than your health. My mother would have made them her way.'

Aai lovingly responded, 'A little fever is nothing. Why fuss over such things? Don't take it to heart. I'll sweat it out after a while and I'll be fine. Better go home now, Venu. Your mother must be waiting for you.'

Venutai refused to go. She continued sitting with Aai. 'Venutai, will you string these flowers? Aai won't be able to,' I said. Venutai wove the flowers into a garland. Then again, she said, 'Aunty, you've got a fever because of me.'

'Don't be silly, Venu,' Aai said. 'You are like family. Like Chandra to me. If your mother's vadis hadn't turned out well, your in-laws would have criticized her. Wouldn't that have upset you? You'd have wept to hear them say nasty things. It would have upset me too. That's why I came. Parvatibai and I are friends. Shouldn't one bear a little pain for a friend's daughter? You think of Shyam as your own family, don't you? And I think of you as mine. It made me very happy to do what I did. I'd never have forgiven myself if I hadn't made those vadis. Now please go home. I'll come over in the morning. I'll have sweated out my fever by then.'

Venu hugged me.

'Come with me, Shyam,' she said. 'My mother has made chawli bean curry. Bring some home. Then aunty will only need to cook rice. Or shall I make the rice for you?'

'No no. Shyam will do that,' Aai said. 'Just send the beans. That's more than enough.' But Venu would have none of it. She lit the fire, washed the rice and put the water on the boil and left only after she had put the rice in. I went with her. When I came back with the beans, I hugged Aai. My eyes were wet. 'What's the matter, Shyam?' she asked.

I told her what Venutai had said: 'Shyam, your mother is a great human being. You must always listen to her. You are fortunate to have a mother like her.' She had stroked my back, bringing tears to my eyes.

'Go, my pet,' Aai said softly. 'Take the rice off the fire if it's done, or it will stick to the bottom.'

I took the rice off the fire. The next day, Venutai left for her marital home. We were sad to see her go.

'Today, neither Venutai's mother nor mine are alive. But I still remember those vadis. Venutai is also gone. But I still remember her love. Love is immortal. People die, but their virtues shine on forever.'

Fifteenth Night

Raghupati Raghav Rajaram

'I was very pious as a young boy. I had heard many holy books being read aloud. The seed of devotion sown in my heart had grown by the day. My schoolmates would gather in our house to hear me tell stories about gods, saints and sages. I had built a small toy temple, decorating its arch with tinfoil. The beautiful Shaligram* I had placed in it seemed to glow with an inner light. King Chandrahasa used to keep

---

* *This is an oval-shaped black stone worshipped by some Hindus as a representation of Vishnu. Shaligrams are found on the beds and banks of rivers, in particular the Gandaki River in Nepal. They are fossils of sea-living creatures called ammonites, which became extinct some 65 million years ago. A myth about Vishnu tells us that he was once responsible for betraying his greatest devotee Vrinda because of which she cursed him saying he would become a stone. Vishnu took the form of Shaligram. The fossilized markings on Shaligrams are seen as the four symbols of Vishnu—shankh, chakra, gada, padma.*

a Shaligram permanently in his mouth. I wished I too could do that.

'Come Sunday, my schoolmates and I would sing bhajans together and sometimes perform *keertan*s. We didn't have a mridangam. But there were empty cans in the kitchen. We would pick up one and beat it loudly to accompany our singing. The entire neighbourhood echoed with our voices.

Flowers for Vithoba / Children sing his praise.
Garlands for Vithoba / Glorious are his ways.

'We danced as we sang. Besides bhajans, we sang invocations that we had learnt from *Bhakti Vijay*. We sang them with folded hands.

'I still remember those songs. I might experience the same deep emotion even today if I sang them. We were just boys then. I was in the fifth, probably about eleven years old. But my devotion was greater then, than it is now. There were no doubts, no questions in my mind; only simple, sweet, sentimental devotion. I would observe waterless fasts and repeat god's name the stipulated number of times. I would have baths as required by our holy texts. One story tells us if we pull our shendi forward from the right side of the head after our bath and squeeze it, the water turns to nectar. There's another story about a prince who dies. A priest revives him by pulling his shendi forward from the right side of his head and squeezing the water into the prince's mouth. I used to believe the story. When somebody in our village died, I said to Aai, "I'll get up early tomorrow morning, have my bath and squeeze the water from my shendi in the dead man's mouth. He'll come alive then, won't he?"

'Aai laughed and said, "You're mad."

'I'm not sure whether the naive faith I had back then was better or worse than the doubts I have today. But let us forget all that. My story this evening is about something else altogether.'

Holy books used to be read aloud in the Ganesh temple every day during the four months of monsoon. Each year, a different scholar would come to stay in the village for this duration. The reading would begin at around four or four-thirty in the afternoon. We were staying at Aai's father's place then and the temple was right across the road from there. If the reading was loud enough, we could hear it in the house. Some people attended the reading every day, while others went only when they could spare the time.

Aai went one Sunday. She never stayed till the end. She would listen for a while, do her obeisance to God and come right back. But while she was away, there were no adults in the house. We had planned to sing bhajans. We picked up empty cans from the kitchen and a pair of cymbals. Soon we were singing and dancing. The cans sounded lovely to our ears. Most sounds are music to children. Besides, it was such fun beating the cans. But what was a source of joy to us was a source of pain to older people.

Shriram Jayaram Jayjay Ram
Our voices echo aloud.
We are drunk, we are drunk,
Drunk on the love of God.

People in the temple couldn't hear a word of what was being read because of our din. It drowned the scholar's voice. 'Just listen to those wretches,' someone said. Another said, 'Shyam is behind this nonsense. He should know there's a sacred reading going on here.' A third said, 'How can his people put up with this? Shouldn't they stop it?' A fourth said, 'Children are pampered silly these days.' While such things were being said about us, we continued singing. We were oblivious to all else, you see.

The devotees called for the *gurav*, the man appointed to look after the temple.

'Go to Shyam's house and tell him to stop the noise.' But Aai had already left, deeply hurt by what people had been saying. We didn't notice her coming in. She stood watching us for a while. Finally she shouted, 'Shyam!' I could hear the anger in her voice. I was startled. We stopped singing. The tin cans fell silent. The cymbals became dumb.

'Yes, Aai?' I said.

'Aren't you ashamed to create this racket?' She sounded really angry.

'Why do you call it a racket, Aai? We are singing bhajans before our god. Look at this Shaligram that you gave me. Look at the crown I have made for him. Why are you angry?' I tugged at her pallu, appealing to her. Just then Bhiku Gurav arrived from the temple. 'Shyam, stop this commotion. Nobody can hear a thing in the temple because of your shouting.'

One of my friends said, 'Do what you like. We won't stop. If someone's reading holy books, we are singing holy songs.'

Aai said quietly, 'Shyam, can't you sing more softly? Why do you need these cans and cymbals? You don't have to be loud to catch God's attention. It's not a bhajan if it troubles others.'

'But even saints and sages used to play the cymbals when they sang bhajans,' I said.

'But they didn't do it to deliberately trouble others. They would have stopped singing if it had disturbed others. Shyam, what do you love more? God's name or beating cans?'

'Beating a can makes singing more exciting. Singing without it makes it a bore,' I protested.

'You can clap softly to keep the beat. Surely that is enough,' Aai said. 'Don't be stubborn now. It isn't much of a prayer if it disturbs others. My puja should never create a problem for another person's puja. My prayer should never disturb another's prayer. If you sang softly, you would still be doing what you want to do, while the people in the temple will be able to enjoy doing what they want to do. Bhiku, you can go. The boys won't make a sound from hereon.' Bhiku Gurav left and Aai went inside the house.

An argument broke out among us.

'These grown-ups think no end of themselves. Why should they ask us to stop? I'm sure God prefers our bhajans to their readings. The people who are listening to the readings now will gossip maliciously the minute they're out of the temple.' We were uncertain about what to do next. Finally I said, 'Perhaps we were wrong. Let's sing softly and clap to keep the beat. We don't have to bang loudly on the cans.'

'Shyam, you're a ninny. I don't like it,' Bapu said.

'Why am I a ninny? We should be proud to think and do what is right. What is so brave about doing something mindlessly?'

My friends were angry with me. They went away in a huff. Banging on cans was more important to them than taking Ram's name. I was left alone. Was I a ninny? I couldn't understand why they had called me that. I sat before God, weeping and singing, 'Raghupati Raghav Rajaram'.

'My friends abandoned me on that day. I was still a boy then. My friends may abandon me again today when I'm a grown man. I will be alone again. But Rabindranath Tagore has said, "You will have to walk alone. Go. Pick up your lantern and walk. The wind of public criticism will blow out the flame. Light it again and keep going. You will have to walk alone."*

---

* *This seems to be Sane Guruji's personal interpretation of 'Ekla Chalo Re'.*

Sixteenth Night

The Runaway Pilgrim

'There is a sweet legend about rivers. It is said that during Simhastha, when the planet Jupiter is in the house of Leo, the Ganga comes to meet the Godavari in Nashik; and during Kanyagat, when Jupiter is in the house of Virgo, the Ganga comes to meet the Krishna in Wai. Festivals are held in both pilgrim centres to mark these rare events. In India, we have endowed nature with feelings. Nature is like a member of the human family. Rivers recognize they are one and come to meet each other. Why should human beings not recognize their oneness? Look how divided we are in our daily dealings. This man is a Gujarati, that one is a Punjabi, this one is a Maharashtrian, that one is a Bengali and that other one is a foreigner. Surely we can be one while still preserving our distinctness. The Ganga merges with the sea, but retains her own being too. Our great forefathers have taught us to see unity in diversity.'

It was the year of Kanyagat. Thousands of pilgrims were flocking to Wai. Even though our village was very far from Wai, many villagers were preparing to go there by bullock cart. One of Aai's uncles, his wife and his friends were also going. Nearly a dozen carts were to leave together, stopping over at Khed and Chiplun on the way. They would camp by a stream at night, cook a simple meal of rice and pithla and set off again in the morning. Travelling by bullock cart is a wonderful experience. A car is faster, but it doesn't let you spend time amidst nature, gazing upon its beauty. Being in the lap of nature is as joyful as lying in your mother's lap, caressed by her hands. So why be miserly with the time you spend with nature?

Nights are particularly magical when you're travelling by bullock cart. Everywhere around you is silence. The moon and stars in the sky peep through the branches of the trees. And from far away comes the sweet sound of cattle bells nudging its way through the silence. Suddenly a tiger appears in your path. His eyes are like fire. You shout and make loud noises till he retreats into the jungle. Joy spiked with fear makes a journey by bullock cart thrilling.

As you know, I was very religious as a boy. I wanted desperately to go with Aai's uncle to Wai. I pestered Aai about it. 'Please let me go. I promise not to throw tantrums. I won't go into the deep. I'll obey Uncle. Tell Bhau I want to go. He won't say no. I've taken all the holy dips recommended in the sacred books. Only the Ganga is left. Don't you want your son to gain such a merit?'

Aai said, 'Shyam, why go now? You can have your Ganga-snan when you grow up. We are poor. We'll need to contribute five or six rupees for you to go. Where will we get that money from, pet? Obeying your parents is like being with the Ganga and Krishna. Remember Pundalik's story? He was massaging his parents' tired legs when God came to his door. But he didn't rise to greet Him, did he?'

'But Aai, Dhruv left his parents and went away. The holy books have both kinds of stories. The Satyanarayan katha says if you have a good thought, act on it immediately. Don't look for a better time. Let me go, Aai. If you talk to Uncle, he'll take me for free. He's hardly going to ask you for money.'

'If he doesn't take money that would be because of his generosity. But should we be shameless enough to expect to be taken free? You shouldn't be a burden on others. You can't take a ride on someone else's back to pray. Flowers plucked from another's garden shouldn't be offered to God. Offer to God what you have earned with your own work. If you want to go to Wai, go on foot. Are you tough enough for that?'

'I'll get tired, Aai,' I said. 'I could walk a couple of miles. But what after that? The carts will move on. What will I do for company then? I'll be scared. If I walk alongside the carts, people sitting in them will feel embarrassed.

They will insist I ride with them. So I'll have to make sure they don't see me while I see them and feel safe in their company. The distance to Wai is 20 or 25 miles from here. How can I walk so far?'

'So when you spoke of Dhruv, it was only big talk, wasn't it? Dhruv wasn't afraid. He believed the snakes and tigers would show him the way, not eat him. If he grew tired and fell asleep and the sun shone on his face, the cobra would spread its hood over him. If he felt thirsty, birds would carry water in their beaks for him. If he felt hungry, mothers would feed him their milk. Everybody is a friend and a helper when you set off to meet God. Do you have Dhruv's faith? Do you have his devotion? Why are you crying now, silly boy? We are small people. And poor. You are still very young. Don't be obstinate.'

I felt terrible. The pilgrims were going to leave at daybreak. I toyed with the idea of following them without being seen. Many doubts troubled me. What would I do when I felt tired and hungry? Why, I could fill my stomach with water. Or pick and eat the tender leaves from trees. If goats could do that, why couldn't I? I decided to eat tamarind and *karvanda* leaves to stave off hunger. I don't know when I fell asleep while these thoughts ran through my head. When I woke up, the carts had already left. It was Saturday. I had a half-day of school. I had a quick bath, did my puja and surya namaskars, watered the tulsi plant, picked up my slate and satchel and set off.

Aai said, 'What's the rush? I'm making pangis. Have one and go. Banya and Bapu haven't left yet. Wait a while.'

'I don't want any pangi-shangi,' I said angrily. 'You want me to eat, but you won't let me go to Wai. I am hungry for Wai, not for food. I'm going to school.'

Aai was angry too.

'Ask for food again and see if I give you any. You want everything to go your way. You should have been born in a king's palace, not in a beggar's hut. Here I am making a good, nutritious pangi for you and you're turning your nose up at it. So don't eat. Not now, not later. Let me see how long you can starve. Big talk . . . "I'm not hungry for food!" Shyam, come back and listen to your mother!'

But I was in no mood to listen to her. I walked away quickly. The boys had not left for school yet, so I didn't meet anybody on the way. I made a stop at the Ganapati temple and prayed to God, 'God, allow my plan to succeed. Help me.' The school was empty. Not a single boy had arrived yet. It hadn't even been opened. I set my satchel down on the verandah and left. I walked very fast to make sure nobody saw me. Soon I had left the village behind. I crossed the river and stood at the junction where three roads met. One road led to Dapoli and the other to Khed. I took the second road. The carts carrying the pilgrims were miles ahead. How was an eleven-year-old boy to catch up with them? I felt confused. The sun had come up and it was getting hot. I began to feel tired. I wanted to cry. Turning back would be too shameful. Even if I did return to the village, where would I go? And if I didn't, where would I find shelter in the jungle and for how long could I stay?

I turned back. My feet carried me towards the village automatically. Tears streamed down my cheeks, but dried instantly under the sun. It was as though the sun's rays were wiping them away. The day had advanced. The sun was directly overhead. I was bathed in sweat. My stomach had been empty since the morning. I reached the outskirts of Palgad, but felt too ashamed to enter. My pride told me, 'Don't go in. Don't go back home.' But my stomach said, 'Go home. Why let your ego stand between you and your parents? Ego and love don't go together. The ego is an offence against love.'

I still didn't have the courage to enter the village. I entered a temple near the river outside the village. It was pitch-dark behind the idol. That's where I hid. But for how long could I remain there while hunger gnawed at my stomach? Finally I swallowed my pride and stepped out. I was walking along the village road now. I could see houses. My head was bent. My feet were burning. My heart was aflame with shame. My eyes were streaming with tears. The tears blurred my sight. Suddenly someone grabbed my wrist. 'Where have you been? We've been searching high and low for you. The noose was round our necks.' It was my uncle. My uncles, my father, the neighbours . . . they had all been out looking for me. They realized I was missing when my friends from school brought my slate and satchel home. The headmaster had beaten me the previous day over my untidy Modi script. He thought I had run away because I was scared of another beating. The headmaster was a violent man. He kept a pile of *nigadi* twigs at hand to thrash students with. He whipped us like cattle. Sometimes he hit us on the knuckles with the iron shaft of an umbrella. He used to smoke ganja and come to school on a high. We prayed to God to get him transferred. Now he was afraid I had run away because of the thrashing he had given me. What if I had jumped into a well and died? When my father went to ask about me after school got over, the boys told him about the thrashing. Bhau was convinced that was the reason I had run away. Neighbours said, 'The headmaster shouldn't have beaten Shyam so much. Where could he have gone? Suppose something untoward has happened? God forbid.' Bhau gave the headmaster a large piece of his mind.

The headmaster said, 'I will never lay a finger on your son again. Does that satisfy you? I beat children only to help them improve. What do I gain from beating them? I will never touch your son again, Bhaurao.'

'That's fine as far as the future goes,' Bhau said. 'But where is he right now?'

Nobody at home had eaten anything. Aai had a feeling I had run away to go to Wai, but didn't mention it to anybody. She couldn't quite believe it herself. Uncle had my arm in a tight grip as we walked back home. My schoolmates had come out to watch the fun, as they would have done if a thief had been caught. Bhau shouted at them. 'Go back home. This is not a circus for you to watch.'

Father didn't scold me. He didn't say a single word. This wasn't the time for scolding. I was exhausted. I threw myself on the bed as soon as I got home. Bhau said to me afterwards, 'Get up, my son. The headmaster has promised not to beat you again. But even if he does, that's no reason to run away. When we were at school, the punishments were worse. They would hang us up by our feet, burn chillies under our noses and beat us with canes. You mustn't let beatings scare you. A teacher is supposed to beat children. What sort of a teacher would he be if he didn't? Come on, get up now. Wash your face. It's as red as a kokum fruit.' He called out to Aai to serve me lunch.

I got up, washed my hands, feet and face. I was feeling a little relieved that my running away had been attributed to the headmaster. I was happy that he would not beat me again; and if he beat the other boys, he would make the thrashing less severe. I had done my classmates a great favour by running away. They should thank me for it. When Bajirao ran away, the Marathas lost their independence. When Shyam ran away, his classmates won theirs, at least from the rule of one colonial monster. And all without Shyam knowing what he was doing.

Only three people knew why I had run away—God, Aai and I. I went back to sleep after lunch. I was exhausted from the walking and the heat. I was still sleeping when dusk fell. It was lamp-lighting time. Aai came to sit by me. She touched my forehead, then called out to me. I opened my eyes. She stroked my face and asked in a voice full of love, 'Don't you feel well? Is your body hurting? You didn't listen to me, did you?' Aai began to massage my body. I put my head in her lap and wept. When I managed to control my tears, I said, 'Are you angry with me for that? I didn't run away because the teacher hit me. You hit me sometimes too. I don't run away then. Bhau thought that was the reason why I ran away. But the reason was what you said yesterday, "If you want to go, go on foot. Are you tough enough for that?" I was trying to test my strength. But I saw the test was beyond me. Your snotty Shyam was nowhere close to Dhruv. Please don't be upset with me. I tend to overreact. I am stubborn. I want to do everything that comes to mind. When I fail, I cry as I'm doing now. Are you upset with me? Please say you're not.'

Aai wiped my eyes, stroked my face and said, 'Why would I be angry, Shyam? I was neither angry nor sad that you had run away. I was just very worried. You are still young. I wept thinking of all the horrible things that could happen to you. I also felt sorry for saying what I did yesterday. But although I was worried and didn't think you should have run away, I was not upset over the reason why you had done it. You didn't run away for a bad reason. The other day I heard of a boy from the village who ran away to join a drama troupe. You didn't run away for that kind of thing. You ran away for God. You wanted to take a dip in the Ganga. How could I be angry with you for that? I would have been proud to announce to the world, "My Shyam ran away for God." So I want you to keep in mind what I'm going to tell you now. Don't ever run away to steal or to tell tales. Don't run away to join bad company. Don't run away out of fear. Run away for God by all means. All our saints did that. I might even pray, let my son run away for God.'

Seventeenth Night

A Lesson in Self-Reliance

Although I had read many sacred texts when I was young, I didn't know any Sanskrit hymns. I only knew a few minor ones, but I had not learnt the incomparably beautiful epic hymn in praise of Lord Ram, the *Ramaraksha*. I had read the *Vishnusahastranamam* several times in my father's book. That is how I had learnt it by heart. But we didn't have a copy of the *Ramaraksha*. My father knew it but hadn't taught me. As a boy I was a great devotee of Ram, so it saddened me not to know this well-known song in his praise.

Our neighbour Bhaskar had a copy of the *Ramaraksha*. He used to memorize one or two verses of it every day. He would come over to our place in the evenings and recite them to us. This made me feel ashamed of myself and angry with Bhaskar. We get angry when our ego is hurt. We are constantly comparing ourselves with others. If we find that we are in any way less than them, we are hurt. When a short man sees a tall man, he hates him. We are sad if someone else is cleverer than us. I used to feel very jealous of Bhaskar because he knew the *Ramaraksha*. I was sure he came over when we were reciting our tables and shlokas to taunt me with his recitation of the *Ramaraksha*.

One day he said to me, 'I have another eight or ten verses left to memorize. Then I'll know the whole of the *Ramaraksha* by heart. You don't know it, do you?'

I lost my temper then and charged at him.

'Bhashya, don't you dare come here to tease me again,' I shouted. 'We know what you know. Don't show off. You have the book. If I had a copy, I would have learnt the whole *Ramaraksha* by heart before you. Big-head! Get out. Don't come back or I'll hit you.'

When Aai heard me shout, she came out to see what was going on. She asked Bhaskar, 'What happened? Did Shyam hit you?'

Bhaskar said, 'Aunty, I only said I will know the *Ramaraksha* by heart in five or six days, and he flew at me. He said get out or I'll hit you.'

'Did you, Shyam? Is that how you talk to neighbours? You'll want to run over to his place before he even thinks of coming here.'

I replied, seething with anger, 'He only comes here to tease me. "You don't know the *Ramaraksha*, do you?" he taunted. Ask him if he didn't. He's acting innocent now . . . Doesn't tell you what he said . . . Liar.'

'All he said was he knew the *Ramaraksha* and you didn't. How is that teasing? He only spoke the truth. You're angry because he pointed out something that you lacked. Instead, why not try and overcome that lack? Bhaskar teases you because he feels that will make you learn the *Ramaraksha*. You read *Ram Vijay* and *Hari Vijay* all the time. Why don't you learn the *Ramaraksha*?' Aai looked me straight in the eye, waiting for an answer.

'Because Bhau won't teach me, and I don't have a copy of the book.'

'Why don't you borrow Bhaskar's copy when he isn't using it? Or borrow it for a day and copy the whole thing down for yourself?' Aai left the room with that.

Bhaskar went back home and I began to make my plans. I decided to make my own copy of the *Ramaraksha*. I got hold of some blank sheets of paper and stitched them up into a notebook. I waited for Sunday to dawn. On Sunday, I went over to Bhaskar's place first thing in the morning. I didn't think he would lend me his *Ramaraksha*. So I went to his mother and said to her sweetly, 'Bhimatai, can you please ask Bhaskar to lend me his copy of the *Ramaraksha* for the day? I want to make a copy for myself and learn it by heart. It's a holiday today, so I can spend the whole day writing it out.'

Bhimatai called out to Bhaskar.

'Shyam has come to borrow your copy of the *Ramaraksha*. Give it to him, please. He's not going to tear it. Shyam, you won't stain the book with ink, will you? Bhaskar, give him the book, there's a good boy.'

But Bhaskar was adamant.

'I won't give it to him. It's my holiday too and I want to learn the remaining verses today. I can't do that if I give him the book.'

Bhimatai was angered by this. 'So today's the only day you can learn the remaining verses? Can't you do it tomorrow or the day after? Shyam is our neighbour, isn't he? Why are you being difficult with him? Give him the book or I'll . . .' Bhaskar knew Bhimatai's temper very well. He marched away angrily and brought me the book.

I took the book home. I needed peace to do the work. So I carried all the stuff, my notebook, inkwell and pen to the cowshed. The cattle were out grazing. I sat there and started copying the book. I had finished most of it by lunchtime. After lunch, I returned to the work and soon it was done. What a sense of achievement I felt. I had copied a whole book with my own hand. This is how books were produced in those days. There were many handwritten books at my grandparents' place. They were written in a bold, beautiful hand with not a single scratch or ink stain on them. This was the practice around the world. Those who had perfect handwriting were highly respected. There were no printing presses in those days. There was a shortage of books. The poet Moropant tells us in his autobiography that he would order books from Kashi, copy them out carefully and return them safely to the sender. Thousands of manuscripts were kept in the ashrams of saints for the public to read. Today you find printing presses at every corner and books in abundance. And yet the level of our knowledge is abysmal. Human heads are still pretty empty. Life has not become noticeably better or more civilized. We have not become more humane, honest and dutiful, nor are we more loving or more ready to make sacrifices. But enough of that.

I was truly happy that day. When I took Bhaskar's book back, Bhimatai said, 'Don't tell me you've already finished copying it, Shyam!'

'I have. See my notebook. I wrote throughout the day so Bhaskar could learn his verses in the evening.'

'Your handwriting isn't half bad. Now start memorizing it. Then Bhaskar won't have a chance to tease you.'

All I did the rest of the day was read the *Ramaraksha*. I was determined to learn it by heart within a week. I would surprise Bhau with it the following Sunday. God alone knows how many times I read my book that week. I would go to it the moment I had even the smallest amount of time to spare. I did not know Sanskrit, but I could still get the gist of what the verses were saying. I felt very happy learning them by heart.

At last it was Sunday again. I had memorized the whole of the *Ramaraksha*. I waited impatiently for Bhau to return home so I could recite it to him. Evening fell and the lamps were lit. Stars twinkled brightly in the sky. I was in the yard reciting the *Ramaraksha* to myself when Bhau came home, washed his hands, feet and face, and went indoors. 'So, Shyam, have you recited your tables and your shlokas?' he asked.

I said in an excited rush, 'Yes, all that's done. Will you hear me recite the *Ramaraksha* now?'

'When did you learn that? Who taught you?' he asked in great surprise.

'I copied it out from Bhaskar's book and learnt it by myself.'

Looking very pleased, he said, 'Let me see your copy.'

I handed over my notebook to him. I had drawn very neat lines and margins. There wasn't a single ink stain anywhere, but my handwriting was a little cramped and uneven.

Bhau said, 'Not bad. Your handwriting is legible. But you should make your letters longer, not squat like this. Now let's hear you recite it.' I recited the *Ramaraksha* without faltering once. Bhau patted my back. I have no words to describe what that meant to me!

When father went out after dinner, I went in to Aai to show her my notebook. 'I didn't show it to you earlier because I was angry with you,' I said. My voice was warm with love now.

'I knew you had finished copying it. I was eager to see your handwriting. But I wanted you to show it to me yourself. I knew you would. You should have shown it to me last Sunday. When you do something good, shouldn't you show it to your mother? She tells you off if you do something wrong. But when you do something right, nobody in the world is as happy as she is. How proud she feels to see her son growing into a responsible human being. You prevented me from feeling that joy and pride for eight days. Every day I would think Shyam will show me his notebook today and I will hug him. But you didn't. You were angry with your mother. But let's forget that. The point is that you've learnt the *Ramaraksha* by heart. Could you have done it if you'd sat around moping over not having the book? Shyam . . . we are blessed by God with strong legs, arms and eyes. We should use them to stand on our own feet. Everything is possible if you have the brains and the will. Working hard as you did helps you grow. Depending on others doesn't. But remember one thing. Never look down on someone who knows less than you. Don't taunt them about their weakness. Give them what you have and try to bring them up to your level.'

Aai now looked through my notebook. She was overjoyed. 'You could put a picture of Sri Ram on the first page. Then your *Ramaraksha* book would be complete. The bales of cloth Mohanya Marwadi gets have pictures of deities stuck on them. You could ask him for a picture of Ram and stick it here. God loves you today, Shyam. Because you copied out this song in His praise with your own hand and learnt it by heart.'

Eighteenth Night

Vegetable without Salt

Raja and Ram were at the river, sitting on a large boulder, when Raja said, 'You know what, Ram, I don't feel like moving from here. Look at this river and all these trees and peacocks. They fill my heart with joy. But the greatest joy is being together with you and listening to Shyam's stories. I love them.'

Ram said, 'Are they stories or are they sermons? Lectures or memories? It's difficult to say what they are. But they are a joy to listen to and they are inspiring.'

Raja said, 'Shyam pours his truest feelings into them. There is not a shred of falseness in them. That's what makes them so sweet.'

'But falseness is what people want,' Ram said. 'These days, that is what they adore. A coin made of pure silver doesn't work in the market. You need to add a baser metal to it for it to ring true and be accepted as currency in the market.'

'I've just thought of an idea. May I share it with you?' Raja asked. 'But promise not to laugh.'

'I promise. Tell me. Why should I laugh at an idea that comes from your heart?'

'Why not have Shyam's memories published? Children would love to read them. They would be very useful for parents too. They are also full of the Konkan culture. What a wonderful picture we get of it from his stories.'

'Shyam won't like that. He isn't very confident about how good they are. Who would want to read these stories, he will ask. People want to read thrilling tales like Laila-Majnu, he will say.'

Even as they were discussing the idea, the bell rang for prayers. The friends got up to go to the ashram. Shyam was waiting for them. When he saw them coming, he asked, 'Why didn't you call me today? Why did you go by yourselves?'

'You were busy reading,' Raja said. 'You work so hard all day . . . It's a pity to disturb you when you've found a little time to read.'

'I don't care as much for reading books,' Shyam replied, 'as I do for reading nature in all her manifestations. It's more important for me to read people and their hearts to try and understand their joys and sorrows.'

'Shyam, you can afford to say that because you have already read so many books,' said Raja. 'You need knowledge to be able to read nature too. Poets describe the joys of a farmer's life. But the farmer who lives that life doesn't have the vision to see it.'

Just then the second bell rang. Everybody sat down for prayers. As was the custom, Shyam began his story as soon as the prayers came to an end. 'Friends, you learn more by example than by reading books or listening to lectures. Action speaks louder than words. It is also more effective than words. How we eat is also part of our culture. My father always said, "Keep your eyes on your plate when you eat. Don't ask for something that you still have on your plate. When the server comes to serve, you will automatically get what you want. Don't be greedy. Don't let a single grain of rice fall outside your plate and eat everything that's on it. Don't ever criticize the food you've been served. If you find a hair or something similar in your food, don't hold it up for all to see. It makes people feel disgusted. Instead, remove it quietly. But if what you find is poisonous, speak out. At the end of a meal, your plate should be shining clean."

'My father would practise all that he preached. I have seen many people eat, but I have never seen anyone leave behind a plate as clean as my father's. It is so spotless you can't believe there was ever any food on it. Not a grain of rice or anything else ever fell outside his plate. If he spotted bits of rice around my plate, he would get angry. "There's enough there to fill one of Mathuri's hens. Clean it all up."

'You never heard Bhau say things like, "This isn't up to the mark" or "That isn't tasty." He seemed to find everything tasty. His favourite phrase was "It's good enough for a king." If he was asked, "How have the vegetables turned out?" he would promptly say, "Good enough for a king." He had no fussy likes and dislikes in food.

'I still remember one particular incident quite vividly.'

It was Bhau's custom to go to the temple after he finished his puja at home. That was the signal for us to lay the plates for lunch. We would serve everything else before he came back except for the rice. When we saw him coming, we would call out, 'Bhau's here, Aai. Bhau's here. Serve the rice.' Bhau would bring back holy water from the temple. We would have that and then settle down to lunch.

That day, Aai had made a dish from sweet potato greens. She used to make tasty dishes from the leaves of all kinds of vegetables like pumpkins and ladies' fingers. She would say, 'Anything can be made to taste good if it's tempered with a couple of spices and the right amount of salt and chilli powder are added.' She was right, of course, because whatever she made did indeed taste good. The culinary deity seemed to dwell in her fingers. She would pour her heart and soul into everything she made.

However, that day was a little different. There was no salt in the vegetable dish she had made. With all the work she had to do, she had simply forgotten to put it in. Bhau didn't mention it, so we didn't either. Bhau's self-control was unbelievable. Every time Aai offered him another helping of the vegetable, he would say, 'This is excellent.' He neither added the salt that was served on his plate nor asked for any. Aai said to me, 'Don't you like the dish? You're not eating it the way you normally do.' Before I could answer, Bhau cut in with, 'Now that he has started learning English at school, he's not going to enjoy these rustic vegetables.'

'Not at all,' I protested. 'If learning English is going to do that to me, I don't want to learn it. Please don't send me to school.'

Bhau said, 'I said that only to make you angry. When you get angry, I know all is well with the world. You like jackfruit, don't you? I'll get one tomorrow from Patil Wadi. If I don't find a tender one, you can have the pods boiled and spiced.'

Aai said, 'Yes, please get one. We haven't had jackfruit in a long time.' Bhau went out to the verandah for his routine walk and prayers. After that he spun yarn for his sacred thread. The spinning disc was made of clay. The house rule was that all of us should know how to spin yarn.

Aai had finished clearing up and had now sat down for her lunch. I was sitting nearby. She took her first mouthful of the vegetable and discovered it had no salt. 'Shyam, there's no salt in this dish. None of you said so. Why didn't you tell me? How could you eat this saltless dish?'

'We said nothing because Bhau said nothing,' I replied.

Aai was very upset.

'How did you eat this?' she kept asking. 'No wonder you didn't have much. Otherwise you would have single-handedly finished half the lot. You like your vegetables. I should have known then. But what's the use of saying it now?'

Aai was full of remorse for her mistake. She believed we should always give people the best we can, whatever it is. She felt she had been careless, not paid enough attention, lost her concentration on the job. She had done wrong and she refused to forgive herself.

Bhau had said nothing because he hadn't wanted to upset her. She had spent so much time at the hearth breathing in all the smoke and fumes just to make food for us. Why find fault? Why not accept what was made as tasty? Bhau believed it was wrong to hurt the person who had cooked for you.

'Friends, it is for us to decide who the finer human being was. Was my father the finer human being because he ate an unsalted dish as if it were the best he had ever eaten in the belief that it was better to control one's tongue than hurt another's feelings? Or was my mother the finer human being because she was upset over serving us something that wasn't perfect, asked us why we hadn't complained and wouldn't forgive herself for her mistake? According to me, both were fine human beings.

Our culture is founded on self-control and contentment as well as on doing work as perfectly as possible. I learnt from my parents that we should aspire to both these virtues in life.'

Nineteenth Night

Rebirth

I was eleven years old when I was sent to Pune to study
English. I was to stay with my Mama, my mother's
brother. My elder brother was already there. But while
I was there, I behaved badly. I ran away two or three
times and snitched on people with made-up stories.
Eventually, Mama sent me home. He didn't want a
disruptive boy like me in the house who might one day
harm himself or somebody else.

When I returned to Palgad, I found things had changed
dramatically. Bhau, who had been jailed for his participation
in the freedom struggle, had served his sentence and come
home. He had grown very weak. So he had gone away to
a relative's place near the sea for a change of air. My elder
sister had come home from her in-laws' place on a short
visit, hoping for a few days of happiness. Instead, she had
fallen ill. Aai had to take care of all the household chores

single-handedly. There was nobody else in the house to help her. To top it all, I had come home in disgrace. Nobody paid much attention to me. I had become the unloved child. All the love was being showered on Akka, who had a baby daughter whom she couldn't breastfeed because of her illness. She had an intermittent fever that was supposed to make her milk poisonous. Poor baby Rangu suffered. Not only did she not get her mother's milk, she was deprived of her touch as well.

One day Akka became delirious. She had never said a word to us about the torture she suffered at the hands of her in-laws. All her repressed emotions surfaced now that she was not conscious of what she was saying. Aai was very sad to hear about these things. They had spent a huge amount of money on their daughter's wedding. Why then should she suffer at her in-laws' hands?

There are two terrible blots on our family life. Brothers fighting brothers is one and ill-treating daughters-in-law is the other. A girl leaves her own home where she is loved, and goes to her parents-in-law's home when she marries their son. Ideally, they should treat her like a daughter. Instead, they treat her like a servant, just to show their power. We have a word for the torture women have to suffer at their in-laws' hands. *Sasurvaas*. That alone proves that this terrible practice has been a part of our culture for centuries.

The songs girls sing describe what sasurvaas is:

In-laws' words are bitter gourd creepers / How can they ever taste sweet?
In-laws' words are webs of deceit / Day and night you weep.

'Women have composed many songs about the lives they are forced to live. Only they can think of comparisons like bitter gourds and webs of deceit. We have still not learnt to be human. A mother-in-law tortures her daughter-in-law. When the daughter-in-law becomes a mother-in-law, she does the same to her daughter-in-law. This is how we have turned a cruel practice that started with our ancestors into a tradition. No wonder we have a proverb that says, "If today belongs to the mother-in-law, tomorrow belongs to the daughter-in-law." A teacher beats a student. The student becomes a teacher. The student beats his student. Teachers ask what's wrong with beating students. We too were beaten. If you observe girls playing house, they copy what they see in life. The girl who plays the daughter-in-law has her hair pulled, is branded and served stale food. When boys play school, they pretend a pillar or a post is a student and thrash it mercilessly. "Will you make a noise again? Do you want more beatings?" they shout. My sister's five-year-old son says to me, "Anna, I want to be a teacher or a policeman." When I ask him why he chooses these two occupations, he says, "Then I can beat everyone. I'll give everybody a good thrashing." This is the idea we have of school. School is another sasurvaas. In reality, both school and parents-in-laws' houses should be like second homes. I know I am rambling. But these things make my blood boil. Why can't we be human? Our culture teaches us to love insects, trees, birds and fish. But today's heirs to this great culture have become worthless. They have forgotten how to be human. My heart burns. My gut is wrenched. But enough of that.'

We had swallowed our lunch somehow and were sitting at Akka's bedside. A small plate of cold water had been placed on her forehead. There were no ice packs to be found in a village in those days, nor eau de cologne to add to the water to bring down the fever faster. Aai was holding down the plate of water. Everybody's faces looked pinched. Suddenly Aai got up, asking me to hold the plate while she went and sat before God. 'Lord Shankar, I promise to cover your *pindi* at the temple with rice and curd for three successive days, but please cure my girl. Bring down her temperature. Let her body cool.'

We were doing all we could to help Akka recover. We were praying without pause. Aai had trust in God. But she was also nursing Akka night and day. God helps those who make an effort to help themselves.

'Shyam, Rangu has woken up. Take her out, will you? I don't want her to start crying here,' Aai said to me. I picked Rangu out of her cradle, held her against my shoulder and carried her out. I walked around with her for a while, but then got bored and took her indoors again. It was almost dusk. The rice pounders had finished their work. The pounded rice had to be measured. The cattle would soon return from grazing. The cowherd would call out 'Your cows are back' and move on. The cattle had to be tethered. I added to these chores that Aai had to attend to by putting Rangu back in her cradle and going out to play. The poor baby began to bawl. What was she saying? What did she want? Was she saying, 'I want to be with my mother? Just put me beside her because I want to feel her touch? I am not hungry for her milk. I am hungry for her touch'? Poor little soul. Little did she know that her mother was burning with fever, that she was rambling in her delirium. Who could understand why the baby was crying? All we knew was that she was crying her heart out.

What was Aai to do? Measure the pounded rice? Light the lamp and show it to the tulsi plant and the gods? Tether the cattle? Milk the cows? Make a potion for Akka? Start the evening's cooking? Play with Rangu? Or sit with Akka? Did she have multiple hands? Women are truly amazing. They work themselves to the bone yet never complain. They toil all day long, dealing with the problems of running homes. The only name that befits their hard work and compassion is Earth Mother.

But there was a limit to how much even Aai could endure. She lost her temper now. 'Where has this wretch gone?' she shouted. 'He's around only to gorge himself. He won't lift a finger to work. He showed his colours at my brother's house and now he's back here to torture his mother. All he had to do was look after the baby for a while. Did he? No. But he'll eat all day, the buffalo. Shyam, you wretch, why don't you pick up the girl? She's crying. She's holding her breath. I wish you'd die. But you won't. You will live to torture me.' Aai was mad with rage and sorrow. I had heard all she had said, but her last words pierced my heart. I began to weep. I picked up the crying Rangu and carried her out, my own eyes streaming with tears. I held her close to me and began reciting shlokas and then the *Ramaraksha*. I kept pacing up and down with Rangu at my shoulder till she finally fell asleep.

Aai's words had woken me up. Suddenly I knew what made life worth living. Sometimes just a spark can change your life. Friction creates sparks. The spark that Aai's words created gave light to my life. The world loves a good, kind person. It has no use for a worthless person. That day I realized that I was of no use to anybody. I was nothing but a burden on my people. That day my life took a turn. I found a new direction. What people say is true. The time has to be right for something like that to happen. The time was right for me that day. I looked up at the sky, now filled with stars and prayed to God. 'God, I have decided to change my ways from today. Please bless my efforts. Please make me a good human being and please cure my Akka.'

Fortunately, Akka's health began to mend. Her body became stronger. At the same time, my heart and mind became stronger with the knowledge that life is worth living only if you pull your weight. We were both reborn. Akka had a new body, and I had a new heart.

Twentieth Night

Hungry for Love

'So shall I start, Govinda?' Shyam asked.

'Can we wait a little? Grandpa hasn't come. It upsets him to miss even a single word of the story.'

'I wonder why. My stories are simple little things. People are silly to give them so much importance.'

'You tell them because you think they are worth telling, don't you?' Bhika asked. 'Or do you think they are worthless? If you do, you'd be wrong to tell them to us. You would be deceiving us. Surely we shouldn't give things to people that we ourselves consider worthless, should we?'

'There's also the question of people's faith, which we should try not to hurt,' said Govinda. 'Your words make people happy. That's why they are so eager to hear you.'

'There he is,' Ram said. 'Come and sit here, Grandpa.'

'No, I'm fine here,' Grandpa replied.

'Let's begin now, Shyam,' Raja said.

Everybody sat up in anticipation. Shyam began to speak, his voice as sweet as a flute.

My father enrolled me in an English-teaching school in Dapoli, about 13 miles away from our village. After my return from Mama's house, where I had disgraced myself, I had stayed home for some time, studying the Vedas and other things. But Bhau wanted me to continue my English studies, in which I had already completed two grades.

Dapoli is a pretty town with a bracing climate. The sea is about 8 miles away. There are extensive parks in the town. There used to be a British encampment there once. That is how the town came to be called Camp Dapoli. That was soon corrupted to Kapdapoli and abbreviated to Kap. This district fell into British hands before any other in Maharashtra. Nanasaheb Peshwa took help from the British to destroy Tulaji Angre's navy. That was a blunder of historic proportions. The Angre navy had kept the British in check. Tulaji had defeated many British and other nations' ships venturing into the Arabian Sea. Shivaji Maharaj had taken great pains to build up the Maratha Navy. Before that, not even the tiniest boat belonging to the Marathas had dared enter the sea. Shivaji, the great man that he was, realized the vital importance of having a navy. He who rules the sea wears the crown. This was Shivaji's thinking as recorded in history. But Nanasaheb made common cause with the British and wilfully removed this hurdle in their path. In return for their help, he gave the British several harbour villages like Banakot along the coast of this district. Ironically, Nanasaheb, who wielded his powerful will like a sword, himself belonged to Velas village in this district. Some of our most illustrious writers and editors, freedom fighters and educationists, mathematicians and legal experts belonged to this district.

The country around Dapoli is covered with thick woods. When the wind blows through a forest of casuarina trees, it sounds like waves crashing against the shore. There are lots of cashew trees too. In the summer, red, yellow and orange cashew fruits sway on the branches like little chandeliers. Every village in the district looks like a veritable birthplace of nature's beauties.

The English school at Dapoli was run by a Christian Mission. At one time, its hostel was famous in the whole of Bombay district. The school, perched atop a hill and surrounded by cultivated mango trees, made a very pretty sight. This is where I resumed my school education.

Palgad was 12 or 13 miles away. Initially, I wasn't sure I could walk the distance. But doing it once gave me confidence. After that, I would return home most weekends. I would start walking around two o'clock on Saturday afternoon when half-day school ended and reach home around the time the lamps were lit. I would spend the whole of Sunday in Aai's loving company, rise very early on Monday morning and be back at school by ten o'clock.

On one Saturday in December, I was feeling rather sad and dejected when I set out for Palgad. I had a sinking feeling that there was nobody for me in the world. I was prone to these moods from the time I was a little boy. This feeling of loneliness overwhelmed me.

'It happens even now and the idea always makes me weep. I feel my heart grow suddenly heavy and my eyes fill with tears. At such times, I feel I am no more than a tiny dot, a leaf that will soon dry and fall. That's why I long for love and sympathy. As a boy, my yearning was so strong it seemed to come from all my previous births, as though I had been hungry for love and sympathy through hundreds of my earlier lives. At a pinch, a person can live without food, but never without love. Love injects life into what is otherwise mere existence. Constant, abundant love nourishes the tree of life. Love should be a continuous flow like the sap that runs through a tree from the roots, through the trunk, to the leaves. Love cannot be like the bubbles in an aerated drink that soon fizzle out and make the drink flat and tasteless. Love that comes and goes like fizz cannot create a life that is fresh, strong and beautiful.

That Saturday, I was hungry for love. I wanted to breathe love. It had to fill the surroundings like air. Lokmanya Tilak used to say, 'I spend two months in Sinhagad breathing its clean, pure air of freedom and live off it for the rest of the year.' I felt that way about home too. Go every weekend, inhale a lungful of love and live off it for a week in the loveless world of the school. Today I know that giving rather than receiving love is the greater joy. But an emerging shoot must not be allowed to shrivel up under a harsh sun. Only when it is watered and tended will it grow into a shady tree. A young child, given love, will grow up to give love to thousands. Those who have been deprived of love as children, grow up to be hard-hearted and incapable of giving love.

My eyes kept filling up as I walked homewards that Saturday. There are many villages along this path and a large jungle midway. There is a well near a village called Karanjani. It is said that an entire group of wedding guests had vanished as they walked past the well one night. I was so scared of the well that I would normally race past it muttering 'Ram Ram'. But I was very thirsty that day. It took all the courage I could muster to climb down the steps of the well to quench my thirst. The well was built to allow horses to drink from it, so the steps were very broad. After a hurried drink of water, I walked swiftly in order to reach home before dark. My heart pounded as I crossed the jungle where tigers were known to prowl.

The lamps had already been lit by the time I reached home. My younger brother was reciting his shlokas. Aai was lighting the *chulah*. Aji was muttering a charm over some ash. When villagers suspected that somebody had cast an evil eye on them, they would knock ash off an ember on to a mango leaf and bring it to Aji. Aji would rub the ash between her fingers as she muttered a mantra. Then she would apply the charmed ash on the victim's forehead.

When my younger brothers saw me coming, they yelled, 'Anna is here, Anna is here,' and clung to me. I went in.

'Why did you leave so late?' Aai asked. 'You should have left earlier. See how dark it has grown.'

'I couldn't walk fast enough. I felt drained,' I said.

'Then you shouldn't have come,' Aai said. 'You could have waited another month and come for Sankranti.'

'Aai, I came to see you,' I said. 'When I see the love in your eyes, I feel strengthened. I go back filled with this strength.' I hugged Aai and wept. That made Aai weep. Then my brothers started weeping. Aai wiped her own eyes and mine with her pallu.

'Here. Here's some hot water to wash your feet with. But wait. Let me massage them with oil first.' I gazed at her as she massaged my feet. I was at the very peak of happiness. Perhaps happiness is an understatement. It was an indescribable feeling. A moment of sheer bliss. I washed my feet and went to sit with Aai near the chulah. My younger brothers said, 'Anna, tell us a story or teach us a new shloka.' Just then Bhau came home, looking tense. Something must have happened to upset him. He did not seem as happy to see me as he would normally have been. He didn't even talk to me. He washed his feet and sat down for his puja.

'Have you finished your prayers?' he asked me.

This was the time I used to say my ritual *sandhya* prayers every evening. They were in Vedic Sanskrit, so I didn't understand a word of what I was saying. But I mumbled the words anyway and followed all the rituals prescribed for the prayer.

'I haven't. I will do it now,' I answered.

'So what are you doing sitting in the kitchen? Get up and do your sandhya,' Bhau said angrily.

'He's only just come,' Aai said. 'He's very tired. He said he was feeling drained. That's why he was resting. Shyam, go do your sandhya.'

I got up and sat before the gods. I smeared ash on my forehead and began to drink sacred water, one sip at a time. The tears in my eyes became my offering to God.

Bhau spoke up again.

'I hope you do sandhya in the hostel. Your hair is like a jungle. Are there no barbers there? You look like a crow. I had told you last time I visited to get your head shaved. Why didn't you do it? You've grown horns, have you? Get hold of the barber tomorrow and get this thatch shaved. Or don't stay here. Get out.'

I came looking for love and stayed to be cursed. I came looking for a piece of bhakri and was served stones. I couldn't control the sob that rose to my throat. 'What are you crying for?' Bhau thundered. 'Has somebody beaten you? Such drama.'

'He'll have his head shaved tomorrow for sure,' Aai said soothingly. 'You'll have to pay for it. Perhaps he couldn't have it done in Dapoli either because he didn't have the money or the time. His school starts at ten in the morning. Have you finished your sandhya, Shyam? Do your aarti. Now wipe your eyes and come here. I'm serving dinner. You must be famished.' Aai's voice remained as sweet as nectar. That day I had a taste of nectar and poison, life and death, summer and monsoon, spring and winter all at the same time.

By the time I finished my aarti, the plates had been laid out, and we sat down to dinner. Aai served me dahi. She served it to me alone, not to my younger brother who was sitting beside me. I put some in his rice when nobody was looking and mixed the rice for him. I felt better after that, though my heart continued to feel fragile. The slightest human touch caused tears to spurt out. My entire body seemed to be made of tears. I had given my brother money before. But that was nothing compared to giving him dahi that day. It produced a sweetness within my soul that was precious.

At night, we siblings lay down to sleep and chatted away. They soon fell asleep, but not me. I continued to weep for a while after, before finally drifting off to sleep. My eyes only flew open at dawn, after my father had left for the fields. Aai was swabbing the floor while singing a song about Krishna.

Krishna, Yashoda's baby boy, lovable and sweet.
Krishna, thirsty for milk, Yashoda nurses him.
Krishna, dark as a cloud, drinks Yashoda's love.

Aai's name was Yashoda and I was Shyam, named after Krishna. Her love was my food and drink. I rose from my bed and hugged her. 'Aai,' I pleaded. 'Please sit beside me and pat me to sleep. Spread your own sheet over me. Come. Please leave that swabbing for a while and pat me to sleep.' What can a mother do when her son insists? When the son has chosen to become a baby? She sat down beside me. She patted me and sang me a lullaby.

The day has broken, the cock is crowing
My little baby, go back to sleep.
The day has broken, the waterwheel creaks.
You are in your cradle, sleep baby sleep.
The day has broken, caw-caw goes the crow.
Sleep baby sleep, do not awaken.
The day has broken, chores must be done
Sleep on little one, your Aai must go.

The lullaby ended. I said, 'Aai, I too must go. I don't want to stay. I yearned to be back home but after the scolding Bhau gave me, I'd like to leave before he returns. Let me go.'

'Shyam, don't be like that,' said Aai. 'Do you think that would be the right thing to do? If he scolded you, it wasn't because he had something against you personally. Perhaps someone said something insulting to him. He must have been hurt inside. That's why he scolded you. We are in a bad situation. You know that, don't you, Shyam? He is depressed. Don't take what he said to heart. He has raised you. Does he not have the right to correct you? He has gone through a lot to bring you up. He has had to borrow money and wear torn dhotis to pay your fees. Should a few angry words make you forget that? He scolded you because your hair has grown. Those who believe in old customs find that hard to accept. He will scold you only while you are young. He's not going to scold you when you are a grown man. Can't you shave your head to make your parents happy? Can't you do that much so that your parents' religious beliefs aren't hurt?' Aai was trying to make me understand.

'What has hair got to do with religion?' I asked.

'Religion touches everything. It touches what you eat and what you drink. But why do you grow your hair anyway? It is a temptation. To resist temptation is religion.'

'Friends, my mother failed to convince me then. But today I understand what she was trying to say. Religion does indeed touch every aspect of life. I don't need to stress this further in an ashram. Religion is about thinking clearly before you act. It is about working for truth, righteousness and the common good. Religion is linked to the way you speak, walk, sit, rise, listen, eat, drink, sleep, bathe, wash, dress. Religion is the air we breathe, the light we see. We need the air and light of religion wherever we go. I grew my hair because I wanted to look good. But real beauty lies in our virtues and in the purity of our spirit. I understand that now. I was about to leave home because I was angry with my father. But my mother didn't let me go. She loved me. But she also pointed out the right path to me. Her love wasn't blind or naive.'

Aai went back to her work. My brothers and I lay in bed for a while longer. When I got up, I called Govinda, our barber. He was our retainer since he shaved our hair in return for a certain quantity of grain we gave him each year. On Diwali mornings, he would give us an oil massage as well. 'Shyam, look at this thatch!' he said.

'Govinda, the barbers in Kap don't have gentle hands like yours. They make me cry.' Govinda was delighted to hear that.

We had our baths afterwards. Bhau came home, bringing tawse with him. Tawse are cucumbers that are old and have dried on the creeper. In the Konkan, they are hung up in the house. They last for a long time, sometimes up to four months. If you hang up cucumbers and pumpkins in the rainy season, they last till the Shimga festival the following March. People believe that they don't last once the Shimga drums are beaten.

Bhau said to Aai, 'I've brought back some tawse to make patole. Shyam likes them. And I've brought turmeric leaves. I see you boys have had your baths. Shyam, can you put some kindling in the chulah? I'll have a bath and go to the temple. I'm going to do repeated readings of the sacred book today. Every fortnight I also make a special offering to Ganapati for you.'

Bhau went out, leaving me feeling very ashamed of myself. Yes, he had scolded me the previous night. But that was nothing compared to the amount of love he really felt for me. He prayed to God so I would do well at my studies and in life. I love patole, so he went searching all over the village for tawse. And me? I had planned to leave in a huff. He would have been so disappointed if he had come home to find me gone. How deeply I would have hurt a loving father's heart. He would have thought of my love for him as weak, my sense of duty towards him as little . . . that I could not stomach the few words he had said in anger. How sad that a few angry words were enough to kill love.

I looked at Bhau gratefully. I put kindling in the chulah outside. I went indoors and clipped the stalks of the hibiscus flowers he had brought home from the field. I arranged them along with the other varieties he had brought, each in a separate heap according to their colour. I arranged the durva grass, the tulsi and the *bel* leaves in the same tray and put a few grains of rice in it. I poured milk for the offering in its little tumbler and put the bowl of holy ash near the low, flat seat. When everything was ready for Bhau's puja, I went to the kitchen to help Aai. I peeled the cucumber and grated it. I wiped the turmeric leaves, making sure no spider's webs clung to them. I began smearing them with the patole batter. I was very good at spreading the batter thin. The batter is made of rice flour mixed with the grated cucumber. Jaggery is added to it and the batter spread thin on one-half of a turmeric leaf. The other half is turned down to make a packet. The leaves are then steamed. When they are done, the steamed patole are peeled off the leaf.

When Bhau's puja had ended, I lit a twig at the chulah and took it out to him to light the little oil lamp for the aarti. We didn't use matchsticks if the chulah was lit. When Bhau left for the temple, I went to the kitchen again to crack open a coconut. Dairy products are scarce in the Konkan. Poor people can't afford ghee, which the rich have with their patole. The poor have theirs with coconut milk. We make it by pouring hot water on grated coconut with a pinch of salt. The juice that comes out when you squeeze the coconut is your coconut milk. Lunch was ready by the time Bhau returned. What a joyous occasion it turned out to be! Bhau said to Aai, 'Serve Shyam another patola. That one's from me.' I was truly happy.

Bhau loved us as much as Aai did. He never beat us. The punishments he gave us were to do ten squats, to weed out grass from the garden, to give a tree four bucketfuls of water or to prostrate ourselves ten times before God.

He would scold us occasionally but never hit us. Aai sat down to dinner after we were done. Then my six-year-old brother came in. 'May I go, Aai?' he asked.

'Where do you want to go, Babulya?' I asked.

'Aai knows. May I?' he repeated.

Aai said, 'Yes, you may. But don't sit there reciting shlokas.' Sadanand grinned and ran off. His name was Sadanand, but we called him Babulya. 'Has he gone to sit on the swing at the Karandikars'?' I asked.

'Nothing of the kind. He wants to do number two. He's such a scamp. He asks for my permission to do that. And he'll sit there reciting shlokas. But when he wants to go play somewhere, he'll run off without a word. Rascal!'

We sat chatting as Aai ate. Aai said, 'Shyam, if you'd gone away today, your father would have been shattered. He wouldn't have been able to swallow a single mouthful of food. If he hiccups or food falls from his hand back into the plate, he says, 'Who could be thinking of me? Gaju or Shyam?' How he loves you. I am constantly unwell. I don't think I'm going to live too long. I will have to leave him one day. He has nobody in the world, neither brother nor sister. Nobody cares for poor people. He can only look to you for his happiness.' Aai's voice grew thick with emotion. 'Shyam, sometimes he says, "The children might care for me or turn on me, who knows?" Please don't turn on him, Shyam. Don't bring death upon him. If death comes, drive it away. Give him some happiness.'

Aai finished her lunch. I wiped down her wooden seat and put it away. I carried the puja utensils out and washed them. Aai scoured the cooking vessels and I rinsed them. Aai put hot milk in Sadanand's little bowl and set it with curd, leaving it behind the chulah to keep it warm. After she finished clearing up, we sat on the verandah. We played the stone game in which Bhau captured all my stones and won without losing any of his. It was such fun. Aai patched my torn dhoti. Bhau told us a lovely story. Night fell. Nobody wanted to have dinner. Aai tempered some buttermilk. We drank that and slept soundly through the night.

We got up at dawn. I bathed while Aai cooked rice, adding a couple of ivy gourds to it because I liked rice made that way. She served it to me with spice powder and a lentil papad. I finished eating my rice and was now ready to leave. I touched Aai's feet. 'Come for Sankranti now,' she said. 'If your legs hurt too much with walking, catch a bus. It's all right to spend a couple of annas on the fare. Take care.'

I touched Bhau's feet. He said, 'Shyam, don't take my scolding to heart. Be a good boy. Study hard.' I hugged both my younger brothers and left. Bhau came with me up to the *behela* tree that marks the boundary of our village, to see me off. He turned back from there and I walked on alone.

I found myself weeping once again as I walked. While I had wept on my way home from Dapoli because I was hungry for love, I was weeping now because I had received so much that my heart was brimming with it. Tears of sorrow and tears of joy. I met a traveller along the way. He said to me, 'Why are you crying, son? Do you not have anybody in the world?'

'I have parents,' I replied.

'Do they not love you?' he asked. 'Have they driven you away?'

'No, I am weeping because they love me too much,' I said. 'I am sad because I am not worthy of their love. I do not know how I will ever repay them for it. That is why I am weeping.'

The traveller looked at me with great sympathy. I walked on, picking up pace as I went.

Twenty-first Night

Durva Aji

An elderly woman who was remotely related to us used to live with us. Her name was Dwarkakaku. She was very fond of my father, which is why she chose to move in with us when Bhau separated from his family. She owned a rice field that Bhau looked after. We used to call her Durva Aji. In the four months of monsoon, women offered one lakh flowers to the gods. That is why the offering was called *lakholi*. Some offered *parijatak* flowers while others offered mogra. Some women chose to offer durva grass that they collected with the help of other women. Aji was always ready to assist in this work. She believed in helping others to do good work. So any woman who needed help to collect durva grass could count on her. If we were asked where she was, pat came our answer, 'She's out collecting durva.' That is how she got her name, something we continued calling her even as adults.

Durva Aji had other virtues too. When water sank to the very bottom of the well during summer, she went down

149

the steps and scooped up mugfuls to fill our large water pot, which Aai then hauled up. Before the harvest, she stayed up all night in her rice field to guard it. She had even caught a thief once. She feared nothing. She knew many spells. She could put a spell on an ember to cure a child who had taken suddenly ill, or a cow that refused to give milk. If she found herself yawning persistently while tending to the ember, she concluded that the evil eye on the child or cow was particularly powerful. People who brought embers to her for unruly cattle also brought along a piece of cattle feed for her to put a spell on. All they had to do then was feed that to the problem animal and all was well.

Durva Aji was a wizard at oil massages; they were guaranteed to cure aches and pains. If your leg was hurting, if you had stomach spasms or if your back was out of joint, you called on Durva Aji to massage the offending part. Once she had administered her massage, you were instantly up and about. Dhanvantari, the god of medicine himself, dwelt in her hands. When my eyes had grown weak, she would massage cow's milk vigorously into the soles of my feet till it was all absorbed. She possessed a huge pipe-like object in which she stored seeds for a variety of vegetables such as ladies' fingers, snake gourd, pumpkin and cucumber. She was an expert at playing games with counters and cowries. She would draw an exact facsimile of a game board on the floor with chalk. She would teach us youngsters other games too. Her favourite was the one in which a child was hidden under a sheet and the 'den' had to guess who it was. She would instruct a stout child to contract his body and a thin child to expand his to outwit the den. Durva Aji knew innumerable songs about gods, goddesses and their glorious deeds.

This story is about the time Aai wanted to make bhajani. Grains, pulses and lentils had to be roasted for it and then ground. Grinding was heavy work. You required two hands at the peg to pull the grinding stone. One evening, Durva Aji suggested they make it the following day. Relying on her, Aai roasted all the stuff that evening. But Aji tended to be unpredictable. The next morning, she was called away by the Khares to whom she was related on her mother's side. Not that blood relationships mattered. She was Aji to the whole village. Whoever needed help would call her and she would go. In this case, a messenger came to tell her that the Khare women were planning to make papads. 'Could you come over to help and stay for lunch?' he asked Aji, who promised she would go.

Aai was upset. How was she going to grind the bhajani single-handedly? She said to Aji, 'What about the bhajani we had decided to grind?' Aji replied, raising her voice, 'What do you mean? Am I bound hand and foot to your work? She's worried about her bhajani. I don't have the strength to turn that grinding stone, understand?'

That set Aai off.

'Oh, so now she can't turn the grinding stone. You have the strength to help others, but your hands grow weak at home, right? She wants the whole village to sing her praises, but she won't lift a finger to help in this house. It would pollute her, wouldn't it? At home it's "Oh dear, such pain. Oh Lord, help me." But outside, she's standing all day pounding rice and running to fetch big pots of water from the well. Such hypocrisy. You're just a sham.'

Now Aji got into battle mode.

'Why shouldn't I help others? Who are you to scold me for that? Am I living off you? I have my own rice field, I'll have you remember. Don't you dare talk to me like that! It won't serve you well. She's complaining that I work for others. They may be "others" to you. I don't think of anybody as "others". You and the Khares are the same to me. How dare you call me a sham? I've never put up with this kind of talk before. You think no end of yourself.'

'Then why did you tell me yesterday we could make bhajani today? I've kept everything ready. I've washed the grinding stone. And now when it's time to work, you're off somewhere else. You're a big one for letting me down. I kill myself working, but you won't lend me a hand, will you?'

'I don't lend you a hand? That's the limit, even from you. So I won't go to the Khares. If it hurts your eyes so much to see me go, I won't. I'm greedy for the world to call me good, am I? Oh no, not at all. It's enough if you call me good.'

'Friends, human beings are complex. When they help others, it might very well be because they are praised in return. Nobody praises them at home for the work they do because it is their duty to do it. My mother was possibly guilty of exaggeration, but there was some truth in what she said. Perhaps Aji had indeed become addicted to praise.'

Such flare-ups occurred occasionally between Aai and Aji, but they did not last. They were like sudden storms that blew around furiously before abating overnight. They served as outlets for the poison that had accumulated in their hearts. Once it had been spewed out, their hearts were cleansed. Storms clear the air. Disease burns the filth in the body. Death brings new life. My mother calmed down. She became silent. Aji continued talking for a while. 'She complains about me working in other people's homes. These are my hands. I'll use them as and where I like. Who are you to impose rules on me? Why are you jealous? Because people call me to help and not you?'

Aai's mouth remained shut. That soon shut Aji's mouth too. A while later, Aai went to Aji and said, 'I was wrong. I said things I shouldn't have. I have no right to say things to you. You are so much older than I am. But this never-ending work, these constant worries and my ill health make me desperate. I lose perspective. I forget who I am talking to. What's the point of this life anyway?'

'What's the point of this life? Why are you saying such inauspicious things? Your children are still young. If you don't live, who will look after them? You must live a long life. See your children married. Let your daughters-in-law come home. Don't you dare think such insane thoughts! When you let your tongue go, mine also acts up. I, too, feel bad afterwards.'

Aai's mood had turned.

'You must go to the Khares. You've promised to go. We can make the bhajani tomorrow. I'll keep the grinding stone as it is. As long as I don't grind anything else on it, it will stay clean. But wait till I make some tea for you. It will give you energy. It's cold outside today.'

There was always some tea powder in the house, for when someone was ill or had an attack of asthma. She made a glass of tea for Durva Aji now. Aji's anger melted away. When she left for the Khares' house, she called out, 'I'm going, Yashode. Please don't be angry. Don't hold any bad feelings in your heart.'

Aai said, 'I hope you won't either. After all, you are family. I am like a daughter or daughter-in-law to you. Please forgive me for the things I said.'

Aji left and Aai turned to her chores. Friends, my mother was not blameless. But who is free of faults? Who doesn't make mistakes? There is only one unblemished being— God. Everybody else must one day stand before the Creator, with all their faults on display. To err is human. To forgive is divine. My mother would commit an error, but immediately make up for it. She did not parade her errors proudly.

Twenty-second Night

Joyful Diwali

Diwali was round the corner. Schools had broken for the holidays. I was studying in Dapoli, but I returned home as soon as the holidays began. Bhau had new shirts made for my younger brothers and me. But his own dhotis were badly torn. Aai had mended them in dozens of places dozens of times. But the cloth was so worn that the mends refused to hold. Despite this, Bhau had not bought himself new dhotis.

This saddened Aai, but what could she do? She didn't have money of her own. She, too, hadn't worn a new sari in years. But that didn't bother her. What bothered her was Bhau's plight. Every day he would try to pleat his dhoti in a way that would hide the mended tears.

People from the Konkan who work in Mumbai and Pune return home for Diwali. The rains stop by then, the sea grows calmer for the ferry service to resume. People bring back firecrackers and toys for their families.

My elder brother, who was staying with our Mama, was not going to come home. But Mama had sent three rupees, as a Bhau Beej gift for Aai, and some sweets for us with someone who was coming from Pune. Aai was very happy to have the money. She asked the visitor if all was well at Mama's place before he left. We crowded around Aai. 'When can we have the sweets Mama has sent?' we pestered her. Mama had sent dried apricots and peppermints. Aai gave us one apricot and two peppermints each. When my younger brother wanted one more apricot, Aai said, 'The sweets are all for you boys. Why finish them in one day? If you eat a few every day, you'll enjoy them for a longer time, won't you?' My brother said, 'Give me one more peppermint then. Take this one back. I want a pink one.' Aai gave him a pink peppermint apart from the extra one. We went out to play *dhabadhabi* with a ball made of rags. Whoever got hit with the ball was out and became the 'den'.

Aai kept the sweets in a cupboard, safe from ants. She called me after some time. 'Will you go to Amrutsethji's shop and ask how much a pair of dhotis will cost? Tell him they are for your father. If he asks whether he is at home, say he's gone away and will be back tomorrow. Tell him you have just been sent to inquire about this.'

I went to Amrutsethji's shop. His sons Mohanya and Badri were there. Mohanya said, 'So Shyam, what do you want? More pictures to stick on your notebooks, I guess.'

'Why would I ask for something you won't give me?' I asked. 'I'm never going to ask you for anything. I've come only to find out how much a pair of dhotis costs.'

'Who are they for? You?'

'No. They are for Bhau. I want finely woven ones of a proper length and breadth. Give me two or three qualities. I'll show them at home and bring them back.'

Mohanya Marwadi showed me three dhotis of varying qualities. Amrutsethji said, 'Bring them back soon, Shyam.'

I said haughtily, 'Don't worry. We aren't going to keep them. And if we do, we'll pay for them.'

'You seem to be loaded. Your father doesn't have a single pie.' Amrutsethji's words hurt me. He said what he did because we were in debt to him. Those who want to live with self-respect should die rather than be in debt.

I brought the dhotis home for Aai to see. Aai liked one pair, which would only cost us three or three-and-a-half rupees. Aai gave me the money and I took the remaining samples back to Amrutsethji. Aai cut the joint pair through the middle to make two dhotis. She put an auspicious vermillion mark on each. The dhotis were kept secret from Bhau for when he returned from his trip. Although we were young, we were part of the conspiracy. Aai was going to give Bhau these dhotis after he had bathed on Diwali morning.

We became busy with the preparations for the following day. Aai made a paste of *takla* seeds to rub on our bodies. We swept the yard clean. Diwali marks the killing of Narakasur, the demon of hell. To my mind, this demon is not half as dangerous as the filth that human beings create. Filth is the root of disease which kills thousands of people. What is the use of making our homes shine like mirrors when we throw garbage out on the streets? We are supposed to put our garbage in the dustbins provided by the municipality. A demon in the street is as bad as a demon in the house.

While we were busy cleaning the yard, Aai made a new planter for the tulsi. She cleaned the little clay oil lamps. We placed them all over the yard and lit them at night. We slept early because it was auspicious to bathe before daybreak on Diwali. Aai was still awake when we went to sleep, preparing the fragrant *utana* to rub on our bodies.

Aai was the first to wake up too. She put kindling in the big chulah in the yard to heat the bathwater. She took a bath and woke us up one by one. She massaged us with utana and oil. She gave us plenty of water for our baths. Bhau had also woken up early. He had already fetched flowers for his puja. He had his bath after we were done. We folded our hands before our house gods and then went to the temple. Bhau finished taking his bath, wore his silk puja dhoti and began performing the puja. He put fragrant oil on the idols and bathed them with hot water while on other days, they shivered under cold water. Aai made some traditional sweets, offering them first to the gods and then giving whatever she could to the mendicants who came around begging. After his puja, Bhau called out to us and gave us the sweets that had been offered to the gods. He did his regular surya namaskars and went to the temple. When he returned, he said to Aai, 'I can't see my dhoti anywhere. Where could it be?'

'Oh, I tore both up and turned them into towels. They were in shreds anyway.'

'And what am I supposed to wear now? They would have lasted another month.'

'Why try their patience for that long? I felt ashamed and sad every time I washed them.'

'Don't you think I felt that way when I wore them? But what could I do? Money doesn't fall from the sky just because we are ashamed.'

'Why not wear this dhoti today?' Aai said, holding out one of the new ones.

'Where did this come from?'

'I ordered it from Amrutsethji's shop,' she said.

'When I asked him for one on credit, he refused. He said, "You still owe me money. I don't know how you're going to pay it. I was stupid to give you credit." So how did you get this? Did you collar Mohanya and talk him into it?'

'I bought a pair. Shyam got it.'

'Where did he get the money from?'

'I gave it to him.' Bhau was taken aback.

'And where did you get it from?'

'Appa sent it to me for Bhau Beej with Krishna.'

'When did Krishna come?'

'Two days ago.'

'You could have spent the money on a sari. Yours is badly torn. Only you have a right to your brother's gift, nobody else.'

'You and I—are we separate? We've lived together for so long, sharing our joys and sorrows, taking the good with the bad. Are we still apart? All that belongs to me is yours, and all that is yours is mine. We have so little between us anyway. When you wear a new dhoti, I feel the same joy I would feel if I wore a new sari. Please wear it. I've marked it with vermillion.'

'Don't you think it will sadden me to have a new dhoti while you are still wearing your old sari? You have taken care of your happiness. What about mine?' Bhau's throat was choked with tears.

'You are supposed to be happy because I'm happy. You live so much of your life in the outside world. You'll be invited to Ganguappa's today to play draughts. You will have to go. I don't have to go anywhere. You can buy me a sari when times are better. So don't feel bad. It's Diwali today, a day when everybody should laugh and be happy. Please be happy so we too can be happy.'

'Why would I not be happy with a life partner like you and sweet children like these? You make me feel richer than the rich. Give me that dhoti. I'll wear it.' Bhau wore his new dhoti and folded his hands before the gods. We were happy to see him in his new dhoti. But Aai was even happier.

The joy you gain when you make a sacrifice for someone out of love is indescribable. You have to experience it first-hand to know how beautiful the feeling is. Do it once and you are hooked.

Twenty-third Night

Ardhanari Nateshwar

It was summer vacation, and I was home. I was in the eighth grade at the time. Aai used to find my presence at home helpful. She was often ill. One day she would have fever while the following day, it would come down. When she had fever, she would lie in bed. When it came down, she would get up and work. She had become very weak. When I was at home, I would help her fetch water and wash clothes. I would sweep the yard and massage her feet.

One day after dinner, when the stars were bright and clear and Aai had finished clearing up and Bhau had gone out, she said to me, 'Shyam, do you think we could do a bit of grinding now? Or are your arms aching? You did a lot of digging this evening to plant *ghol*. If you can't manage the grinding, we'll leave it.'

'My arms are fine,' I said. 'When our hands turn the grinding stone together, mine gain strength from yours. I'll bring the grinding stone out.'

I set up the grinding stone in the yard on a length of jute cloth. Aai fetched the dals for grinding. She was going to make ambolis the next day. I loved ambolis. We began to grind while the moon bathed us from above. A cool breeze blew. Aai sang *ovis*[*] occasionally weaving my name into the verses. I was thrilled. I loved helping Aai with the grinding. I had been doing it ever since I was a boy. I had even learnt how to feed in the grain at the right moments during the process.

Hearing the sound of the grinding, Janaki aunty from next door walked over.

'Oh, Shyam is grinding with you, is he? No wonder. I didn't think you could be doing it alone. I came over just to see. Shyam, what is this you're doing? You are studying English now, aren't you?'

'Am I not supposed to help you grind then?' I asked Aai.

'Janakibai is joking,' Aai said. 'She has come over only because she is fond of you. Nobody criticizes a person for working. And there is certainly no shame in helping your mother. Only the uncivilized laugh at a boy for helping his mother. Remember the story where Lord Krishna helps Sant Janabai grind grain?'

---

[*] *This is a song sung by women when they grind grain or put a baby to sleep. The metre of an ovi fits exactly the three-and-a-half rounds of the grinding stone needed to turn a fistful of grain into flour.*

'Yes, of course! But did those things really happen? Did Krishna really help Kabir weave shawls, and Janabai grind grain and wash clothes? Did he really stand behind Sant Namdeo when he performed keertans, accompanying him on the cymbals and dancing? Are these things true?'

Before Aai answered me, she said to Janakibai, 'Why don't you sit down? You've been standing all this time.' Then she turned to me and said, 'God helps those who have faith in Him and always have Him in mind as they go about their work. If you are helping me now, it is because God prompted you to. When the May vacation starts, God comes to help me in your form. God takes many forms to help me. Sometimes he comes as Shyam. Sometimes as Janakibai.'

'Aai, will I ever meet God?' I asked all of a sudden.

'He reveals Himself to those who merit it. You must help others and amass a lot of merit. You are sure to meet God then.'

Janakibai said, 'Shyam, you aren't planning to become an ascetic, are you? Why study then? You're studying English to find a good job. Then you can take your mother away with you.'

I turned my attention back to Aai. 'I do want to become a sadhu, Aai. I want to be a lifelong devotee. Do you think I'll meet God if I do nothing but chant "Om namo bhagvate Vasudevay" as Dhruv did?'

'Son, Dhruv had already collected an enormous amount of merit and possessed a resolve that was unbreakable. Even when his father offered him a kingdom, he did not return to claim it. Such a staunch rejection of worldly desire is uncommon. Try and be the best you can in this life, Shyam. Then perhaps you might meet God,' said Aai.

Janakibai piped in, 'Shyam, let go now. You must be tired. I'll help your mother.'

I looked at Aai.

'Aai, you let go. Aunty and I will grind. Aunty, I know how to feed in the grain. I can do it with my eyes closed. I'm an expert now. Aai, please let go for a while.'

I freed Aai's hand. Aunty and I began to grind. 'Look, aunty. Just look at how fine the flour is. You could put it in your eyes and not feel a thing.'

Janakibai said to Aai, 'You've turned Shyam into a proper woman, haven't you?'

'Is there anyone else in the house to help me?' Aai asked. 'If Shyam doesn't help, I won't have any help at all. Janakibai, women are often forced to do men's work. Do they feel ashamed to do it? Shyam helps me pick rice and lentils, washes vessels and clothes. He even washed my sari once. I said to him, "Shyam, people will laugh at you." He said, "Aai, I'm particularly happy to wash your sari. I sleep under its fourfold, so why can't I wash it?" Shyam feels no shame in doing these things. You say I've turned him into a woman. Shyam doesn't mind that one bit.'

'Friends, I still remember Aai's inspiring words. Men become complete human beings only when they have learnt the so-called feminine virtues of tenderness, selflessness, endurance and hard work. Similarly, women become complete human beings when they learn to manage their homes efficiently, be courageous and even hard-hearted when required. Ardhanari Nateshwar symbolizes the union of the masculine and the feminine. When these two halves of the human race meet and merge, they become two complete individuals.'

Twenty-fourth Night

No Moon Monday

Whenever a no moon night occurs on a Monday, married Brahmin women who have taken the vow of Somavati worship the peepal tree. It is a day when 108 pieces of anything—pedhas, saris or whatever a woman can afford—are offered. It is a form of charity. The offerings go to the family priest. However, he does not keep all 108 things for himself. He distributes them among his fellow priests. So it's a form of sacrifice that ensures that there is no jealousy or competitiveness among priests.

My mother had taken the vow when we were still living with my father's extended family. We were well off then and she had made valuable offerings like 108 four anna coins, pedhas and paans. But when we became poor and she did not have a proper sari to wear, how could she make an offering of 108 saris? When she herself did not have enough to eat, how could she offer 108 pedhas? But a vow, once taken, can't be abandoned midway at will. And yet how could she even ask her husband for 108 of anything? What did he have to give?

It was Christmas vacation and I was at home. I said to Aai, 'What will you offer this Somavati? Janaki aunty says she's offering 108 tender betel nuts.'

'I offered those a few years ago myself. Your aunt Sita had sent them to me.'

'So what will it be this year? There are only two days left to Somavati. Suppose you want to give jaggery or oil. How would you measure 108 of either of those?'

'You can give 108 cans of oil or 108 compressed cakes of jaggery. But units can be calculated in terms of cups or spoonfuls too. Any measure is acceptable. Depends on what you can afford,' Aai said, lost in thought.

'Then what about 108 one-eighth parts of a cake of jaggery?'

'Shyam, there isn't a single pie in the house. Not even to buy poison or rope to hang ourselves with. Where am I to get a cake of jaggery from? We don't have a tree in the garden that sheds money when you shake it. We are desperately poor, Shyam.'

'Maybe you can give 108 sour berries.'

'I've offered them once already, my pet. Your father had brought them from Sovali. You remember Tukaram from Sovali? He had sent them.'

'Would 108 tamarind seeds do?' I was laughing now.

'Why should they not do? But . . .' Aai hesitated.

'People will laugh, right? So let them. All it means is that they expose their teeth. It's easy to laugh. Those who laugh don't come to help us. So why bother ourselves with them? As long as God doesn't laugh. As long as He isn't upset.'

'God is never upset. Remember how He loved the broken rice Vidura served Him? He wiped the plate clean and wanted more. God ate Sudama's pohe greedily as though He was starving. He refused to give Rukmini even a small fistful. God is always starved for love. Only one devotee in a lakh serves Him with real love. Whatever you give God, if it is given with love, it is more precious to Him than an ocean of milk. Remember the berries Ram ate after Shabari had bitten into each to make sure they didn't have worms? You've read all these stories. God accepts anything if it is given with true devotion and a tender heart. Even tamarind seeds. Why, you can give Him pebbles with love and He will find them as sweet as sugar candy. He will suck on them for aeons as though they were a rich sweet. But I don't think my devotion equals Draupadi's or Shabari's. My tamarind seeds will not have the same value as their offerings. I am not so worthy.'

'So what will you offer? You must have planned something.'

'I'm going to offer 108 flowers. That's what I will do. Nothing is as pure as flowers. After all, our offering is for God, not for the priest. If the priest believes that any offering made at God's feet is transformed into a blessing, he will take the flowers. Otherwise the flowers will stay at God's feet. What's to be done if we can't offer anything else? We give God what we can.'

'So which flowers will you offer? We don't have the best varieties in our garden. Why not offer leaves instead?' I said. 'Our gods seem to prefer leaves to flowers. However many flowers you offer, you still need to include a tulsi or a bel leaf or durva grass with them. Your puja isn't complete unless Vishnu is offered tulsi leaves, Shankar bel leaves and Ganapati durva grass. Why is that?'

'Because they aren't difficult to get. They grow everywhere. Give them a little water and they grow all the year round. It's different with flowers. They blossom only in their own season. That is why our saints and sages told us that gods love leaves too. That removed a big hurdle in the path of worship. In the process, it also ensured that a poor woman like me would not feel embarrassed to offer god a simple leaf. She would not envy women who offered money, choli pieces and coconuts. She would not feel ashamed of her poverty. Nor would the rich feel overly proud of their offerings. So, however expensive their offerings, they would still have to add a tulsi leaf to complete them. I will offer 108 tulsi leaves some other time.'

'So what flowers will you offer this time? You aren't telling me that.' I was getting impatient.

'I told your father two days ago that I'd decided to offer flowers this Somavati. I can find marigolds and white champakas here. But it would be nice if I could offer flowers with a sweet scent. I asked him if he would get me some.'

'Oh! So that's why Bhau has gone away!'

'Yes. He's gone to Jalgaon. The Barves have a large garden with a number of *nag chafa* trees. "How wonderful it would be," I said, "if he could collect 108 nag chafas." Jalgaon is miles away. But he said, "We may not have money. But we do have legs to walk distances."'

'Friends, there are many varieties of *chafa*—white chafa, green chafa, *sone* chafa and nag chafa. The sone chafa has a heady scent. The fragrance of the nag chafa is sweet. It is a beautiful looking flower too, with broad white petals on the outside and a cluster of stamens within.

'Although we were poor, my mother believed in living with dignity. She wasn't one to upset her husband by demanding things that he couldn't afford. She wasn't one to make him feel small, to force him to lower his head in shame. She asked for nothing more than flowers, but she wanted good flowers for which he would have to travel far and for which he would have to make an effort to find. She taught her husband the value of idealism and the need to wear himself out in the service of God. She was a saint.'

Twenty-fifth Night

God Loves Everyone

It was nearing five o'clock in the evening. It was vacation time and I was at home. Aai had gone to the temple. When she returned, I asked her, 'May I go out either to Kamalya's or Banya's? If Bapu comes, tell him he'll find me at Banya's. May I go?'

'You may, Shyam, but I want you to do something before you go. There's a Mahar woman sitting outside Baldada's gate. She's very old and looks ill and weak. The bundle of firewood she was carrying on her head has fallen down. She can't get up with the load on her head and needs some help. Please help her with the bundle. I'll give you a bath afterwards.'

'Aai, people will curse me if they see me doing that. They'll beat me up. They will crowd around me, baying for my blood. You really want me to do it?'

'Tell people you are going to take a bath afterwards. How long can the old woman sit out in the sun waiting for another Mahar to come by and help her? She has to sell the firewood before she returns to her colony. If anyone questions you, say your mother instructed you to do it and will give you a bath.'

Aai's word had to be obeyed. That was all I knew. I started walking down the road, pretending I was off for my own work. I was careful not to let on that I had come out specially to help the old woman.

'What's the matter? Do you need help with this?' I asked her, raising one end of the bundle.

'Don't touch that, brother. You're a Brahmin. I'll be beaten up if someone sees you. Please, brother, go your way. Someone is sure to come by from the Mahar colony, selling fodder. He'll help me,' she pleaded.

'Don't worry. I'll go home and have a bath, all right? Take this.' I put the bundle of firewood on her head and helped her up.

Just then, Shridharbhat appeared from nowhere and began yelling at me.

'Shyam, don't you know she is a Mahar? You touched her! You've become a sahib with your English studies. I must tell Bhaurao about this.' Hearing Shridharbhat's comment, a neighbour, who had been relaxing on his verandah, also started to scold me. 'Shyam, you've gone too far now. You've lost all sense of right and wrong.'

'I'm going to have a bath. I'm not going to barge into the house without a bath and pollute it. How long could this old woman have waited for help? It would have been nightfall by the time she crossed the river and reached home. A bath will cleanse me.'

Back home, Aai said, 'Call the old woman over. How will she walk through the village balancing that heavy headload? She'll drop it somewhere again. We're out of tinder anyway. Go call her.'

I called out to the old woman. She came in through our gate. Aai settled how many measures of rice she would take for her entire load of firewood. I measured out the rice from the bin and poured it into her sari. Aai asked her, 'Are you ill, old woman?'

'Yes, mother. It's a fever. But what can I do? The stomach needs food,' the old woman said.

'I have some leftover rice from lunch. May I give it to you?'

'Please do, mother. God will bless you. Nobody cares for the poor,' the old woman said pitifully.

Aai brought the rice on a leaf plate and gave it to her. She moved to a corner of the yard and ate it.

'Can I have a drop of water, brother?' she asked. I poured water into her cupped palms. She drank it thirstily and went on her way, calling for God's blessings upon us.

'Come, wash yourself, Shyam,' Aai said.

I stood on a flat stone under the banana plant. Aai poured water over me from a distance. Then I moved to another stone, washed myself and went in. I told Aai about an experience I had had. 'You remember the wedding at the Khers that I attended? When we were having lunch, a poor Mahar woman stood outside the pandal begging. We were having puran polis. The hosts came round repeatedly, pressing us to have more. They pressed Bhaskarbhatji so relentlessly, he lost his temper and was about to get up and leave. But Apte uncle persuaded him to keep sitting. It was unbearably hot. The hosts sprinkled water on hand fans and fanned the guests. The water they served was scented with cool khus grass. The poor woman stood outside under the blistering sun begging. "A morsel of food, please," she called. But nobody gave her either a morsel to eat or a drop to drink. Not only that, there was a man there whose name I don't know. He works in Mumbai. He was wearing a silk dhoti and serving us. All of a sudden, he marched out of the pandal and barked at the woman, "Aren't you ashamed of begging at such a time? We haven't finished lunch yet. Come back for the leftovers once we are through. There are Brahmins eating inside and you stand here shouting. You people have become too arrogant. Now, will you get going or shall I fling my slipper at you?" The man actually did pick up his slipper to throw at her. The woman said, "No, brother, please don't do that. I'll go." And she went away. Aai, these people eat in restaurants in Mumbai where people of all castes eat. They are happy to lick their boss's boots. But they come to the village and show off. What that old woman said a while ago is so true. Nobody cares for the poor.

I'm sure if a Mahar man came here as a government official, these same people will give him lunches and dinners, spray rose water on him and garland him with flowers. Their dharma is to worship money and power. Those are their real gods. Picking up a slipper didn't pollute this silk-dhoti-clad man. They wear animal hides on their feet and walk about daintily, holding up their silk dhotis. Those slippers don't pollute them. But the man who has made those very slippers is supposed to pollute them. Not even his shadow must fall on them. What do such ideas mean? How can this be dharma? Does God approve of it?'

Aai said, 'You are right, son. Money and power do count for a lot. Remember the story of Pandharinath? He was poor and people always addressed him as Pandya. Then he went to the city. He studied, became an advocate, earned money by the shovelful in Varhad and Khandesh. He returned to the village once. He held a huge celebration for the village deity Someshwar. Suddenly people were calling him Pandharinath Baba. He was invited to somebody's place for a grand dinner. He was offered a wooden stool to sit on. He pushed it away and sat on the floor. He said, "Tatya, you haven't laid out this stool for me but for my wealth. So I'll lay the thick gold wristband I'm wearing on this stool and sit on the floor. You respect money, not the individual. Not the God in a man's heart. Not the riches of his mind. What impresses you are these white and yellow stones. What you worship are paper notes."

'We keep Mahars and Mangs at arm's length because they are poor. If they were rich, we would be deemed Mahars and Mangs instead. Shyam, whoever a needy person may be, Mahar or Mang, we must help without discrimination. We can come home and have a bath afterwards. Even that is only because we still have to live in this society and don't have the courage to face its censure, not because they are sinners or because their touch is polluting. As far as sin goes, we are all sinners.'

'Truly. Who has escaped sin? Who can put his hand on his heart and say I have never sinned. I would say that the Mahars and Mangs who earn their bhakri by honest labour and the sweat of their brow are the ones with merit. Isn't that true, Aai?'

'Shyam, that field of ours near Vithana actually belongs to a Mahar. I know the whole story. We had loaned him half a maund* of grain. We compounded it twofold or threefold and when he couldn't pay it, we took over the land.' Aai looked deeply dejected. 'In God's court, we are going to be declared sinners. We are going to have to stand before Him with lowered heads.'

'Lord Vitthal transformed himself into a Mahar for Damaji's sake, didn't he? If he thought Mahars were

---

* *A maund was a unit of weight in many Asian countries, particularly in India where it was used till the middle of the twentieth century. It was equivalent to today's 37 kg.*

defiled by their very birth, why would he have assumed that form?'

'For God, every living form is sacred. He went through ten avatars. First He was a fish, then a turtle, then a pig, then a half-lion half-man. What this means is that all these forms were sacred to Him. God resides as much in a fish or a Mahar as in a Brahmin. God runs to help the elephant. He tends to horses. He takes cows out to graze. He loves Kubja and He loves Shabari. He loves Guh the spider, Jatayu the bird and Hanuman the monkey. He loves us all because we are all His, just as I love you because you are mine. Just as you try to live in a way that will please me, we must try to live in a way that will please God. A person who doesn't love his parents, his brothers and his sisters, will find it impossible to love Mahars and Mangs. You must begin by loving the people at home. When love begins to spill over from your heart, it turns towards everybody around you. This I know, although I am not educated. You are studying now. You will know much more when you grow up.'

It was already time to light the lamps. I heard someone call me, so I went out.

'Friends, let us bury our ideas about high and low once and for all. Let us simply believe that whoever serves others is a sacred being. Until we arrive at that state, I will continue to believe what I have said in this verse:

178

> *God does not dwell in my Bharat*
> *Darkness pervades the land*
> *Why would God live in a place*
> *That extends no friendly hand?*
> *Why would God live in a country,*
> *Which shows neither love nor pity?*
> *No God in the temple, no God in the heart*
> *God is dead in my Bharat.'*

Twenty-sixth Night

Lessons in Brotherly Love

It was the summer holiday and all of us siblings were home that year. My elder brother, who lived with my Mama in Pune, had also come home. He came only once every two years whereas I was free to come home every weekend if I wished, since I was close by. My brother had had a severe attack of smallpox between his last visit and this summer. His condition had been so bad that not even the tiniest sesame seed would have fitted in between the blisters on his face. The illness had left him feeling very weak. Even after a patient has recovered from smallpox, his body retains a lot of the heat that the disease has generated. He needs to eat cooling foods to ease it. Rose petal preserve known as gulkand was supposed to be the best. But it was expensive and naturally, we didn't have any. So my mother discovered a poor man's home remedy: onions. They are cheap and nutritious. Doctors say they contain phosphorus. My mother half-steamed some onions, peeled the top layers and steeped them in jaggery syrup. She would give my brother a couple of spoons of this onion preserve every day.

One day, I said to Aai, 'You never give me any of that preserve. Dada gets everything—onions, ghee on his rice, extra helpings of dahi. No such things for us. We are like common birds. We fly home every chance we get. Why should anyone care about us? Those close at hand are hidden from sight. Those at a distance are bathed in light. Dada is lucky. Maybe I should have had smallpox. Then I'd have got onion preserve and milk and dahi and ghee.'

My words saddened Dada. His heart was pure and honest. He had had to bear many hardships to get an education and he had borne them without a word of complaint. He wasn't a wicked mischief-maker like me. He was quiet and steady. If he was insulted, he would bury the hurt deep in his heart like fire in the belly of an ocean. He wouldn't utter a word about it to anybody because he did not want to upset them with his sad stories. So now Dada said to Aai, 'I feel bad having these things that my brothers aren't getting. Could we all have the same things from now on, please? I've recovered from smallpox. So let's share what's left of the onion preserve.'

Aai said, 'Shyam, are you my stepchild? Why do you say such hurtful things? Don't you know that his eyes and his soles burn? He spends sleepless nights tossing and turning. The onions cool him down a bit. We aren't born to eat, are we? How can you wish for a terrible thing like smallpox on yourself? God has given you a strong body. Instead of being grateful for that, you come out with this monstrous idea. You're not a child any longer. You read stories about gods and saints. What use are they if they don't affect your life? Stop reading them then. You've read about Laxman's and Bharat's great love for Ram. What difference has that made? Dada is your blood brother, isn't he? Forget brothers, you should care even for strangers if they are ill. Don't I massage the soles of your feet with oil when you walk home from Dapoli? Don't I make a special sweet for you? Don't I pack sweets for you to take back to school? Don't be jealous of your brother. Otherwise a day will come when you won't be able to stand the sight of each other. Don't let that ever happen, Shyam.'

Dada interjected, 'Aai, don't take it so seriously. I don't think Shyam meant what he said. Come now. You said you were going to make pangis. Shall I go get banana leaves?'

'You go, Shyam. Don't touch the tender leaves. Take the leaf cutter and get us the old leaves from the top.'

I went out and cut down the leaves at the top. I carved neat pieces out of them and carried them in. 'Give me a leaf spine to split and make a click-clack with,' clamoured Babulya.

Aai made pangis. She served them to us straight off the fire, smeared with home-made butter, which made them tastier. She said we could also help ourselves to the butter and sugar she had offered to the tulsi in the morning, something she did at daybreak without fail. Dada fetched the jar of onion preserve and served it to us.

Aai said, 'Shyam, don't ask for any tomorrow, will you? Don't grudge it to your brother. Do you hear me, Shyam? Please learn to be good.'

I decided to sulk for the rest of the day. I had not spoken properly to anybody since the morning. Dada had asked me to play *viti-dandu* with him. I had refused. So he played bow and arrow with Babulya, who had scraped the spokes of an umbrella smooth to make arrows. Dada aimed them at a tree. When he hit the target, sap would run out of the tree. I said to him angrily, 'Why are you hurting the tree? Sap is its blood.'

Dada said, 'Will you play viti-dandu then?'

'Get lost. I don't have time to waste.'

I marched off in a huff. I felt no love for Dada, even though suddenly I felt a great love for the tree. I was deluding myself. If you can't love your brother, you can't love a tree.

After lunch, Dada lay down to rest. He was rubbing his soles because they were burning again. Even today, so many years after his attack of smallpox, his soles still burn. Ordinarily, I'd have helped relieve his pain by standing on his feet and rocking gently. He liked that. But since I was sulking, he didn't ask me for the favour. He only cast pleading looks my way. But I was determined not to give in. I had become cruel. Every bit of love in my heart had died.

I had turned to stone. When Dada could not bear the pain any longer, he called out to me. 'Shyam, can you massage my feet, please? I hate troubling you every day. Once I'm back in Pune, I won't. But while I'm here, please help me. Can you massage my feet, please?' Dada's words melted my heart, but not my ego. They say love can melt the hardest ego just as the sun can melt a mountain of ice. But love failed that day, because I had willed it not to succeed. I did not budge from my place.

Aai was in the middle of lunch. She had heard Dada. She rose, washed her hands, saw that I had not got up and said to him, 'Gaju, come, I'll massage your feet. Don't bother him. As the saying goes, "Blood brothers, ill-wishers".'

Aai began to massage Dada's feet. Her lunch was still half-eaten, the kitchen had to be cleaned, a cartful of vessels had to be washed. But Aai set everything aside. She closed the kitchen door to keep stray dogs away and came to help Dada. My loving, self-sacrificing, hard-working mother. My proud mother. She did not say a single angry word to me. She simply did what she had to. This deflated my ego. I went to her. 'Aai, let me do that. Please go back to your lunch. And your work.'

Aai said, 'If you want to help, please be gentle. Massage his feet till he falls asleep. Then you can go out to play. Shyam, remember he's your brother.'

She went back to the kitchen. She finished her lunch and took a pile of vessels out to the backyard to wash.

I stood lightly on Dada's feet, using my toes to press his soles. Soon Dada, my brother who had always been totally without ego, fell asleep.

My anger had ebbed away. As the sun disappeared over the horizon, my temper vanished with it. Dada, Purushottam, Babulya and I were sitting out in the courtyard. Aai joined us when she finished clearing up after dinner. The pot over the tulsi plant was still dripping. In the summer, when the plant could dry up in the heat, we would suspend an earthenware pot over it. Water dripped on to the plant through a hole all day and all night. When the pot ran dry, we filled it up again. An oil lamp was always lit before the plant. But that night, no artificial light was required. The moon was shining as bright and pure as my brother's heart. After Aai came out, Durva Aji also joined us and so did our neighbour, Janaki aunty. Aai had soaked field beans that had sprouted. We had to peel them. Our hands flew as we pressed them down on a stool with both thumbs to make them pop out of their skins.

'Aai, please sing that song about Abhimanyu,' I requested. 'You know the one. It comes when Krishna and Arjun go looking for him on the battlefield and hear a soft voice repeating Krishna's name. They find him on the ground, near death. The song goes, *There lies brave Abhimanyu, felled by the cruel chakravyuha that Drona devised*. It is such a lovely song. Please sing it Aai.'

'I think Aji is going to sing us a nice song today. Isn't that right, Aji? Sing the *Chindhi*. I haven't heard it in an age.'

Durva Aji knew many songs. I had never heard her sing the *Chindhi*. Chindhi actually means a strip of old cloth. I took the song to be literally about that. So I protested, 'No, Aji. No strips of ragged old cloth, please. Sing about silk.'

'Shyam, listen to the song. It is all about silk dhotis and saris,' said Aji, laughing. She began to sing in her sweet voice. When she sang, she paid full attention to the words. She emphasized them in the right places to underline their meaning, gesturing with her hands to bring out the emotion. The refrain of the song was, *What a perfect brother was Narayana to Draupadi*. The song is about the mutual affection and concern that Draupadi and Krishna share. The poet starts the song by questioning why Krishna loves his adopted sister Draupadi more than he does his own younger sister Subhadra.

Answering his own question, the poet recounts a story. Narad Muni who moved constantly between the three worlds—the divine, the human and the subhuman—came to Krishna one day, holding his veena against his shoulder and singing songs of devotion. Because he met so many kinds of people on his travels, from the finest and purest to the coarsest and most barbaric, he had a great stock of experiences. He went around the three worlds doing his work. He would praise a great person here, teach an egoist a lesson there and if he found an undiscovered flower in some corner, spread its fragrance in all directions. Everybody held him in high regard because he was selfless and strove hard for the welfare of others.

When Narad Muni arrived at the Pandavas' home as a guest, Krishna sprang to his feet to embrace him and ask after him. Narad Muni said, 'Lord, I am here today to lodge a complaint against you. Wherever I go, I speak of your impartiality, your equal view of people. But one person said to me, "Stop praising Krishna. He loves that adopted sister of his more than his own sister. What kind of equal view is that?" I had no answer to his charge. So I decided to come to you for an answer. Now tell me. Why do you love your younger sister Subhadra less?'

Krishna said, 'My dear Narad Muni, please understand that in myself I am totally inert. I go where I am pulled. Take, for example, the breeze and a man who keeps his doors and windows shut. Would this man be right in complaining that the breeze does not enter his house but goes only to houses that keep their doors and windows open? Both wind and light enter homes that keep their doors and windows wide open. I am pulled towards Draupadi perhaps because the rope she pulls me with is stronger than Subhadra's. I have no control over my movements. I am without desire to possess, I am without a will to act. That would be an exact description of me. Would you like to test what I am saying? Then run to Subhadra, tell her Krishna has cut his finger and ask her for a strip of cloth to bandage the wound. If she does not have a strip to spare, go to Draupadi and ask her for it.'

Narad arrived at Subhadra's place. She inquired after him, asked him to make himself comfortable and tell her about happenings on Mount Kailas, in the world of the gods and asuras. 'You have a great life, wandering about everywhere. I don't think you ever get bored. You see a new country and new people every day. Nandanvan today, Madhuvan tomorrow. Please sit down. What's the hurry?'

Narad said, 'Subhadratai, I have no time to sit and chat. Krishna has cut his finger. It is bleeding badly. Give me a strip of cloth to bandage it with.'

Subhadra said, 'Where can I go looking for a strip of cloth, Narad? Here's a silk dhoti, a memento of Arjun's victory in the north. Here's a heavy silk sari, a present from King Kuntibhoj. And here is this very expensive Paithani sari. I don't have any old cloth to tear a strip from.'

'That's fine. I'll ask Draupaditai,' Narad said and left.

Draupadi was stringing flowers for a garland, with Krishna's name on her lips.

'Come in, Narad,' she said. 'Let me welcome you with this garland. I know you are in these parts for my Krishna. He is here so all you bees are bound to come buzzing around him. But don't steal the whole of him. Leave some of him for me.'

'Draupadi, I have no time to joke,' Narad said, his voice full of fear. 'Krishna has cut his finger. Give me a strip of cloth, quick.'

'Really? Is it very bad?' Draupadi asked and instantly tore a strip from the yellow silk sari she was wearing to give to him.

Aji ended the song with the line, *She tore a strip from her rich silk sari / What a perfect brother was Narayana to Draupadi.* Aji had sung the song so beautifully and so lost was I in it that my hands had forgotten to peel the beans.

'Did you like the song, Shyam? Were you listening carefully?' Aai asked.

That is when it dawned on me.

'Shall I guess why you wanted Aji to sing this particular song today, Aai?'

'Go on. Guess.'

'This afternoon, I refused to press Dada's legs. At lunchtime I would not let him eat onion preserve alone. Subhadra was Krishna's sister, but she didn't give her brother a strip to bandage his wound. I too didn't help my brother when he was in pain. You wanted Aji to sing this song to shame me. Isn't that right? Admit it.'

'Not to shame you, but to teach you to love.'

I got up and went to Dada. I took his hand in mine and said tearfully, 'Dada. I will always do what you ask me to. I promise to love you. Please forgive me for my behaviour this afternoon.'

Dada said, 'Come on, Shyam. Why are you asking to be forgiven? I have already forgotten what happened this afternoon. Your temper is like the clouds. They are there one moment and gone the next. Don't I know your moods? But I also know that your heart is as clear as crystal. Aai, don't worry. We will never part. We might quarrel, sure, but we will make up the next minute with a hug.'

'Our happiness lies in your love for one another,' Aai said. 'Your mutual love will make God happy too.'

Twenty-seventh Night

A Father's Generous Heart

One of our cows had calved. Aai had made kharwas from the colostrum. I loved this sweet. When I was still living at home, Radha, the dairywoman, used to bring me kharwas whenever one of her cows calved. Sadly, Radha had died prematurely. Aai could not help but think of me the day she made kharwas.

'We could have sent Shyam some kharwas, if somebody had been going that way,' she said to Bhau.

'Why somebody? I'll take it to him,' Bhau offered. 'It's made from our own cow's milk. That makes it a special treat. I could leave early tomorrow morning. What shall I carry it in?'

'I'll steam it in a can with a tight lid. You can carry the can itself,' Aai replied. The next morning, Bhau left on foot for Dapoli, carrying a can of Aai's delicious kharwas.

School had broken for the lunchtime recess. We, its caged birds, had flown out and were flitting about freely in the open outdoors. The school was surrounded by trees. The branches of cultivated mangoes grew very close to the ground. Boys were having a great time swinging from them and jumping off them happily like monkeys. They were doing other things too—eating from snack boxes their families had sent them, sitting on trees, singing and playing games. My friends and I were sitting under a tree playing *antakshari*. I knew lots of shlokas and poems. I could always find one to recite starting with the last letter of the opponents' song. I would also recite poems I had composed in classical metres. I was generally pitted alone against the rest of my friends and still won every round. The boys used to call me Balkavi after the well-known boy poet Thombre.

In the midst of our game, a boy came running to say somebody was looking for me. Before I had time to wonder who it could be, Bhau was standing before me.

'Why did you come all the way, Bhau?' I asked. 'The break will soon be over. I would have been home in a couple of days.'

To tell the truth, I was ashamed to see Bhau dressed haphazardly in his old bedraggled clothes. I was studying in an English school. My friends were from well-to-do homes. I had still not learnt what to value. I valued showy clothes. I did not see the love of a father who had walked six kos* to

---

* *This was a unit of distance measurement in ancient India that was used particularly by village folk, well into the early twentieth century. One kos equalled roughly 2.25 miles, which is roughly 3.5 km.*

meet me. Instead of giving me better vision, my education had made me blind. Instead of my heart growing bigger, it had contracted. Instead of learning to look beneath surfaces, I was busy looking at surfaces themselves. Education isn't what its name says it is if it fails to open your heart to other people. Education should have taught me to look at every individual and every object as a temple of knowledge. I should have been able to see the great expanse that lay below what we saw on the surface. The heart plays a vital role in lending beauty and sweetness to life.

Bhau had walked six kos just to bring his son a special sweet. It had given him joy to do this for me because he loved me very much. That is what love is. It makes hard work and hardship seem sweet and beautiful. As a boy I was lucky to receive such love. Today I might find fault with it. Perhaps they could have given the kharwas to a poor child in the village. Why did they not think of every child as a version of Shyam? Why did they feel only this particular lump of flesh with this form, colour and name was theirs?

Such an evolved vision of love takes time to develop. One grows into it slowly, moving away from a life of desire to a life of detachment from desire. Because my parents poured so much love into me back then, I can give at least a little of it to people today. My parents sowed these tender feelings in my heart without being conscious of it. That is why my life isn't an arid desert, but is touched with joy and fragrance.

But in that moment, it bothered me that my schoolmates would laugh at me.

'Is that your father?' they would wonder. 'Look at his turban. And that coat.' Only my discomfiture mattered to me. We are all self-centred. We are concerned about our honour, our happiness, our opinions, our prestige. Life is all about us. That is why we remain stunted. How can a person who cannot see beyond himself love anybody?

Bhau said, 'Shyam, your mother has sent you some kharwas. Share it with your friends so I can take the can back.' He handed the can to me. The other boys were sniggering. I was feeling thoroughly ashamed. Bhau said, 'Shyam, why are you gaping? Why are you feeling embarrassed? Come on, boys. Eat. Shyam is feeling too shy to eat by himself. He shouldn't eat by himself anyway. We should always share what we have.' Many of the boys went away. Only my friends stayed back. One stepped forward boldly, opened the can and said, 'Come on. Let's wipe this can clean.' Then all of us pounced on the kharwas. Bhau moved away and sat down to rest. He refused to eat any of the kharwas although we kept pressing him to. 'No, no. It's meant for you boys. I'm enjoying watching you eat,' he said.

We polished off all the kharwas. It was absolutely delicious. Meanwhile, my tired father's eyes had closed. Just then the bell clanged its call. Bhau got up with a start. 'Are you through?' he asked. 'Give me the can. I'll wash it when I get to the river.' Bhau got ready to leave. 'Study hard,' he said to me. 'And look after yourself. The new calf is lovely. It's a male.' He left and we returned to school.

I was feeling thoroughly ashamed of myself. I was an ungrateful child to my parents who were so full of love. What had happened could not be erased. It had left a bad taste in my mouth. How would I ever repay the debt I owed to a father who thought nothing of walking six kos for me and a mother who had sent him with kharwas? The only way I can free myself of the debt is to give my innumerable brothers and sisters the same genuine love I have received, given without expecting anything in return. If I don't, I will remain permanently indebted.

Twenty-eighth Night

Samb Sadashiv, Give Us Rain

After a good bout of rain one year, it suddenly stopped. Gradually the mud in the fields began to dry up. Water vanished from the canals. Grass shrivelled on the plains. People grew anxious. Farmers' eyes were fixed on the sky, keeping a lookout for a black cloud.

Rain is our greatest support. The world runs on rain. Without it, nothing can exist. Indeed, water is life. The Sanskrit word for water is *jeevan*, which also means life. The man who proposed the word jeevan for water must have had a very fine mind. We have given water other sweet names too like *amrut*, which means nectar. Could there be a more appropriate word than that for water? Sprinkle water on a wilting flower, let it nourish a stunted tree, let a few drops of dew fall on dried grass and see how life returns to them. Drink a few sips of water and your fatigue vanishes. You are instantly refreshed. Our old sages called water *mata* or mother. They compared the life-giving qualities of water to motherly love. I won't go into all the virtues of water here, except for one. It's that water is formless. It has no colour, smell or shape. We lend it these attributes. In that sense, water is like God.

That year, the rain just would not come and the crops would not grow. Drought was almost upon us. There is an old custom in our village. When there is a drought, we 'imprison' Lord Shiva to bring rain. There is a Shiva temple in the village where we drown the Shivaling in water. The whole of the inner sanctum is flooded and kept that way. The priest chants a vedic hymn as villagers come with pots of water to pour over the Shivaling. This ritual continues night and day till we get rain. A roster is prepared for villagers to bring water turn by turn and another for those who know how to chant the hymn.

The Shiva temple, which is always crowded during drought, resounds night and day to the sombre recitation of the *Rudrasukta* chant. This hymn is solemn, radiant and sublime. The poet who composed it must have seen the entire universe in his mind's eye. He must have seen nature in all its forms unfurl before him, including man and his needs. The poet must have become one with the universe. My father knew the *Rudrasukta*. His turn to chant it used to come after midnight.

Aai said to me one day, 'Why aren't you going to the temple? You must also carry water there.'

'Our water-pots are too heavy for me to lift. They are huge,' I said.

'We have a small one. Take that. Even a mugful will do. You can carry many mugs of water one after the other. The Ganapati well has footholds that will make climbing in and out easy. Go. Take the mug.'

'That little mug? Why not our little spouted oilcan then? Or the set of ladles we use for puja? People will laugh me out of the temple.'

'No, they won't. They'll laugh if you try to lift a regular water-pot. It is silly to do things that are beyond your strength, but wicked not to do something that is within your powers out of sheer laziness. This work is for the whole village. You can't recite the hymn because you don't know it. But you do know how to carry water. Pull your weight by doing that. We must all do our bit without shirking our duty. Krishna might have lifted Mount Govardhan single-handedly, but his cowherd companions also put their sticks to it. Why do you read all these stories if they don't touch your life? Your brain might as well be stuffed with cow dung. There is the other story about Ram's *setu*, the bridge he built to cross over to Lanka. The mighty monkeys, Maruti, Sugreev and Angad, were transporting mountains. But the tiny squirrel wanted to lend a hand too. It was sacred work. To get rid of Ravana was vital for the well-being of the world. The whole world had to participate in the work. So what did the squirrel do? She rolled about in the sand and shook the grains caught in her fur over the bridge. She did what her strength let her do. If you cannot carry the large water-pot, take the small one. If not that, take a mug. If even that is too much for you, take a tumbler. But go, Shyam. How much more coaxing do you need?'

I got up reluctantly. I took the small water-pot to the temple. Many children were carrying water, helping to 'imprison' Shiva. The atmosphere was grave with the flooding and the chanting. Even children younger than me were carrying mugs of water. I joined them, feeling a little embarrassed at first. A priest said to me, 'Good to see you here, Shyam. Were you feeling shy because you are studying English?' I did not answer him. The little children were singing their own mantra while fetching water. Not a Sanskrit mantra but one in Marathi. It went:

Samb Sadashiv, give us rain
Let the rice fields bloom again
A paisa, a payli, we'll buy the grain.
Samb Sadashiv, give us rain.

Let the rain come, let the corn ripen, let prices fall, they prayed. Although I was embarrassed to chant the mantra with them initially, their enthusiasm was enough to drive any feelings of shyness away. Soon I, too, began to sing 'Samb Sadashiv, give us rain' loudly. My voice merged with the other children's voices and I danced with them, matching step for step.

Aai taught me that one should always do one's bit for a common cause. There is no need to feel embarrassed. An ant should work like an ant. An elephant should work like an elephant.

Twenty-ninth Night

I Stole to Become a Great Man

'The village of Latvan is located not too far away from our village. The Phadkes are its most important family. Inamdar Phadke still lives there. He belongs to the well-known Sardar Haripant Phadke family. There used to be much coming and going between our families once. Balwantrao Phadke of Latvan would visit my father often. He used to talk to us children with great affection. He had no airs. He was a very simple and trusting man. I used to take the ring off his finger. He would say to me, "Shyam, would you like to have the ring?" When he said that, I would try it on each finger in turn. But it was too big for all of them and kept falling off. He would laugh at that and say, "You must grow fatter. Only then will it fit you."'

I was home from Dapoli once when Balwantrao came to visit us with another gentleman. I had become an avid reader at school at this point. But good books were hard to come by.

I used to read books published by the Dabholkar Mandali, although I didn't understand much of what I read. I remember having read a biography of Spenser. It was around this time that Bhaskarpant Phadke had begun publishing *Ramtirth* in several volumes. I have been deeply influenced by Phadke's writings. I am charmed by his simple, luminous Marathi prose style. I have since read all the volumes of *Ramtirth* and know them practically by heart. But back then, I could not lay my hands on a single one. I remember a relative of ours had a volume that I picked up greedily when I visited, but he snatched it away. 'You think you'll understand anything that's in this?' he scoffed. I was very upset. I was sure I would have understood more than he ever would because I shared the poet's sensibility. I too had a poetic bent of mind. My parents had nourished my heart and mind. I had read the scriptures and was filled with love and devotion.

I wanted to buy all the volumes of *Ramtirth*. But where was the money? I didn't even possess all the books I needed at school. I was studying English but did not own a single dictionary. I would manage somehow by guessing the meanings of words. But I was determined to buy the whole of *Ramtirth*.

I saw that the gentleman, who had come with Balwantrao, had a thick wad of notes stuffed in his pocket. *Why not slip one out*, I thought.

I knew it was a sin to steal. But I was stealing to read a good book. That would earn me merit. Immediately after

I had taken a note, I started teaching my younger brother a shloka, *I yearn for you to give me a pure mind*, while here I had just stolen money. At some point, the visitor began counting his money and found that he was five rupees short. 'Bhaurao,' he said. 'There's one note missing here. A five-rupee note.'

'Have you checked all your pockets?' Bhau asked. 'Did you give it to somebody?'

I stopped teaching my brother the shloka. A thief is never at peace. Aai was having her lunch in the kitchen. I went and sat with her.

'Aai, how can this little bit of rice fill you? Did we not leave you enough?' I asked.

'I have little appetite these days, my pet,' she said. 'I shove some food down so I have the strength to work. I am only waiting for you boys to grow up.'

'Don't worry, Aai,' I said. 'I'm going to study a lot, read a lot and become a great man.'

'Study and become a good human being. Sometimes education spoils people. That's what I fear. I always pray to God to make my children good, no matter if they are not highly educated. I don't care about greatness. I want you to be kind and good.'

How sweetly she spoke. I was always amazed at how eloquently my unschooled mother could speak. People would often say to Muhammed, 'If you are indeed God's prophet, show us a miracle.' Muhammed would say to them, 'Nature is itself full of miracles. I don't need to show you anything else. Is it not a miracle that your tiny boats skim the sea with the aid of the wind? Is it not a miracle that, tiny as they are, they have the courage to dance and sway on the immense chest of the ocean? Is it not a miracle that your cattle, sheep and goats go out to graze in the jungles and return home every evening? Is it not a miracle that you come upon fresh springs in the desert and sweet dates grow in the arid sand?' Then Muhammed would say, 'Is it not a miracle that He made it possible for the Quran to be spoken through an illiterate man like me?'

'Friends, it was He who was speaking the Quran through my mother, so to say. I take the Quran to mean the utterance of a full and loving heart. My mother's words too came from a full and loving heart. They were the words of the sacred Shivaling hidden in the sanctum of her heart.

'"Grow up to be a good man, not necessarily a great man," she had said. The words stung me like scorpions, bit me like serpents. Friends, they say that during the reign of the Tudors in England, secret police used to prowl around everywhere. One historian has said, "It was like having a scorpion under every pillow." There was no place in that kingdom where a man could lay his head in peace. There are scorpions in the heart too that will not let you sleep. They are with you all the time. Wherever you go, even when you die and go to hell, you take your scorpions with you. They are your secret police, your conscience.'

'This is a mystery,' said my father. 'No outsider came here.'

'Ask Shyam if one of his friends came,' Balwantrao suggested. 'Young boys have become very wicked these days. They can't do without bidis and paan. Shyam . . .' he called out to me.

'Yes?' I said, coming forward.

'Did any of your friends drop in? We are missing five rupees.'

'Nobody came,' I replied. 'I went out to play and came back in the evening. Nobody came after that.'

Bhau looked at me and said, 'Shyam, I hope you didn't take the money. Admit it if you did.'

'Nonsense,' Balwantrao said. 'Why would he take it?'

Aai washed her hands and came out. She had heard what had happened. Bhau was upset that a visitor's money should have gone missing in his house. He asked me again, 'Shyam, are you sure you didn't take it? To buy a compass box? You were asking me for money for a compass box the other day.'

Aai spoke up immediately.

'Shyam would never do such a thing. He has a temper. He sulks. But he doesn't touch other people's things. That's one good thing about him. And if he does something wrong, he always admits it. That is the other good thing.

He pinched a piece of candy a long time ago. As soon as I asked around, he said, "I took it, Aai." He won't take what he shouldn't. And if he does, he'll always come out with it. You haven't taken the money, have you, Shyam?'

How completely my mother trusted me. How could I betray her trust? Tukaram has said in one of his *abhangs*, 'The one who can be trusted is the best of humankind.' The wall that had propped up my deceit came crashing down. My mother's simple, trusting words had razed it to the ground. My eyes began to stream. Aai said, 'Don't cry, dear. I didn't accuse you of taking the money. I know you wouldn't do such a thing. Hush, little one.'

Her gentle words brought down the last of my resistance. I ran to her. Clinging to her, I said, 'Aai, it was I, your Shyam, who took the money. Here it is.' After this, all I could do was sob, 'Aai, Aai.' Aai was deeply hurt. Her trust and pride in her son had taken a beating. But all was not lost. God had saved some of her honour. She had sworn that her Shyam would not steal and if he did, he would say so. I had not cleared the entire test, but I had passed one-half of it.

'Shyam, never do that again, will you? Let this be the first and last time. But I am happy you confessed. Now hush, my son,' Aai consoled me.

Balwantrao appreciated my honesty and gave me a rupee as reward. I promptly gave it to Aai.

'Shyam, can you tell me why you took the money?' Aai asked me later.

'To become a great man. To read books and become knowledgeable.'

'But didn't you read the lesson "Never Steal" in your first standard book? You haven't learnt that lesson yet. Then why read other books?' What Aai said sounded simple, but it was actually profound.

'Friends, the great sage Patanjali is supposed to have said, "If you have fully understood even one word, you will attain salvation." What does that mean? It means that when you truly understand something, you assimilate it and live by it. A child wants to touch the glass of a lantern. It is hot. His mother says, "Don't touch it, you will hurt yourself." But the child returns to the lantern. The mother says, "Go ahead. Touch it then." The child touches it and burns his fingers. He doesn't touch hot glass ever again. This knowledge is now firmly lodged in his head. Socrates calls knowledge a virtue. In Sanskrit, knowledge is called *anubhuti*, lived experience.

'I had merely read the words "never steal" but not understood them. Truth, compassion, love, non-violence are words we use glibly. But it takes entire lifetimes for them to become our lived experience.'

Thirtieth Night

You Have Grown . . . Not in Age But in Heart

The summer vacation was over. School reopened just as the monsoon set in. Clouds cool the heated earth. When showers fall, the hot earth exudes a warm fragrance. The fragrance that the first shower brings is special. The phrase 'the scented earth' makes total sense then. I believe that flowers and fruits also draw their scents from the earth.

This time I had returned to Dapoli with a plan. One day, during the vacation, my younger brother had thrown a tantrum, asking for a new shirt. Talking him out of it, Aai had said, 'When your Dada and Anna grow up and begin to earn, they will make you a new shirt. Don't cry for it now.'

In those days, people didn't own as many clothes as they do now. We didn't even know what a coat looked like. As for shirts, we got a new one once in two years or so. During winter, we went to school with a folded dhoti around our necks. We possessed neither scarves nor jackets nor warm coats. City dwellers have always had these things, but now even villagers do. I believe it is good to have as much air and sunlight touch our skins as possible. I believe God Himself touches and cleanses us in the form of wind and sunshine. But we do not allow nature to come anywhere near us.

My brother's shirt was torn. Aai had sewn patches over the tears. My plan was to take home a new shirt for him. But where was the money to come from? My father used to come to Dapoli quite often to fight the cases that his creditors had filed against him. He was becoming poorer by the day, but that didn't stop him from defending himself in court.

Some people cannot live without the law courts. It is like an addiction. It's not always their case that is being heard. Perhaps that has even been settled already. But they are there to help someone else win theirs. The deal is, 'If I manage to get a judgement in your favour, you give me a certain sum of money. If I fail, I bear the expenses of the case.' I have seen people take contracts to fight other people's cases.

Whenever Bhau came to Dapoli, he gave me an anna or two for snacks. My plan was to save some of that money. School had started in the month of Jyeshtha. Ganesh Chaturthi was three months away. I calculated that at the rate that I was saving money, I would be able to save a rupee till then. That would be enough to get a shirt or a coat stitched for my brother.

With my eyes set on my goal, I would count the money I was saving again and again. By Ganesh Chaturthi, I had collected a rupee and two annas. I went to the tailor. A boy from school who was more or less the same size as my brother accompanied me on this trip. I told the tailor to make a coat to fit the boy. I bought two yards of fabric and half a yard of cloth for lining. The total cost was going to be exactly as much as I had saved. When the coat was ready and I went to pick it up, my eyes filled with tears that fell on the coat. I realized I was leaving a mark of love on the coat where normally we put an auspicious spot of vermillion.

The day I left for home, the rain was coming down in torrents. The family with whom I lived said, 'Don't go in this rain. The rivers and streams will be full. You won't be able to cross over either at Pisai or Sondeghar. Listen to us.' But I was in no mood to listen to anybody. With love flooding my heart, I wasn't afraid of any brimming streams. And so, I left with the new coat tied up in a bundle. If I had had wings, I would have flown home. I was dreaming of Aai's joy when I noticed a *naneti* jumping right next to me. A naneti is a green-coloured snake that moves in a series of jumps. That gave me a bit of a scare. Now I looked carefully about me as I walked. The stream at Pisai was raging. The current in this stream had always been very strong. I hesitated a moment, then took my mother's name and entered the water. I was carrying a stick. I would plant it firmly before me and only then take a step forward.

Even then I was almost carried away by the current at one point. I managed to hold on somehow and at last I was on the other bank. Perhaps my love kept me afloat. This stream was rushing to meet another. Surely it would not drown me when I was rushing to meet my brother.

With the soil washed away, stones stuck out of the path, sharp as needles. They hurt my feet, but I hardly noticed. I was trying to get home before it grew dark. Even then, night fell while I was only halfway there. Lightning split the sky and, a moment later, thunder split my ears. The rain continued to pour down. I was walking in the company of all five elements.

At long last, when I did reach home, I was drenched to the skin.

'Aai,' I called from outside. Bhau was doing his evening puja and Aai had just put some coals in the chulah. My brother opened the door and shouted, 'Aai, it's Anna. He's home.'

'Why did you come in this pouring rain, Shyam? Look how wet you are,' Aai said with concern.

'Wasn't the Sondeghar stream overflowing?' Bhau asked.

'It was,' I said. 'But I managed somehow.'

'It carried a woman away the other day.'

'He's here by Ganapati's grace,' Aai said. 'Now take off those wet clothes and have a hot bath.'

While I was having a bath, my brother opened the bundle. Like any boy, he was looking for a small gift. A sweet or a toy or a picture book. But what he found was a brand new coat. It was not a coat. It was a heart. It was love. It was the fruit of my mother's teachings.

'Anna, whose coat is this? Who is it for?' my brother asked, holding up the coat.

'I'll tell you later. Take it to the kitchen,' I said.

'Aai, look at this coat. It isn't Anna's size. It's my size. Do you think he has brought it for me?'

Aai handed me a dry dhoti. I sat by the chulah warming myself. 'Whose coat is that?' she asked.

'Is it to be delivered to Moru Joshi's?' Bhau asked. 'Mukya from the Camp must have sent it.'

'No. I had it stitched for Purushottam,' I said.

'Where did you get the money from? Did you borrow it or spend your school fees?' Bhau asked.

'I hope you didn't take somebody else's money,' Aai's voice trembled as she asked.

'Do you think I've forgotten what you said when I did that once? You said, "This is the first and last time you will touch someone else's money." No, I did not borrow or steal or spend the school fees.'

'Then you took credit from the tailor, did you?' Bhau asked.

'No, Bhau. I saved up from the money you gave me for snacks every time you came. In three months, I had enough to have the coat made. Aai had said to Purushottam that he would get a new shirt when his Dada and Anna grew up and began to earn. But why wait till then? I decided to give him a coat for Ganapati. Purushottam, try it on. See if it fits.'

Purushottam put it on.

'See, it fits perfectly,' he said. 'And look. There's a pocket inside. Now I won't lose my pencil.'

Aai was very moved by what I had said.

'Shyam, you have grown . . . not in age or wealth or education, but in your heart. I hope you will continue to love each other all your lives, my sons. May nobody's evil eye fall upon your love.'

Bhau stroked my back. He did not say a word. But his hand on my back said everything.

'Aai, shall I put a vermillion mark on this?' Purushottam asked.

'No, little one. Fold it up and put it away for now. Tomorrow, you can put vermillion on it, fold your hands before God and wear it. Tomorrow, you will wear a new coat when you bring Ganapati home.'

Thirty-first Night

To the Temple at Ladghar

Raja was leaving that day. He was sad that he would not be around to hear the rest of Shyam's stories. But he resisted the temptation to stay back. He had duties to perform. It is not only bad things that tempt you. Even good things do. Both temptations have to be avoided when duty calls.

'I don't know when we'll meet again, Shyam,' Raja said. 'I will miss hearing your stories. They sound simple, but they are lessons in dharma. Yashoda saw the universe in Krishna's tiny mouth. We see our entire culture in your stories. You have shown us how much love and joy we can pour into our daily lives. Love between siblings, love for animals, love for birds, all these can make our lives richer and more beautiful. How often I've wept to hear you speak. You are like an embodiment of Krishna himself.'

'Raja, you always exaggerate. You see all these virtues in me because you love me. I admit to having only one virtue. Genuine emotion. When I perform a keertan, I make up for my weak musical skills with strong emotion and an eagerness to communicate. What else do I have? Nothing. I am just a chatterbox. I only tell stories. I am devoted to words. But you, Bhika, Namdeo, Ram, you are devoted to hard work. I respect you deeply for that. However much you praise and adore me, I know I am nothing. It's like smearing sindoor on a stone and turning it into a god.'

Just then Ram walked in. 'Is the cart here?' Shyam asked.

'No. Plans have changed. Daji said they won't leave now, but at night after this evening's story. Don't worry, Raja. You'll still get there on time.'

It was evening. The sky was filled with a flamboyant display of colours. Every shade of red and yellow and blue was splashed across the firmament. Shyam and Raja were sitting on the bank of the river. First they chatted, but then fell silent. Soon they noticed the cowherds returning home with the cattle. Some rode on the backs of buffaloes. Others followed behind, playing on their flutes.

'We should go back,' Raja said.

'I suppose we should. But when you see nature in all its splendour, you don't want to wrench yourself away. You want to sit still, allowing nature's silent song to absorb you completely.'

Shyam's lips trembled as he spoke. At that moment, he was pure emotion. Pure yearning. At last the two friends rose and returned to the ashram. People had begun to gather on the terrace. The stars too had begun to gather one by one in the sky above. Soon the terrace was filled from end to end with people. When the prayers ended, everybody sat with their eyes closed for a few moments. Then Shyam began to tell his story.

When we were still boys, Aai had begun to suffer from joint pain. We had asked the Goddess of Ladghar for a boon to cure her. Ladghar is a beautiful village near the sea in Dapoli district. There is a holy place nearby known as Tamastirth, or 'fiery' pilgrim site. It is called that because the water there has a reddish tinge. Over time, Aai's joints had improved. Although she wasn't completely fit, she could move around the house and do her chores. But she had to wait for a long time before she could return to Ladghar to redeem her pledge to the Goddess with an offering of a wooden doll, kumkum, a blouse piece and a coconut. At long last it was decided that she would come to Dapoli and I would take her from there to Ladghar by bullock cart.

I was eager for her arrival. She had not been out of Palgad for at least twelve years, neither for a change of air nor for a holiday. It was already night by the time Aai arrived. I had engaged a cart to take us to Ladghar. It was three kos away, roughly three hours by cart. Aai and I got up at cockcrow. The cart driver arrived on time and called out to us. I gathered all our stuff together and we climbed into the cart. A distant cousin of ours lived in Ladghar.

We were going to halt with her and were expecting to reach her place by seven or eight o'clock that morning.

As soon as the cartman got into the driver's seat, the pair of bullocks set off at a clip. They seemed happy to be trotting along. It was a silent time of day. There was no sound except for the sweet tinkle of bells around the bullocks' necks. They sounded like a call to morning prayers in nature's temple. The lovely Krittika star cluster was still on display in the sky. Flowers had opened, a cool breeze was blowing and birds had broken into song. Although I was about fifteen years old at the time, my mother still saw me as a little boy. No mother really believes that her child has grown up. I too thought of myself as a child and lay with my head in Aai's lap. Aai stroked my head and ran her gentle hands over my arms and back.

'Just look at your shendi, Shyam,' she said. 'It's like straw. Don't you ever oil it?' I paid no attention to her words. I was in seventh heaven. Aai and I had never travelled together before. We had never been so free and independent. That day, the world belonged to us. I dreamt happily of the time I'd be an adult and make sure Aai didn't lack anything. I promised myself she would live in a heaven of happiness.

'Why aren't you saying anything, Shyam?' Aai said.

'Because I have everything I want. I desire nothing more than to lie with my head in your lap and have you look at me lovingly as you stroke my hair. I want to be a

little boy. I want you to pat my head and sing ovis to me.'
Aai really did all of that.

Between Dapoli and Ladghar, one passes through dense jungle. It is so thick with trees that not a single ray of sunshine can enter. There is a site in the jungle where water cascades down the side of a mountain. It is a sight that awes you into silence. Lining the path on both sides as we passed were mango, jackfruit, cashew nut and banyan trees. Several kinds of birds flitted busily through their branches, chirping and singing. While nature was waking up, I wanted to fall asleep in my mother's lap. Sleep eluded me, but I lay with eyes closed anyway. Aai was singing ovis to me, inserting her own lines in the middle of traditional ones. She sang:

> *In a dense jungle where a cascade does roar*
> *May God be with Shyam*
> *Now and forever more.*

I knew this one was composed by her. I shot up immediately to see the cascade she was singing about.

'Why have you got up, Shyam?' Aai asked. 'I don't mind your lying in my lap. My legs don't hurt.'

'Aai, you've just invited God into my life with your ovi. God's presence must bring about an awakening. I can't sleep if He is with me.'

We now heard the distant rumble of the ocean. Soon the jungle cleared and we caught a glimpse of its surging waters. We needed to move just a little bit past human civilization to see serenity laid out before us like a feast.

The neat and pretty village of Ladghar came into view just a bit further. By the time we entered it, little boys could be seen driving waterwheels with their bullocks on every plantation. We could hear the wheels creak even as we entered the village. Water rushed through the canals to the betel nut, coconut, banana and pineapple plants. Every house had its own plantation. It was a lovely and happy little village with the sea beside it, abundant water and several species of flowers, fruits and trees growing luxuriantly all around.

We weren't sure exactly where our cousin lived. As we drove through the village, we stopped to ask for directions. We passed a school on the way. The schoolchildren stared at us in wonder. It is always so with children. Their curiosity is awakened when they see something new and unfamiliar. At last we found Subhatai's house. The cartman untied the bullocks, tethered them and fed them grass. I had never seen Subhatai before. Even Aai was seeing her after many years. My mother was much older than Subhatai. Subhatai could have been her daughter. She was excited to see Aai. Looking at me, she said, 'And who is this?'

'This is Shyam. The one who used to throw tantrums and fight with everybody. Surely you remember him?'

'You're a young man now, aren't you?' she said. 'Are you studying English?'

'Yes, I'm in the fourth,' I replied.

Subhatai's house was filled with love and we immediately felt at home there. Subhatai said, 'Why don't you go down to the sea for your baths now so you can be back by ten or eleven? We can go to the temple after lunch and you can leave in the evening. I wish you were staying for a few days. We haven't met for so many years. For me it would be like having my mother come to my in-laws' house. Won't you stay?'

'I can't,' Aai demurred. 'This cart has been hired for the day. And I've left my little children at home. There's nobody to look after them. Shyam can't miss school either. It's lucky we've been able to meet at all, even if it is for a day.'

We picked up our clothes and went by cart to the sea. Subhatai's husband accompanied us. The bullocks set off at a quick pace. The sea was not too far away. The road ran parallel to it. We were headed for Tamastirth. I could not take my eyes off the sea. I was drinking it up with my eyes. The ocean spread before us, an ageless force that had neither beginning nor end. It was a limitless stretch of blue with another limitless stretch of blue overhead.

Our cart reached the spot we were headed for. We climbed down. Subhatai's husband showed us where we could take our dip. It was a spot where the waves seemed to rear their heads and the sand around it was reddish in colour. I asked Subhatai's husband, 'Why is the water red just here and nowhere else?'

'Let's call it God's miracle, what else?'

Aai said, 'Perhaps God killed a rakshasa here, turning the water red.'

Subhatai's husband said, 'That sounds likely.'

I entered the sea in my langoti. I played with the small waves near the shore. I did not go too far in. My acquaintance with the sea was limited. Aai sat down in knee-deep water and began to scrub herself. The sea tickled me with a hundred hands. With every retreating wave, it drew away the sand from under my feet. It was lovely to gambol about in this great creation of God. Although the water was salty, Aai drank a sip as holy water. She made me drink a sip too. Then she proceeded to worship the sea, offering it flowers and haldi-kumkum. She also offered four annas to the sea, which actually held piles of valuable pearls in its stomach. It was an expression of gratitude. Devotees worship the creator of the sun and the moon with small oil lamps. We always look for some outward expression of the feelings in our hearts. The sight of the limitless ocean made us want to give something in return.

We changed out of our wet clothes and clambered back into the cart. It was noon by the time we reached home. We were ravenous. Subhatai had already laid out our plates for lunch. Her husband's daily routine was simple. He would finish his bath and religious rituals at daybreak and then go out to work in his orchard and plantation.

We sat down to lunch, which was a simple yet delicious meal. For the sweet dish, Subhatai had taken the trouble to make khandvi from rice semolina. She had extracted coconut milk to go with it. She served us a vegetable dish of brinjals and radish pods. And there was coconut chutney on the side. In fact, coconut had been added to everything and gave a delicious taste to the food.

'Shyam, please recite a nice shloka,' Subhatai said. I recited a Sanskrit shloka, which her husband appreciated greatly. 'You go to an English school, but you aren't ashamed of reciting a Sanskrit shloka. Most boys these days don't even know any shlokas. What's your rank in class?'

'Second.'

'Clever boy.'

Subhatai had two children. Her son Madhu was five and her daughter was two. Madhu, who was sitting next to his father, also recited a nice shloka.

'Shyam, have more khandvi. Don't feel shy,' Subhatai urged me.

'Shyam is the shyest boy on earth. You don't need to feel shy here, Shyam,' Aai said.

After lunch, Subhatai cracked open a tender betel nut for Aai. I too had a bit of the kernel. I went with Madhu to the plantation while Subhatai and Aai cleared up and lay down for a while to rest. Many of the banana plants had borne fruit. I was fascinated to see how the petals of the large banana flowers opened, revealing the comblike prongs sheltering within, which would later grow into bananas. Many of the combs had fallen to the ground. While they made excellent chutney, who would care to pick them up when there was such an abundance of them? There was a guava tree too, which I climbed. Some parrots were sitting on it, pecking at a delicious guava. I plucked it and Madhu and I ate it. Just then we heard Subhatai calling.

'Shyam, can you pick two or three pomelos off the tree, please?' she said. 'We'll eat a couple here and you can carry one back with you to have in the cart.'

'Where's the tree?' I asked.

'Come, I'll show you,' Madhu said and pulled me by the hand. There were several brilliant yellow pomelos hanging from the tree, each as large as a coconut in its husk. There used to be a pomelo tree at our place, but it never bore such big fruit. I climbed the tree, knocked down three pomelos and carried them indoors. I had an idea. I suggested we take the fruit with us when we went to the temple and have it in the jungle. It would be fun to sit under the trees and eat pomelos. But Subhatai had other ideas. 'We'll eat these here and have tender coconut and pohe in the jungle.'

It was soon time to go to the temple. I woke the cartman up and all of us except Subhatai's husband found a space to sit comfortably in the cart.

The temple was on the outskirts of the village at the foot of a hill. Aai worshipped the Goddess, placing all our offerings at Her feet. We put holy ash on our foreheads and carried some back in a twist of paper for the people at home. We drove into the jungle where we had a picnic of tender coconut, pohe and jaggery. It was great fun. The jungle always gives you a sense of freedom. No walls enclose us there. We are in nature's open house where there is nothing to constrain or limit us.

Once we were back at Subhatai's home, we got ready to leave. It would be night by the time we reached Dapoli. From there, Aai had to go on to Palgad. I touched Subhatai's and her husband's feet.

'We are quite close to Dapoli. You should come here once in a while instead of going all the way to Palgad for the weekend. Are you listening, Shyam?' Subhatai said.

Her husband, too, said, 'Yes, you really must come. We are not strangers, are we? Relationships don't grow unless we visit each other.'

I nodded. We bowed before the family gods and offered them a betel nut. Subhatai gave us tender coconuts, betel nuts and pomelos to take home.

'I wonder when we'll meet again,' Subhatai said, choking a little.

'Only God knows that. This is the first time in twelve years that I've stepped out of the house. Where could I have gone anyway? I have brothers in Pune and Mumbai, but they are busy with their own lives. They don't remember their sister much. There's also this fever that has been troubling me on and off. I lie down when it rises; get up and do my chores when it abates. There's nobody at home to help me. The poor should not fall ill, you know. It's a sin. There's no taste to my tongue. I push some food down my throat somehow, helping it along with a piece of ginger and a slice of lemon for taste. It's God's will. We can do nothing except endure. Live from one day to the next. There's nobody I can talk to about it either. I am saying this to you now because I know there's love in your heart for me. You are like a daughter to me. You and Chandri used to play together. I have bathed you as a little girl and stitched long skirts for you. I feel close to you, otherwise I wouldn't be telling you my woes. Sharing them makes me feel lighter. The only other person I speak to is God. I tell Him everything.' As she spoke, Aai's eyes filled with tears. Subhatai too put her sari to her eyes.

'You must come for Madhu's thread ceremony,' she said. 'When Shyam and his brothers grow up, they'll make sure you won't want for anything. Your kids are the best gift God could have given you.'

'That is true. When Shyam comes home during his vacations, he helps me with my work. They say he's good at school too. It is God's grace.' Aai gave a rupee to each of Subhatai's children and a choli piece to her.

'Oh, you shouldn't have,' Subhatai said. 'They are just kids.'

'So what? Who knows when I will meet them again. I'm not a rich woman. This was all I could give,' Aai said, stroking the children's backs.

We were back in the cart and it began to roll. The bullocks tried to go fast, but the incline was against us now. We had been going downhill on our way to Ladghar. Now it was mostly uphill, which slowed down the animals. It was almost evening and the entire ocean had turned into a fiery red. The sunset was captivating. You could actually look at the sun. It had turned into a red ball. The sea surged as though to bathe the sun, exhausted after the day's journey. Going, going, gone. For a moment the sky turned blue and green, before the sun sank into the waves. It would rest all night, snuggling down in the water to rise again to a new day.

We now entered a dense wood with trees on both sides of the path. Crickets chirruped. We could still hear the rumble of the sea in the distance. Riding through a jungle at night is always a sombre experience.

'Aai, I wonder when the two of us will travel together again. To be alone with you gives me a very special sense of your love,' I said, taking her hand in mine.

'Once you have grown up, I will travel with you on your money. You can take me to all the pilgrim centres, Pandharpur, Nashik, Kashi, Dwarka. But right now my Kashi and my Pandharpur are beside my tulsi plant. You know what they say, don't you? Even repeating over and over again that you will go on pilgrimage one day brings you as much merit as actually going. When we pour water over our bodies in the bath, we say, "Har har Gange". All the holy rivers are right there in our yard. It is a convenience made specifically for the poor. But how can we even think of going anywhere under the present circumstances, my pet? The debtors are at our door every day. I don't feel like living. Enough of this world, I say. There's no need to go on pilgrimage. This life itself is the biggest pilgrimage. All I want is to complete this journey with my marital ornaments and my honour intact.'

We were now near the roaring cascade. Tears were streaming down my mother's face too. I clung to her.

'Aai, we want you to be with us forever. We have nobody else but you. I am studying for you. If you weren't there, who would I study for or even live for? God is not going to take you away.' I held her tight as though I was fighting off death that had come to fetch her.

'God does what is good for us. All I want is that you should grow up to be a good human being,' Aai said.

We were silent for a while. I had put my head in Aai's lap. I felt my heart overflowing with love, devotion and gratitude. After a while, I said, 'Aai, remember you used to tell us a story about a little beggar boy who would sprinkle a few grains from his bag on the road and in the morning found them turned into a golden feather? I'm sure we will not always be poor. We will also see good days.'

'Shyam, nothing is impossible for God. He turns day into night, poison into nectar. Did God not give Sudama a city of gold? But we are ordinary people. We are not so worthy.'

'They say God's blessings are always with us. Poverty, humiliation, suffering—they are all to be seen as blessings. Is that true?'

'Your illiterate mother doesn't have answers to such questions, my child. All I know is that whatever God does is always for the best. I have beaten you as a boy, but wasn't that for your good? One must trust in God, because He is more compassionate than I am most times. Whether He gives you a cup of nectar or poison, have faith in Him.' Aai was preaching from the Book of Faith. Just then something caught my eye.

'Aai, look . . . it's a tiger,' I whispered, my voice trembling with fear. How his eyes shone. How magnificently ferocious his face looked. And how elegant his gait as he walked out of the jungle on the right, across our path and into the jungle on the other side. Was this proof of God's compassion? But it was also true that birds and animals loved my mother, whether it was cows or buffaloes or cats. Cats are called the tiger's aunts[*]. If cats love my mother, why wouldn't a tiger? Perhaps he only came for a darshan of her. Surely that is why he walked away humbly?

We were nearing Dapoli now. The town lights twinkled in the distance. We reached home at nine in the night.

---

[*] *The cat is called the tiger's aunt because in a folk tale, when the tiger's mother was dying, she called the cat to her, and taking her paw, she said, 'When I am dead, you must take care of my child.' The cat answered, 'Very well.' Then the tiger's mother died. However, the cat did not keep her word. The story goes on to narrate how she cheated the tiger who threatened to eat her up. That is why cats are terrified of tigers.*

Aai changed her plans. Instead of leaving for Palgad that very night, she left the following morning.

'Friends, that day and night became an enduring memory for me. Never again did we travel together anywhere. It had been a sublime pleasure to spend the day with nature's bounties, the great ocean and jungles dense with trees and vegetation. It was a time for us to communicate with nature and with one another, with our hearts full of love. After that day, my mother's life was nothing but hardships and calamities. God was putting her through fire to turn her into pure, unalloyed gold. Friends, my mother was like a goddess living under a curse.'

With this line, Shyam quickly left the terrace. His listeners sat in silence. Then, coming to themselves, they rose and dispersed to their respective homes.

Thirty-second Night

Indebtedness Is a Living Hell

It was the day the moneylender's henchman came to our house to collect his dues. Whenever he came, my mother died another death. Indebtedness kills happiness. It is a living hell. It's better to starve than to borrow money. Better to die than to borrow money. When you borrow money, you smile for a while. But once the borrowed money is spent, your tears begin flowing. Borrowing makes you a beggar. It leaves you with neither pride nor honour. It forces you to lower your head in public. It makes you wretched. Abject.

Oh, the moneylender's man! My father used to be most hospitable to him. He had instructed Aai to make a special vegetable and kadhi for his lunch. Use curry leaves in the kadhi, he instructed. That will give it extra aroma. He had picked banana leaves to serve lunch on before he left for the field. The man sat on the verandah. Aai made tea for him. She had run out of tea leaves, so she borrowed some from next door. After he had had tea, Aai gave him hot water for a bath. The clerk had his bath but did not wash his dhoti. He was the moneylender's man after all. Even a rich man's dog is to be respected. The poor are expected to kiss the cur.

'I read a story once. A rich man's dog was about to bite a farmer. The farmer beat him off with a cane. The rich man filed a case against him. The farmer was found guilty and fined twenty-five rupees. After all, he was only a farmer. A farmer can hardly be considered a human being. He is only a slave who must toil for the world. He is a species of animal that must work to feed those who don't have a care in the world. How dare such a creature beat a rich man's dog? Friends, in India, animals and birds are given greater respect than human beings. Dogs and crows are allowed into a temple but not a Harijan. Parrots and mynahs are welcomed in homes, but a Harijan is not. A country of monsters who love birds and animals but hate human beings can never be truly happy or free.'

And so, my mother had to wash the moneylender's clerk's dirty dhoti. A virtuous woman had to wash the dhoti of a corrupt man. Perhaps God willed that her pure touch should inject some virtue into the wearer. God's ways are inscrutable. There is no saying how and through whom He will do His work of turning evil to good.

Bhau returned from the field and asked after the clerk's comfort. The man replied that he had been satisfactorily taken care of, and was only waiting for Bhau to arrive. 'I will discuss your accounts with you and leave for Visapur, where I will stay the night,' he said.

'Very well,' said my father. 'Please relax. I'll have my bath and join you.' After his bath, Bhau did his puja. He asked Aai in a whisper, 'Did you give him tea? I hope you borrowed tea leaves to make it.'

'I've given him everything,' Aai said. 'I've even washed his dhoti. It's drying on the line. Just let the pestilence go.'

Aai was angry, upset. Bhau did his puja peacefully. He looked calm on the outside, but signs of his inner turbulence flashed occasionally. After he prayed to the family gods, he went to the temple. Purushottam had now returned from school. He set the plates for lunch. Soon Bhau returned from the temple and said to the clerk, 'Please wash your hands and feet, Vamanrao. Let's have lunch.' Then he said, 'Please come in. Sit here. Never mind if you're not wearing a purified dhoti.' Bhau who was strict with us about the rules of purity and impurity was willing to put up with an improperly dressed man beside him, as though he was God himself. Bhau's job was to say yes to everything the clerk said and flatter him to the skies.

'What had brought about such abjection, such a lack of self-respect, such obsequiousness? A single loan. Why had he needed to borrow money? Because he had overspent on family events like thread ceremonies and weddings. Because we had tried to live in the old family style, taking false pride in the past. Because we had stretched our limbs beyond the size of our blanket. Because of family quarrels and brothers crossing swords. Because of Bhau's never-ending visits to the law courts to fight against his creditors' claims. Because of our refusal to repay our debt as quickly as we could, allowing it to keep mounting instead. Because we coveted our land so much that we refused to sell a piece to pay off the debt. Friends, if you don't want your family's honour to be trampled upon in public, don't ever touch that thing called a loan. If you are in debt, sell off everything you have—land, ornaments, everything—and free yourself from it before you do anything else.'

Lunch was served. Bhau and the clerk sat down to eat. Bhau said to Purushottam, 'Recite a nice shloka for Vamanrao. Something he will applaud.' Purushottam obeyed Bhau and recited a shloka. But Vamanrao's heart was not large enough to applaud. Living in the company of the moneylender had made him hard-hearted, haughty and ungenerous.

'Please don't feel inhibited, Vamanrao. Have some more vegetable,' Bhau said. Then turning to Aai, he said, 'Serve him another helping, go on.' Vamanrao was not saying much. Perhaps he did not find the simple meal to his taste. It was not spicy. But at last, the lunch was over. Vamanrao and Bhau moved to the verandah. Vamanrao was offered betel nuts and cloves. He asked for fresh water. Purushottam went to the well to fetch some. Vamanrao drank the cool water. Aai sat down to her lunch in the kitchen.

'So, Bhaurao, time to pay up the interest,' Vamanrao said. 'You promised to pay it today. I expect at least seventy-five rupees. Don't let my visit go waste. I've come because you asked me to.'

'See, Vamanrao,' Bhau began. 'I had about ten maunds of rice and some millets. Together they fetched twenty-five rupees. I have kept it packed and ready for you. I don't have more today. Please placate your master. Say something on our behalf. Tell him I'm not going to sink his money. Let the boys grow up. Let them start earning and we will repay it in one go. Clear it once and for all. The elder one is already in college. Look at it this way, Vamanrao. Do insects crawl in dung forever? Even they fly away.' Bhau was pleading his case with the man.

'I'm not interested in all that,' the man said. 'I'm not going to budge until I have the money. You had money to build this new house. You have money to send your son to an English school. The only thing you don't have money for is to pay back the moneylender. If he doesn't get his money, we servants don't get ours. Nothing doing. It embarrasses me to face the master empty-handed. Just pay up. That's it.' Vamanrao was speaking in anger, not a trace of respect in his voice. Why would he not? He too was only a slave to his master's orders.

'What can I say about this house, Vamanrao?' Bhau said. 'The roof is old thatch and the walls are unfired bricks. I built this cowshed of a house at my wife's insistence. But I had to sell her gold bangles even for this.' Bhau's voice was filled with shame.

Bhau was pleading with the clerk on the verandah. In the kitchen, the rice on Aai's plate was turning wet with her tears. Her grief was too enormous to contain; the rice too hard to swallow.

Outside she heard the clerk say, 'You sold your wife's bangles to build a house. Now sell her off to pay the moneylender,' Vamanrao said this without a shred of shame.

Aai shot up like lightning. She washed her hands and stormed out, her eyes blazing with rage and sorrow. She stood trembling on the threshold of the verandah. 'Get out. Leave this house this minute,' she said. 'Are you not ashamed to talk of selling wives? Do you have no control over your tongue? Do you not have a wife yourself? Get out of here. Go tell that moneylender he is free to auction the house and everything in it, but we will not tolerate this kind of talk. Go beat a drum. Confiscate the house. But don't let your tongue speak such evil before my children.'

'Fine,' the clerk responded. 'We've been waiting to do just that. If I don't have your house and land confiscated by the end of the month, I'll change my name. Bhaurao, how can you allow a mere woman to insult us like this?'

'Go in,' my father said furiously to Aai. 'Do you hear me?' Aai heard. She went in meekly and sat weeping. What other support did she have besides tears? Back on the verandah, Bhau was busy pacifying Vamanrao. After much pleading, the clerk agreed to take twenty-five rupees and leave.

Bhau flew into the house the minute he left.

'You women don't have even a paisa worth of brains. How tactfully I'd been handling him since the morning. How much time I'd spent pleading my case. And you . . . you should just sit by the chulah and cook. That's all you're good for! If death is coming tomorrow, you will invite it today. Is anger any way to handle these things? You have to be soft-spoken. You women have no idea how we are pushed and pulled in the outside world just to survive.'

'I don't mind dying today if living means being humiliated every day,' Aai said. 'Is life worth living if you're treated like street dogs? Let them confiscate everything we have. We will learn to live as labourers. Even labourers won't let people say such obnoxious things to them. Let's start living on daily wages. We can sleep on hard earth, drink from springs and eat leaves off trees.' Aai was pleading desperately with Bhau.

'Easy to say, hard to do. You'll know better when the blistering sun shines on you at noon.' Saying so, my father walked out.

My younger brothers sat by Aai. 'Don't cry, please. It makes us cry,' they said. 'We'll do any work you tell us to, but please don't cry.'

The children were trying to console their mother in the same way that flowers might hope to support a tree. It was heartbreaking.

Thirty-third Night

Poor People's Dreams

Shyam had been looking rather sad lately. Could it be the effect of the stories he had been narrating about his mother? Was he lamenting over the hard, painful life she had lived?

'Shyam, you rarely smile these days,' Ram said. 'You always look so sad. What is the matter with you? Is something troubling you?'

'When I talk about my mother, I think of our country, its indescribable suffering, misery and poverty. Our country is sinking in wretchedness, debt and slavery. Her children have nothing to eat and drink. They have no work and no education. I can't bear to see their condition. It breaks my heart. How much loss we have had to suffer under foreign rule. Wherever you look, you see drought and famine. Babies die even as they are born. Not a single face glows with health and contentment. It is as if the very springs of life have dried up. This alien rule devours and destroys. What you see in India today is death, not life; grief, not joy;

ungratefulness, not gratitude; greed, not love; beastliness, not humanity; darkness, not light; disorder, not harmony; fear, not courage; shackles, not freedom; customs, not reason. This monstrous, all-encompassing sorrow burns me up inside. There are millions of mothers like mine whose golden lives are turning to dust. What can I do if not weep?'

Shyam fell silent. Ram spoke now. 'Shyam, when you face grief, you must rise to banish it; when you see darkness, you must try to bring in light; when you see shackles, you must move to break them. Why lose hope? The more challenges a warrior faces, the more spirited becomes his fight.'

'But I am not a warrior. You are warriors. I envy you. I would love to be like you, never feeling gloomy, never giving up the fight. But the thread by which my hope hangs is weak. It snaps. My hope is false, a pretence.'

'To lose hope is to forget God. To despair is a sign of losing faith in Him. When you believe in Him, you are confident that all will be well, that light will overcome darkness,' Ram said.

'Even if dawn follows night, night always returns, doesn't it? The world still seems to be where it always was. I can't see any progress. Never mind. It is best not to delve too deep into this. One must do what one can. Lift a stone, pluck out a thorn, plant a flower bush, sweep a road, speak civilly to people, smile sweetly, sit with the sick, wipe the tears of the grieving. We are of this world for a short span.

What more can someone like me do? How many patches can a weak man like me stitch on to this frayed sky?'

'Why can't we bring people together, spread new thinking, defeat misery, work for human welfare? I find hope dancing in every nerve end of my body,' Ram said.

Just then the bell rang for prayers. People gathered in the prayer hall. A silence descended. The prayer that evening was from the Gita. Ram was going to sing a bhajan after that. He sang a song of sublime hope, one that was familiar to Shyam. A small smile played on his lips. It was a song he had written in a different time. Where was that hope now that had inspired him then? He had become a conflict zone between hope and despair. If he smiled today, he was sure to weep tomorrow. If he jumped around today, he would be sure to lie still tomorrow. He had become a conundrum.

The song was over. It was time for Shyam's story. 'Friends, I had returned home from Dapoli in despair. I had something to say to Aai,' he began.

'Aai, it isn't possible for me to continue in this school. Bhau can't pay the fees and I don't qualify for free education. Bhau says I should stand up in class when the question of freeship comes up. When I stand up with the other poor students, the teacher says, "Shyam, you are not poor. Sit down." People only remember that we were once rich. They don't know that we don't have enough to eat now.

They don't believe me when I tell them. My classmates laugh at me. So I sit down.'

'I think you must leave school altogether, Shyam,' Aai said quietly.

'But I've only passed the fifth. What can I do with that if I leave now? Of what use will I be? Do I have a skill that will help me earn?'

'Your father was saying he will find you something to do in the railways. He is helpless. He complains about having to pay your fees. It would help if you left school. Do whatever work you can find.'

'Why should I start working now? Why should I take on the burden of a job at this age? I have so many plans, so many dreams. I want to be highly educated. I want to become a poet, a writer. I will give you a happy life. Are you asking me to drown my dreams? Tear my castles down to dust?'

'Shyam, the castles that the poor build in the air have their natural end in the dust. The poor have no right to self-esteem. They must do what falls to their lot. Many pretty buds are eaten by worms before they bloom.'

'Aai, you disappoint me. You don't seem to feel for me at all. Do you feel it is right that your children's lives should turn to mud? Do you not wish for me to grow into a respected man?'

'Of course, I would like my son to grow up to be respected, but not at the cost of his father's happiness.

Not by drowning his father in worry. If he wishes to depend on his father, he must do as he says. Otherwise, he must stand on his own feet and climb as high as he wants to in life.'

'How can I do that, Aai? Show me the way. You have always been my guide. Tell me what I can do.'

'Dhruv left his parents and went into the jungle. You too can leave the house. Go into the wide world. He put himself through austerities to find God. You must do the same to get an education. You can gain nothing without working hard for it. Stand on your own feet. Starve. Toil. Get your education. Grow into a worthy human being and then return home. Our blessings will go with you. I will always be with you in spirit wherever you are. There is nothing more I can say to guide you.'

'Shall I really do that, Aai? You have articulated exactly what I had been thinking of doing. You live in my heart. That's why you know what I'm thinking. I have heard of a princely state called Aundh, which has very low fees. May I go there? I can live off alms. Nobody there will know about us. Nobody will laugh at me. I can work in people's homes to support myself. You have taught me to do so yourself. As long as I am out of sight of people who know us, I will be all right. May I go?'

'Why not? It isn't a sin to beg for alms, especially not for a student. A poor student has the right to go from door to door asking for food. But don't steal. Don't carry tales. Pride is bad, but pride in truthfulness isn't. Be as helpful as you can. Speak sweetly to people. When your tongue is sweet, the world turns sweet. Always smile. Make friends. Don't spurn anybody. Don't hurt anybody. Give your studies all you have. Always think of your parents, brothers and sisters. Thinking of them will keep you on the right path. Go. You have my permission. Dhruv found God and saved his parents. Pray to the Goddess of knowledge and save us.'

'Will you bring Bhau around? Will you get me his permission?'

'I will. Don't worry. He himself has hinted at something similar.'

We had sat down to dinner. Aai had made kulith pithla and served dry mango pickle to go with it. She said to Bhau, 'Shyam was saying he wants to go somewhere far away for his education. Do give him permission.'

'Where is he going? I'll have to send money there too. It's become impossible now to spare even a single paisa. There was a time when these very hands counted out thousands of rupees. But why talk of that now? I feel numb. I am helpless. Otherwise, why would I not want my boys to acquire knowledge? Which father would want his clever, talented, hard-working boys to not study? But I have no choice.' Bhau's voice was filled with sadness.

'He won't need you to send him money where he is going. He says education costs nothing there. He will beg for food from door to door. You only need to give him ten rupees to get there,' Aai pleaded.

'I have no objections then. If he is ready to fend for himself, he is free to go. I will not insist on his taking a job. Only, I no longer have the strength to support him. But he has my blessings.'

We had finished dinner. We were sitting together talking. Young Purushottam said, 'Aai, does that mean Anna will go away from us? So far that he won't come back to see us?'

'Yes, my pet,' Aai said. 'First he will study, then he will help you to study. He is going far away only because he wants to make sure you can go to school.'

It was decided that I would go to Aundh. Bhau looked in the almanac for an auspicious date. As the day approached, the turmoil in my heart grew. It was going to be a long, long time now before I would set eyes on my mother again. In the old days I was like a bird, flying home whenever I felt lost or lonely. I would fly home even for a weekend just to feel Aai's gaze on me. Now I might not be able to do that even in the long vacations. Who would bear the cost of the journey? One had to count coins for every single thing one wanted to do. As it is, Bhau had had to knock on several doors to borrow the ten rupees I needed to go to Aundh. The only thought that kept my spirits up was that I was going for my education. That was going to make me more worthy of my mother's love. Even more importantly, it would assure my parents of a life free from care. But even as this thought helped me dry my eyes, another thought made me sad again.

Who will help Aai as I did when I was home? Who will massage her legs for her? 'How cool your hands are, Shyam,' she used to say to me. 'Please put them on my forehead. It is burning like a furnace.' To whom will she say that? Who will wash her sari, sit and chat with her while she has her food, coaxing her to eat more? Who will help her with the grinding? Who will carry wood from the shed for her? Who will say to her, 'Aai, I'm stacking wood in the fuel pit'? Who will fetch dung for her to plaster the yard? Who will draw pots of water from the well for her? I used to do all these chores for her whenever I came home from school. Now I will not come home for who knows how long. But then, who was I? Who was I to think I was responsible for my mother's happiness? Why should I be proud of that? God is the Supreme Carer of all three worlds. He worries about everybody. He is the compassionate one, the caring one. He alone was the ultimate support for my mother and for the entire universe.

I was busy packing. The bullock cart was to leave at night. Aai laid out two thin quilts and a rough blanket for me. 'Don't give me the blanket, Aai,' I said. 'Give me a length of gunny cloth. I'll spread that with one quilt on top and the other to cover myself with. Keep the blanket. You'll need it when you have a fever and start shivering.'

'You are going to an unknown place where you know nobody. What will you do if you fall ill? Keep the blanket. Listen to me. We'll manage here somehow.' Aai rolled the blanket into my bedding. She made a little chivda for me and gave me a piece of solid kokum oil to keep my lips from chapping in the cold. She also gave me some amla squares to stop me from being seasick and some home remedies for common ailments. My loving, hard-working mother was thinking of all the little things that would help me when I was on my own.

The cart was to come at nine in the night. Before that, I stuffed dinner down my throat somehow. My stomach was already full with emotion. Aai served me dahi with rice. After a while, the cart arrived. Bhau put my things in it. I said to my little brother, 'Don't throw tantrums now. Aai has only you to help her.' I bowed before the family gods. I bent to touch Bhau's feet. He choked over his words but lay his hands on my back. I put my head on Aai's feet and bathed them with tears. She went to the chulah for ash and put it on my forehead. I went next door to touch Janaki aunty's feet. I said to her, 'Please look after my mother. Help her when she falls ill, won't you?' She said, 'Don't worry, Shyam. We are there for her.'

Purushottam clung to me. Aai said, 'Take care.' I merely nodded and got into the cart. Bhau followed the cart on foot. I got off at the Ganapati temple where he and I took darshan. I bowed before the idol. I took *tirth* and put it to my eyes. I took the sindoor off Ganapati's feet and put it on my forehead. I asked Him to look after my parents. I touched Bhau's feet once again. 'Take care, my son,' he said. Bhau stood where he was for a few minutes long after I had gotten into the cart and the cart had trundled away. Then he turned to go home.

The bullocks ran. The cart rolled. The journey of my life had begun. I was entering the vast ocean of the outside world. Would I sink, swim or dive in and fish out pearls? Whom would I meet? Who would come close to me? Who, having come close, would move away? Where would my boat hit a sandbank and get stuck? I was entering the great unknown. My mother had pushed me out with her inspiring words. I was flying on the wings she had provided. She had said, 'Do what Dhruv did.' But how could I—her weak, erring, scatterbrained son—be compared to Dhruv, that shining embodiment of resolve?

I sat weeping, unaware that we had crossed the village river and left Palgad far behind. Memories crowded my mind and brimmed over. I told myself that as long as Aai's blessings were with me, I would not give in to fear. Her blessings were the only protection I needed. I was wearing that invincible armour. She had encouraged me to learn swimming and had now pushed me into this vast ocean.

'In the years that followed, I often came close to drowning in the ocean. I got stuck in sludge, sank into the sand, was knocked down by waves. But I always resurfaced somehow . . . It is not as though all dangers are over even now. But my mother's blessings have kept me afloat thus far. They will keep me afloat in the life ahead. My mother is no longer alive. But even after a mother passes away, her blessings remain with us. They do not die. We continue to receive her love even after she is gone.'

Thirty-fourth Night

No Money, No Respect

Shyam began his story.

Our debt increased by the day. We weren't even able to pay the interest on the loan, and it kept mounting. We had several pieces of farmland. If Bhau had sold off even a couple of these, we could have paid off the entire amount and still had enough land left to give us our daily rice. But Bhau did not think it right to do that. He saw selling land as sinful. As humiliation.

One night, Aai's father came to visit. We used to call him Nana. He had come to have a talk with Bhau. He wanted to try and change Bhau's mind if he could. Nana was a clever and careful man. He was practical, punctilious and principled. Unfortunately, he was vain when it came to his mental abilities. He could not tolerate anybody differing from him. People who have sharp brains look upon others as brainless. They think they were born with all the brainpower available in the world. Nana was a bit like that. It didn't help matters that he was also short-tempered.

Bhau was sitting on the verandah on a piece of jute cloth. He had just finished dinner. Aai was having hers in the kitchen. As soon as Nana arrived, he began to speak his mind. 'Look, Bhau, I have come to give you an ultimatum. I have spoken to you several times before, but you have paid me no heed. Now you're in deep water. You must act before it is too late. Sell off your lands. Pay off that moneylender first. We'll see what to do about the other people you've borrowed from. They won't mind waiting and their interest rates are not as high either. The main debt is that man's. It rises from one day to the next. Soon it will drown you. So listen to what I'm saying.'

'Why are you so worried about me?' Bhau demanded. 'The whole world rushes to advise a poor man. Is a poor man incapable of knowing what to do? Please understand, Nana, that I know what to do with my debts. You don't have to flood me with fountains of sympathy.'

'Bhau, I have rushed here because I couldn't stay away any longer. The love in my heart brings me here. My heart is trapped here. I have trudged through mud this late at night because a piece of me, my daughter, is here. I have come to see if I can ensure that my beloved grandsons have a bit of home, a bit of land left to their names, so they don't have to leave their ancestral village to go begging around the world. Your properties will soon be confiscated.

Land sells at knock-down prices in auctions. There's a man in Visapur who is offering fifteen hundred rupees for your land at Payrey. Sell it to him. You won't get that price again. You can pay off the moneylender with it.' Nana was pouring his heart into his advice.

'Nana, how can you tell me to sell the farm at Payrey? We grew up on that land. We helped it grow, made it what it is today. We spilt our innards breaking huge boulders. We blew up the plateau with dynamite to turn it into cultivable land. Earlier it used to yield almost 375 kg of grain. It has begun to give us almost three times as much now. We dug the well there. And you tell me to sell that land. The boys love that piece of land. They used to live there with Durva Aji on weekends, sharing meals of rice and brinjal bharta with her. How many mango trees we have planted there and how many flowering bushes. And talk about fertile soil, that land is capable of yielding gold. Such are the bonds we have with it. Bits and pieces of it have been disappearing over time. Should I not hold on to what is left? It is beyond me to sell any part of it. Is it possible to cut out a piece of one's heart? Can one's hands sell a piece of one's heart? That would be as big a sin as selling one's mother or the cow in one's shed. That piece of land is our mother. It has fed us.'

'Bhau, your big talk doesn't help you in the practical world. Talking about food doesn't put flesh on your bones. So that land is your mother and you can't sell it. But you can buy another, right? Or grab it. Whose mother is that, then?

Don't give me tall moral tales. There was a time when you confiscated land, auctioned land, abducted it. Land is sold. Land is bought. You have to think practically. When the boys grow up and, by the grace of God, find jobs, they will buy land. If not this, then another piece. But how do you intend to keep your land while there's a debt on your head? The town crier will announce to the world that your land is to be confiscated. The police will come, the land will be auctioned, they'll seal your house, you will be publicly shamed. Does that strike you as a happy picture? Or would it be better to act now, sell your land and preserve your home and honour?'

'I will look after my honour. My honour isn't yours, is it?'

'Of course, it is mine too! That is why I am here. You seem to have forgotten that you are my son-in-law. Will people not say that the land belonging to so-and-so's son-in-law has been confiscated? My daughter's honour is my honour. Think about that. It is stupid to hold on obstinately to your ideas.'

'Call me stupid or whatever else you please. You and the whole world have the right to call me names. So call me stupid, call me bonehead.'

'I certainly will. Why should I not? You claim to be an aristocrat. You have a noble lineage. That is why I married my daughter to you. Gave you a dowry. I gave it to help my daughter live a comfortable life. I didn't marry her to you for her honour to be shredded and hung out in the public square. Is this what you call aristocracy? Not a sign of gold or even a proper sari on your wife's body and not enough to eat. Is this your aristocracy where moneylenders stand at your door and say what they please about your wife? You have no home to live in and you talk of being aristocrats. You've lived thirty years without acquiring a shred of sense. Your own people cheated you and drove you out. Open your eyes, Mr Nobleman. This is beggary, not aristocracy. Fine. You have no sense yourself. Then listen to others. You won't do that either. What nonsense is this? What is one to say about this idiocy? Bhau, stop being an ass. Do what I say.'

Aai could no longer bear to hear what her father was saying. She was shattered. She came out to the verandah and said, 'Nana, please don't say such things. Our situation is already so bad. People have been shaming us. Now you are doing the same. These things happen. There are ups and downs in everybody's lives. If I have lived in peace and had enough to eat, it is because of Bhau. Our luck has turned now, yes. But with God's grace, we will face whatever is coming our way. Your advice may be practical and correct. But perhaps everything in life isn't about money. Try to understand Bhau. He has told you what the piece of land that you want him to sell means to him. He isn't out to ruin his children. He too is looking for a way out. In these bad times, we need your love and blessings, not your anger and accusations. I hope you will never again speak to Bhau the way you have spoken today. I ask for your blessings instead.' So saying, Aai bent down and touched her father's feet.

'Bayo, stand up. Since you wish it, I will leave this minute. I will not step through your gate again. Do you understand? What's it to this old man?'

'Nana, please don't misunderstand me. Don't be angry. I want you to keep coming. But I am his wife just as I am your daughter. I must consider everybody's feelings. I want you and I want him. Nana, our luck has abandoned us. Our kin have abandoned us. Will you abandon us too? Please keep coming. Come to meet us with love. Come to see your Bayo. You will, won't you?' Aai's throat was choked.

'No, I will not. Why should I come to a place where my word carries no weight?'

'Is your word more precious to you than your daughter?' Aai said, but Nana had already left. 'He's gone. What can we do?' Aai turned to Bhau. 'Please go and lie down. Do you want me to massage your head with oil? It might calm you down.'

'What good is oil for a life that is shattered? Go away. Leave me alone.'

Poor Aai. She went indoors. Purushottam was asleep. She straightened the covering on him and went away. Away? Where to? To the tulsi plant, of course. There she sat shedding tears. The massive mango trees stood around her solemnly. The wind had fallen. The sky was still. My mother sat weeping. Debt had turned her life to tears. Debt was making her weep day and night.

Thirty-fifth Night

A Life of Anxiety

'I had gone to Aundh for my education, but God wanted to drive me out. I will not talk about how I had been eking out an existence there. The poor have always had to face hardships. But I want to talk only about my mother. I will talk about myself only when my memories of her involve me.'

My youngest brother Sadanand had been staying with my mother's sister in Pune. We believed Yashwant had taken birth again as Sadanand, and entered our lives. Then suddenly, one day, he died of the plague. He had been repeating God's name. 'There He is, calling me. I must go,' he said and died.

I was in Aundh at the time. The plague soon arrived there too. When Aai heard of this, she grew anxious. She had lost one son to the plague. The second was far away and quite alone. The grief of Sadanand's passing was still fresh. For days afterwards, her tears had refused to stop. Even as that sorrow was slowly healing, anxiety about me began to consume her. Her life became one long stretch of anxiety.

The school in Aundh closed as soon as the plague arrived. Out-of-town students were advised to leave. But where was I to go? I had no money. I sold my thin rug and the few good books I had. They fetched me five rupees. I left Aundh since the school was expected to remain closed for two or three months.

I got off the boat at Harnai and took a bullock cart to Palgad. I reached in the early hours of the morning. Eagles had descended on a banyan tree and were waking up the village with their loud call. Morning hymns and Veda recitations could be heard from around the village. I paid off the cartman and entered our gate. I was utterly depressed. I feared that my brother's memory would return when Aai saw me and she would begin to weep. I made my way across the yard slowly and on to the verandah. Aai was in the kitchen churning buttermilk and singing a song about Krishna in a soft voice. It was a sweet song full of love.

As a boy you stole milk and butter
None knew then you were God, no less.
Radha alone went mad over you,
Saw you in your glorious fullness.

I stood on the verandah listening to her sing, waiting for the courage to enter. But how long could I continue

256

standing there? At last, I knocked on the door and tried to push it open.

'Who is that?' Aai asked.

'It's me. Shyam.'

'Shyam! My little boy. Wait, I'm coming.' She hurried to the door, opened it and held me tight. 'Go bow to the gods. I'll put some jaggery before them. Oh, how I've waited for you to come. God took one away. I wasn't sure I would ever set eyes on the other.' Both she and I were moved to tears.

When Bhau came into the yard after his ablutions, Aai hurried forward and said, 'Our Shyam is back. He's just come.' Bhau washed his feet and came in. I touched his feet. 'Shyam, I was reciting Ganapati's name for you. You've come at last. I hope you are well. Your brother is no longer with us.' So saying, he put his shoulder cloth to his eyes.

Aai said, 'Why don't you lie down for a while, Shyam? It's quite cold.' I washed my face, changed and lay down on Aai's mattress. I pulled her folded sari over me. It was like covering myself with her love all over again.

Soon I had settled into my old routine. Purushottam filled me up on everything that had happened at home and in the village in my absence. And I told him about my days in Aundh. I told him about my amusing misunderstanding over the word 'kavath'. There was a kavath tree in Aundh. We don't have those trees in the Konkan. For us, a 'kavath' is a hen's egg. So when a boy asked me one day, if I liked kavaths, I lost my temper with him and all the boys laughed at me. I also told Purushottam about how I almost drowned in a pond once, and about the Yamai Temple and the peacocks in the woods. He in turn told me about a man from Patil Wadi who had gone to Pasara, was bitten by a snake and died; and about a cow that died grazing on leaves she should not have eaten.

Time went by, but the school in Aundh remained closed. My father refused to believe that. He began to get suspicious. He thought something must have gone wrong there and I had had to return empty-handed. Over time, the doubt in his mind intensified. One night, Purushottam and I were lying side by side under one coverlet chatting about everything under the stars. Soon Purushottam fell asleep. A while later, so did I. Suddenly I was startled out of my sleep. I had dreamt that I had fallen from a great height. As I lay awake, I overheard the following conversation.

'He's back because he hasn't been able to cope with his studies there,' my father said. 'The plague was a good excuse. Why should the school remain closed this long?'

'But why would he lie?' my mother said. 'His life there is hard, but he still plans to go back. He hasn't come here for easy meals. I would not allow that.'

'Gopal Patwardhan was ready to find him a job in the railways. That would have been a great help. Where are jobs to be found these days? But you two, mother and son, had different ideas.'

'He doesn't want to work just yet. Let him study. He'll soon go back to school. He's not planning to be a layabout, just eating without working.'

'For you, your children can never do wrong. But see if I'm not proved right. He's back because he couldn't cope. It'll all come out one day.'

I could not restrain myself any longer. I sat up in bed and said, 'Bhau, I did not mean to eavesdrop. I woke up suddenly and overheard you. I'll leave tomorrow whether or not the plague has abated. Why should I stay here if you don't trust me? I didn't come here to laze about and eat. Despite the plague, I had planned to stay on there. But they would not let out-of-towners stay. I was forced to come home. But I'll leave tomorrow.'

Aai was upset. 'Don't take what he said to heart. Let the plague die down and then go. Listen to this foolish woman.'

'I refuse to stay. I'll leave tomorrow. Unfortunately, I'll have to ask you for ten rupees again, Bhau. Please do me that favour. Don't worry about me, Aai. Nobody dares kill if God means to save. If He wishes to, He will save you even in the midst of a raging disease or keep you afloat even in the vast ocean.'

'You are his son after all. Just as stubborn as you always were. Go if you must. Be happy wherever you are. That is all I want. I don't know why this wretched woman's eyes won't close forever. God takes away little children and leaves us behind to weep.'

When morning dawned, I said to Aai, 'I have made up my mind to go. I would have had to anyway in a month or two. Please give me your permission.'

She gave in. She never imposed her will on others. She understood their viewpoint. Her love was not of the possessive kind. It set one free. Made one independent.

I was leaving out of anger against my father. She could only weep. She had lost a child to the plague. Another was now choosing to jump into it. What could she do but weep, crushed as she was between the will of a father and a son? I touched my parents' feet, took their blessings and left.

'Friends . . . that was the last time I saw Aai alive. After that, I only saw her form turned to ashes on her funeral pyre. I had no idea then that I was seeing her for the last time; that I was hearing her nectar-sweet words for the last time. But I was fated to experience the hard truth that God's will often crosses human desires. And I did.'

Thirty-sixth Night

If We Had Oil, We Had No Salt

'Today's cotton twists are not well-made. The yarn keeps breaking. The cotton hasn't been combed properly. Govinda, did you comb it?' Bhika asked.

'No. Shyam did, and he also made the twists today,' Govinda answered.

Just then Ram came in and overheard the conversation. 'These days, Shyam is always sad,' he said. 'His mood interferes with his work. If you want to do good work, you have to be happy. Tukaram says, "If you seek fulfilment, seek contentment first."'

'Where is Shyam?' Ram inquired.

'He was upstairs a while ago,' Bhika said.

'He was supposed to visit Ailabai. They say she's very ill.'

'What sort of a name is that? Ailabai!' Bhika remarked.

'It's the colloquial way of saying Ahilyabai,' Ram explained, just as Shyam entered the room.

'What are you people doing, Govinda?' he asked.

'Nothing much. How is Ailabai?'

'They've sent her away to her village.'

'I hope she'll recover there. Her children are still very young,' Bhika responded.

'Who knows? But there's nothing we can do.' Shyam glanced at the cooking vessels. 'Bhika, you haven't scoured these vessels properly today. Your mind wasn't on your work.'

'As yours wasn't when you combed the cotton.'

'Why? Weren't the twists good?' Shyam asked.

'The cotton wasn't fully cleaned of muck,' Bhika explained.

'But my yarn wasn't breaking.'

'Perhaps you were using the first batch of twists,' Bhika said.

'No, I made my twists from the cotton I combed.'

'But I swapped your batch with mine,' Govinda explained. 'The first batch had come to me. But I put it in your share because you spin at night and the batch you had would have tried your patience.'

'Shyam, you shouldn't stay awake so long,' Ram said.

'What can I do? I can't sleep. What's the point of just lying in bed? So I spin.'

'Why aren't you able to sleep? We sleep like logs.'

'You work hard. Hard work in the day brings sound sleep at night.'

'As if you don't work hard. You swept around the well today.'

'I meant to but didn't. Bhika, Govinda and Namdeo wouldn't let me. You boys don't allow me to work. You want to work and earn all the merit yourselves, and not let me earn any.'

'They didn't let you sweep because you weren't feeling well today,' Ram pointed out.

'I see people have begun to gather. We must ring the bell,' Govinda said.

The bell was rung and the prayer began. After that, Shyam forgot about the conversation and started to narrate that evening's story.

Dire problems had begun to dog the home. If we had oil, we had no salt. If we had salt, we had no chilli. One day there was no firewood for the stove. Another day there were no cow-dung pats. Aai would go looking for sticks and twigs in the backyard. At times, all she found were dried mango leaves. So she made do with them as fuel. Sometimes she could not temper the vegetables because there was no oil. Perhaps her tears provided the taste. What could she do but weep? She was trying her best to live with honour. Aai's parents no longer lived in the village. They were with their sons in Bombay or Pune. Their place was locked. Aai did not leave the house now. She was ashamed to go out. She spent all her time indoors.

Around that time, an elderly couple had come to stay next door to us. They had no links with the village. They had come to Palgad because the climate was good, a large community of Brahmins lived there and the gentleman, a retiree, had great faith in our Ganapati. They had bought a plot of land next to ours and built themselves a pretty bungalow.

Aai got to know them gradually. Radhatai was a kind and affectionate person. Aai used to visit her and she too would drop in to see Aai. One day Aai said to her, 'Radhatai, if you have any work for me, please tell me. I could grind your flour for you. It would be a great help for me.'

Radhatai had lived in a city. She was accustomed to paying for services like grinding. She promised to give Aai her grain to mill. Aai had very little strength left in her. But there was no help for it. As soon as Bhau left in the morning, she would set up the grinding stone. Purushottam would help her till it was time for school. After that she would grind the rest, stopping at intervals. She often thought had I been there, I would have finished the whole lot. That reminded her of how I had left the house in anger. And that made her weep some more. Her eyes wet and her heart heavy, she would somehow complete the task. She would buy oil and salt with the little bit of money she earned, and that helped her tide over a few days.

As Diwali approached, she realized she would need a little more oil and other ingredients. She would have to light at least two oil lamps. There was a time when we used a whole pitcherful of oil for lamps every evening during Diwali. Hundreds of lamps would be lit. But these were only memories. How was Diwali to be celebrated now? She asked Radhatai if she could wash her family's clothes. 'Or let me do some other work.'

As it happened, Radhatai's daughter had come to stay with her mother. She had just delivered a baby boy and then fallen ill. Her name was Indu. She had become very weak and the change of air was expected to help her. Radhatai said, 'Could you give Indu her oil massage every day and massage and bathe the baby?'

Aai said, 'I'd be very happy to. It is work that I love. Many years ago, my daughter Chandri had come to stay. I used to give her a massage every day.'

Aai began to go over at first light to give Indu her massage and to bathe the baby. She put her heart into the work. She thought of Indu as her own daughter. Rubbing oil on to the soft spot on the baby's head was a special pleasure. Putting him on her outstretched legs and pouring water over his soft little body brought out all her motherly love. Soon the baby began gaining weight. Indu too lost her pallor and acquired a glow.

Radhatai had great faith in Aai. At the end of the month, she gave her two rupees. 'Why two?' Aai asked. 'One would have sufficed.'

'Please take it, Yashodabai,' Radhatai said. 'Diwali is coming. You have poured your heart into the work. You can't put a value on that, can you? One shouldn't assess that kind of work in terms of money.'

Aai returned home and prayed to God.

'Dear God, you are the guardian of my honour.'

She spent the money she had earned on a little oil, a little ghee and a coconut. She made a few karanjis and anarases. She lit two oil lamps outside the house during the four days of Diwali. On the day of Bhau Beej, Purushottam went over to Indu's. Indu greeted him with an aarti. Purushottam put four annas in the aarti salver as a gift from a brother to a sister. Aai made him a pipe through which he could blow little *trisul* berries. They made a small explosive sound as they emerged. When the trisuls were over, he made a leaf pipe and blew through it to make a cracking sound. He did not insist on having real fireworks.

Aai was already very weak and worn out. How much longer could she live with all the hard work she had to do? She started getting a fever every day. She was also falling short of breath. She kept pushing herself for as long as she could. On the last day of Diwali, Purushottam brought home amlas, tamarinds and marigolds from Ghorivade village. Aai offered kumkum and haldi to the tulsi plant and prayed, 'Tulasadevi, please let my eyes close now. Take me away as a married woman with my honour intact.'

Thirty-seventh Night

Honour in Shreds

Shyam began to speak.

Ultimately, the moneylender filed a case against us. He made a claim for four thousand rupees, which he had calculated as the sum of the principal and interest on his loan. Hearings began. The court decided in favour of the moneylender and ordered all our possessions to be confiscated and auctioned.

It was the day the town crier was going to beat his drum and make the announcement in the village. For two days, Aai had not been able to swallow a single morsel of food or sleep a wink. She prayed to Goddess Jagadamba, 'Dear Mother, must these eyes now see our honour torn to shreds? Must these ears hear the town crier's cruel announcement? Why don't you take me away, Mother? I don't want to live.'

Purushottam was at school when Aai's fever came on. She lay in bed tossing, turning and weeping. It was around nine in the morning when the town crier, always a Mahar according to village customs, began walking through the village. He stopped at intervals, beat his drum and made his announcement, which began thus: 'This afternoon, Bhaurao's house is to be confiscated.' Those who find joy in other's distress were happy. The more civilized felt sad.

When the Mahar stopped before the school and made his announcement, the children began to tease Purushottam, aping the announcement: 'This afternoon, Purshya's house is to be confiscated, *dhamdhamadham*'. Purushottam began to sob. He went to the teacher for permission to go home. The teacher said, 'Why do you want to go now? Go sit in your place. School will soon be over.' How could the teacher not see what was happening in my brother's heart?

School ended at ten o'clock. My brother was now like a lamb before a pack of wolves. They pursued him chanting 'dhamdhamadham' all the way home. He ran into the house and clung to Aai. 'Why are the boys teasing me, Aai?' he asked. 'They are saying our house is going to be confiscated. You'll have cow-dung lamps on your house, they say. What does that mean?'

'It means everybody will know we are bankrupt. It's God's will, my child. What else can I say?' Aai held Purushottam close to her heart as she lay in bed weeping tears of sorrow. A long time passed. Then she said to him, 'Go now, my child. Wash your hands and feet and go to Radhatai's house. Indu has asked you over for lunch.'

Purushottam was too young to understand what was happening. He went next door for lunch. Bhau did not eat all day. He took his bath, did his puja and, although he was feeling ashamed, he went to the temple. He went with his head lowered and returned the same way. Not even a dog took notice of him in a place where once he had been called Sardar, where he had been a member of the village committee, where he had been honoured wherever he went. In this very village, he was now followed by little boys making fun of him. Aai was forced to pick up dung where she had once picked flowers. She had fought bravely to live with honour, but God had wished to put her through test after test. God had shown her the heights of glory. He now wanted her to see the depths of humiliation. Total joy and total grief, full moon and no moon—the Supreme Carer wished to acquaint the little mother with both extremes of life.

That afternoon, the police, clerks, village accountant and witnesses gathered in our house. They collected all the cooking utensils save a few, and stacked them in one room. There was no ornament on my mother's body except the black beads and single gold bead of her marriage necklace. There was nothing else of value anywhere in the house. Whatever there was had been collected in that room. The moneylender put his lock on the room and the police sealed it. Two rooms were left for our use as a favour.

Aai had been standing throughout the time that the people were there. She was running a fever and trembling violently. She was consumed by a fire inside out. When the people left, she collapsed to the ground. Purushottam burst into tears. Bhau picked her up and carried her to her bed. A little while later, Aai came to her senses. 'What I had feared has happened,' she murmured. 'Now whether I live or die makes no difference.'

Thirty-eighth Night

Aai's Last Illness

Shyam had fallen ill. He was running a fever.

'Would you like me to massage your legs for you?' Govinda asked.

'No, no. You don't have to nurse me. You have work to do. What's the point in sitting with me? I'll lie here quietly, taking Ram's name.'

'Shyam, don't we visit other people when they are ill? Why should we not sit with you when you are ill?'

'I am not that ill. Only your love prompts you to sit with me. When I finish eating, you accuse me of not having had my fill. When I'm feeling well, you think I'm ill. That's crazy. It's almost as though you would rather have me ill than well. You can sit with me if I become delirious. Right now, I'd feel better if you returned to your work. Please go, Govinda. You too, Ram. Go comb the cotton.' Shyam's tone was so firm that there was no arguing with him.

Shyam was feeling better by the evening. He was sitting up in bed, spinning and singing a shloka in his melodious voice.

I want and love none other than you / I am at your feet for eternity / I never want this addiction to end / As I sing Govind Hare Mukund / May you be my life's obsession / May all strife and conflict end / Leaving for me your love's sole bond / As I sing Govind Hare Mukund.

While he was spinning and singing, some children entered. A small boy asked, 'Are you going to tell us a story today?'

'Of course, I am,' Shyam replied. 'Do come in the evening.'

'See, we've brought you some nice stones. We went for a walk on the hill. We found them there,' the child said, setting the stones before Shyam.

'How beautiful they are. Come, let's make pictures with them. I'll make a parrot,' Shyam said. He arranged the stones as the children handed them to him one by one.

'Now I need a very small red stone for the beak.'

'Take this. It is just right,' said another child. Shyam put the stone in its place and the pretty parrot was complete.

'Now make a peacock,' another child said.

'Why don't you make it?' Shyam suggested.

'Ours won't be as nice.'

'But don't you think you should go home now? You'll come back after dinner, won't you?'

An older child said, 'Yes, we should go home.' And so the little birds flew away.

Shyam continued to gaze at the multicoloured stones before him. How much beauty God had poured into the little things. Each was a tiny image of the sublimely beautiful Almighty Himself. Shyam realized that this was how a devotee saw God's image in everything in his surroundings. The thought brought a soft glow to his face.

When Govinda, Ram and Namdeo arrived, Ram asked, 'What have you got in your hand, Shyam? A flower?'

'I don't touch flowers with my sinful hands. I fold my hands before them.'

'So what's in your hand?'

'An image of God.'

'But didn't you give away your Ganapati image to Babu?' Bhika asked.

'Yes. But I have others.'

'Let us see them,' Govinda said and opened Shyam's fist. What he saw were rubies and pearls.

'These are my gems, my gods. People say pearls are found on the seabed and diamonds in the womb of the earth. But I find gems on every riverbank and hilltop. Just look at these colours.'

'Are you going to tell us a story today then?'

'Yes. Some children came to me with these stones. I told them to come back after dinner. They have given me so much joy. I can speak for hours now. Is it time for prayers?'

It was indeed time for prayers. When the prayer was over, Shyam began to speak, his coverlet wrapped around his shoulders.

Durva Aji was not at home the day the house was sealed. She had gone away to another village. When she returned, she saw that Aai had taken to her bed. Her fever would come and go. There was nobody to nurse her. Aji did what she could. Radhatai would come over once in a while with amla preserve or something similar to take care of Aai's nausea. Janaki aunty and Namu aunty would visit too. But who was to do the housework? Who would bathe Indu's baby boy, Sharad? Aai couldn't earn her two rupees now. When father came home, Durva Aji would mutter angrily, 'How am I supposed to cook? There's not a stick or a piece of dried cow dung to put in the chulah. There's no oil or salt for the vegetables. I can't just boil them with the rice.'

'Give us plain boiled rice, Dwarka Kaku. We've already lost our honour. Please don't make it worse,' Bhau said quietly.

That day, Aai said to Purushottam, 'Son, please write to my sister. She's the only one who can help me in my last days. Write to her. She'll come. I've asked Radhatai to give you a postcard. Run over and fetch it. Or just tell Indu I need her. She'll write a good letter. Go, my pet. Ask her to come.'

Indu came across with a postcard.

'Are you feeling worse, Yashodatai? Shall I press your forehead for you?'

'No, Indu. It just makes me happy that you asked. My head hurts more if it's pressed. I asked you to come because I wanted you to write to my sister. Tell her about my illness. Say I want her to come. I don't need to tell you how to write the letter. You know better.'

Indu wrote the letter and Purushottam posted it. She hurried back home because her son had woken up.

'Can you get me some water?' Aai said to Purushottam. He got ready to pour water into her mouth. 'Not that way, son,' she said. 'Use a spoon. If you can't find one, use the small puja spoon.' Purushottam did as he was told.

Janakibai came to visit a while later. She too asked if she should massage Aai's legs.

'No, Janakibai. My bones hurt more when they are massaged. Please sit with me. That is enough.'

'Shall I bring you a piece of dried amla? It might bring the taste back to your tongue,' Janakibai said.

'That would be nice,' Aai said in a weak voice.

Janakibai took Purushottam with her to bring back the piece of amla. Aai sucked on it. 'Go play outside now,' she said to Purushottam. 'But don't go to school. Not till I feel a little better. There's nobody here otherwise.'

Purushottam went out to play. Aai's childhood friend, Namu aunty, came over. She was also married to someone in the village. The two girls had played many games together, swung on swings, sung songs and been each other's companions during their respective Mangalagaur pujas. But Namu aunty couldn't visit Aai because her house was at the other end of the village, and she, too, was often ill.

'Come, Namu,' Aai said, welcoming her. 'How is the swelling on your feet now?'

'Better. I fomented them with champaka leaves. That brought the swelling down. But how are you? You're looking like a skeleton. Won't your fever come down?' Namu aunty touched Aai's forehead.

'Namu, please let me send Purushottam with you. There isn't a drop of oil in the house. Can you send a bit with him? Durva Aji keeps screaming about it. You know how things are. I needn't tell you. I know you don't have much for yourself, but you are close to me. That's why I have dared to ask you.'

'Don't worry. It's nothing much. Don't take it to heart. Your real illness is that you take everything to heart. The children need you. So hold on to your courage.'

'I have no desire to live now. I'm through with all the festivities of life.'

'You shouldn't speak such nonsense in the evening. I'll make you some soft rice tomorrow. Would you like that?'

'I just want my eyes to close forever. What a shameful, humiliating life this is.'

'Stop it. You're going to be fine and your fortunes will change soon. Gajanan and Shyam are growing into fine young men. Has Gajanan found a job?'

'Yes, a month ago. But the salary is only nineteen rupees. He has to survive on that in Bombay. What can he save to send home? He does a private tuition in addition to the job. He sent his father five rupees a couple of days ago. He must have skimped on something to do that.'

'Have you told Shyam you are ill?'

'I told his father not to write to him. He's busy studying. Why should we add to his worries? And where will he find the money to come home? He'll need some more to go back. Going and coming costs money now. When he was in Dapoli, he could come whenever he wished. But he had to go away for his education. All I want is that God should keep him happy.'

Soon it was time for Namu aunty to go.

'There's kumkum and haldi in that niche. Please put some on.' Namu aunty took the container from the niche, put kumkum and haldi on her own forehead, then on Aai's, and left.

A few days later, the postman delivered Sakhu aunty's letter.

Purushottam ran in with the letter.

'I can read the whole letter,' he said excitedly. 'Shall I read it out to you?' He did. Sakhu aunty had a clean, legible hand. She said she was coming.

When Indu came over, Aai said, 'Sakhu is coming tomorrow. Remember the letter you wrote to her? That's her reply. Give her the letter, pet,' Aai said to Purushottam.

Indu read the letter and said, 'Finally, I will meet her. You've told me so much about her. I've been longing to meet her.' When it was time for her to go, she said to Purushottam, 'Come with me. Mother has made semolina halwa. I'll give you some to bring back.'

Purushottam hesitated. But Aai said, 'Go, my pet. They aren't strangers, are they?'

Bhau was sitting beside Aai. He said, 'I am responsible for all your suffering. I haven't even been able to feed you properly. What a miserable creature I am. But what can I do?'

'Please don't say that,' Aai pleaded. 'If you go on like that, what is little Purushottam to do? Men mustn't allow their spirits to break. You don't have to feel bad. You once gave me a life full of riches and happiness. I lacked for nothing. Yes, these are bad times. But they will pass. I may not be around to see the boys do well. But you will be. And I will see it all through your eyes.'

'But you are going to get well. Sakhu is coming. She'll make sure you recover.'

'Why give me false hope? This tree has been hollowed out from inside. It's bound to fall one day. I see my death as a golden end. I will go as a married woman. The only thing that saddens me is that you will be left alone. What more would I want otherwise, than to die with my head in your lap? Other joys are nothing beside this bliss.' Aai put her burning hand on Bhau's knee. She felt exhausted after this long speech.

'Please, can you give me some water?'

Bhau poured water into her mouth, one drop at a time from a small spouted can.

'To have you give me water is to have the holy Ganges in my mouth. This water is sweeter to me than nectar. Please sit with me. Don't go anywhere. I will close my eyes and meditate on you.'

Aai took Bhau's hand in hers, closed her eyes and began to meditate. They made a picture of sublime love.

When Radhatai came and saw Bhau sitting with Aai, she was about to go away. But Bhau called her back. He said humbly, 'Please don't go,' and left the room. Radhatai stroked Aai's hair into place and said, 'So your sister comes tomorrow morning, doesn't she?'

'She does. Indu read the letter.'

'She told me about it. That will be really nice. It is so comforting to have your loved ones around you at such a time.'

'You are all my loved ones. Shyam's father is near me. You are a neighbour. What more can I ask for?'

Our aunt was expected to arrive early next morning. Purushottam had woken up at the crack of dawn. His ears were pricked for the sound of the cart. This was the time for carts to bring passengers who had got off the boat at Harnai harbour. Each time he thought he heard a cart stop at our gate, he would run out to check and come back when it had moved on. At long last, one cart stopped at our gate. Durva Aji, who was swabbing the floor, called out, 'It's here.' Purushottam ran out. Bhau followed. Our aunt had indeed arrived. Purushottam carried her basket in, Bhau her trunk, aunty herself her bedding. She paid off the cartman and came in. Purushottam was shaking Aai awake in great excitement. 'Look, Aai, aunty has come. Really. Look.'

Aai half woke from her dream.

'Has she? Now my way is clear,' she said. The sisters were meeting after several years. The sight of Aai turned to skin and bone brought tears to aunty's eyes. 'Oh, Akka,' she exclaimed. All her love and care were poured into those two words.

'Are you here, Sakhu? I've been waiting so impatiently for you,' Aai said. 'I was holding on to life till you came. Waiting to put my children in your care and go.' Aai was in tears.

'Akka, stop saying such silly things. I'm here now and you're going to get well. Once you have recovered, I'll take you and Purushottam back with me. I have a job now.'

'I don't want to go anywhere. I just want to go to God. Let me breathe my last in this hut. I insisted that Purushottam's father build us an independent home. I want to lay down my body here, in my palace, with my head in his lap and you near me. Don't we have a saying, "If the mother dies, the aunt must live"? That will come true. You have no children. God decided to end your marital life, as though He had created you for my children. Please take care of them. Be their mother.'

'Why are you saying such things, Akka? Don't speak now. It will exhaust you. Lie quietly. I'll pat you.' Aunty took out the blanket from her bedding and pulled it over Aai, who had not known anything other than a fourfold sari or thin quilt as covering for a long time now.

Aunty sat beside Aai, patting her gently. Their love was like that between the Ganga and the Yamuna. The scene was as solemn as dawn meeting night.

Thirty-ninth Night

Live Together and Love Each Other

Shyam had begun his story. Dogs barked in the distance. They belonged to the itinerant stone hewers who were camping outside the village.

Sakhu aunty nursed Aai night and day. She seemed to have been born with nursing skills. First and foremost, she made up a clean bed for Aai to sleep on. She covered it with her own sheet and put a clean pillow under Aai's head. She put some ash in a bowl and placed it beside Aai for her to spit into. She covered it with a piece of wood and cleaned it out every day. She would also close the doors and sponge Aai down with a napkin dipped in hot water. She had brought a thermometer with her to keep an eye on her temperature. If it started to rise, she would put pads soaked in eau de cologne on her forehead to bring down the fever. She spread a rubber sheet and paper underneath her and persuaded her to answer nature's call in bed. Then she took away the soiled paper and put a fresh one in its place. She did not give Aai rice. Instead, she would set bowls of curd day and night, churn and dilute the curd with water and let Aai have that. She had brought some sweet limes with her. She used them thriftily so she could give Aai a little juice every day. Aai had never been looked after so attentively in all her life. She had suffered hardships throughout, but aunty made sure she did not suffer in her last days. Aunty was the very essence of love and service, which she provided with total selflessness and utmost care.

'Mathi has been mewing all day. Have you not given her rice?' Aai asked. Mathi never touched our milk vessel on the sly. She was perfectly content with the few drops of milk we gave her. She was a very well-behaved cat.

'I did give her rice, Akka, but she just sniffed at it. It was good rice mixed with ghee and milk. She'd probably eaten a mouse or two before.'

'She could be suffering from a stomach ache. Poor dumb creature can't tell us.'

Aai's health was crumbling from one day to the next. Her illness was advancing rather than retreating. My elder brother had taken four days' leave and come from Bombay to see her. He had just found a job. It took a lot of pleading for him to get a leave. The sight of Aai's condition brought a sob to his throat. 'What a state you've been brought to, Aai,' he said. 'You were working yourself to the bone here, with not a morsel to eat while we were having our fill.'

Purushottam had given him a detailed account of Aai's hardships and the town crier's announcement. Dada's heart split in two.

'Dearest, it makes little difference to this body whether it is fed or not fed,' Aai said. 'This machine will work only while God wishes it to work. Don't be upset. You haven't been living it up either. You also work hard. I was very moved when you sent us five rupees. Your father was so happy to receive the first money order from his earning son. I have no worries now. Raising you boys was my only task. You have both turned out well. Whether you earn good money or not, I don't care. You have a wealth of goodness in you. Shyam is busy studying. Your aunt will take care of Purushottam. I hope you will always love each other and be mindful of each other's needs.' Aai was winding up the business of life.

'Shall I stay with you, Aai?' Dada asked. 'Why do I need a job? What use is a job if I can't serve my mother? I don't crave a job for itself. Truly, I don't. Your feet are worth more to me than the boss's boots. To serve you will be my happiness, my salvation, my all. I have brought my letter of resignation with me. Shall I send it off? I'll do as you wish.'

Aai thought about it for a while. Then she said, 'Gaju, I have Sakhu with me. Jobs are hard to come by. Hold on to the one you have found after so much effort. Send five rupees to your father every month. Even two rupees would do, but just remember to send it regularly every month.

If you serve him, you would be serving me. I'm not going to die just yet. I am not so fortunate. I will pine away gradually till I die. If it gets really bad, I promise to send for you.'

Dada got ready to leave for Bombay. He did not know it then, but that was the last time he was to see Aai. He put his head on Aai's feet. He moved closer to her. She stroked his face and hair. Her hand was thin, but her touch was filled with love. 'Go, my son. Don't worry. When you write to Shyam, please tell him I am fine. There's no reason to worry him needlessly. Live together and love each other. Never turn your backs on one another.'

Dada left with a heavy heart. He went as a matter of duty. Life is full of hard choices. And that's the truth.

Fortieth Night

The Final Days

'Water that lemon tree, will you? Or it will dry up. Water the new jackfruit sapling too.' Aai was telling us these things in her delirium. She had planted those trees. Even when she was ill and weak, she had never forgotten to tend to them, to water them, to look out for insects. She had planted many trees in our back garden. When I was in Dapoli, I had taken home sandalwood saplings. The ones that others had planted had died. Only the one she had planted survived. Are fingers green when they are filled with love?

It was dawn when Aai became delirious. She muttered illogically. One moment she was talking about trees, the next about the town crier. 'He's shouting. Let me block my ears.' Purushottam was asleep. The rest of the family sat around Aai, their faces pinched and wan as though death had already entered and was sitting with them.

'Look there. Shyam is perched on that peg. Come down, you scamp. He was always stubborn. Come here.

With whom can a child throw tantrums if not his mother? But that's enough. Come down.'

'Akka, Akka,' aunty called out softly, hoping to bring Aai to her senses. 'Namu, I haven't returned your oil. Forgive me. Come, Shyam. Put your cool hand on my head.' Everybody sat absolutely still and silent, their eyes moist. 'Your lap is my honour. Town criers and their announcements! Who cares? I have his lap. I have the kumkum on my forehead. Who can take away my honour? Which moneylender? Ha! Honour isn't in ornaments and houses and land. His lap. That's where it is. I want his lap.'

Aai struggled to get up. It was difficult to hold her down. But they managed. She lay down again. Bhau lifted her head on to his lap. 'Water, water,' Aai mumbled. Aunty dripped water into her mouth. 'Akka,' aunty called. Aai lifted her weak hand and gestured, 'No, nothing.' She lay quietly for a while. Then she asked, 'Is my head on his lap?'

'Yes, I'm right here,' Bhau answered. 'Now rest. Don't speak.' Soon she started again.

'Why have you come to meet me? Has Chandri also come? But you shouldn't have left your studies. I'm always with you. Come now. Don't sulk, Shyam. Is it because I made you grind with me? No more grinding now. What do you mean? Of course he's there. I can see him. You don't know him. Only a mother knows her child.'

She went through that day and night in delirium. A new day broke. Aunty asked Purushottam to run over to

287

Radhatai's for *hemagarbha matra*. 'We might need it.' This matra is given in the last moments of life to extend it by a few minutes. Aunty had read signs in Aai's eyes of a sudden decline. They had sunk deep overnight. It was Sankashti Chaturthi that day. Bhau used to fast in the old days. But now that he had grown weak, he had taken to a partial fast. 'Isn't it Chaturthi today? Go take your bath and have some semolina. You must look after yourself.' Aai was speaking painfully in short, jerky words. Bhau took his bath, went to the temple and returned with Ganapati's tirth, which he put on Aai's tongue.

Aai held Purushottam close. Caressing his face, she said in a weak voice, 'My little one, be a good boy. Don't sulk for things. Dada and Anna are there for you. Aunty will take care of you. Be good.' Aai kept stroking his back as he wept.

'Sakhu, has everybody eaten?'

'Yes, Akka, we have.'

'They are all yours now. Let mother die, but let aunt live. All my children are now your children.'

'Yes, of course.'

'Shyam is meek. Talented. Gaju, Chandri . . . God is there for them. He is there for everyone.'

Looking at Durva Aji, she said, 'Forgive me for the things I have said.' Aji's heart melted. Aai's words now came one at a time with long pauses in between. 'Sakhu, tell Nana to forgive me. Tell him to forgive his Bayo.'

Aai fell silent. Then her pupils went round and round in her eyeballs. Her eyes closed. Then she said, 'Shyam.'

'I'll write to him today, Akka,' aunty said. She said to Bhau, 'I think you should call the priest and give away the cow.'

They say you should give away a cow before you breathe your last. If you don't have a cow, give money. The practice is called *gopradan*. It was now performed at Aai's hands. Sometime later, she lost her speech. She looked at people wordlessly. But she kept stroking Purushottam's back all the while. Then she pointed upwards to say she was going to God. A long time later, she mustered all the strength left in her body to say to Bhau, 'Take care of yourself. Don't neglect yourself. I am at peace with my head on this . . .' She could say no more. The village vaidya came, examined her pulse and pronounced sadly, 'A few minutes more,' and left. Janaki aunty, Radhatai, Namu aunty and Indu were all there. There was a sombre silence in the room. Everybody sensed that Aai was about to leave them.

'Shyam and Chandri couldn't meet her. Only Gaju came,' Bhau muttered. Aai's lips moved. Did she want to say something? Were the lips saying Ram or Shyam? Radhatai prepared some hemagarbha matra paste on a rubbing stone. She placed a dot of the paste on Aai's tongue. The tongue was being sucked in rapidly. 'Do you want to say something?' Radhatai asked loudly in Aai's ear. Aai lifted her hand to make a negative gesture. But a while later, she mustered her strength once again and said, 'Take care, all of you. God is with you.'

The signs of a life ending were all there. Aai was on her way to meet God. It was an auspicious day. Radhatai put a couple of drops of Ganga water in Aai's mouth, and then a tulsi leaf. She was lifted on to a rough rug. When you go to God, you go as an ascetic.

A while later came a sound.

'Ram.' Aai had taken Ram's name. Aai had left us.

Nobody can reject the call when it comes. I had lost my mother. Bhau had lost the very source of the merit he had accumulated. Purushottam had lost his shelter. Shyam and Gaju had lost the saint who had inspired them. Chandri had lost her *maher*, her mother's home. Nana and Aji had lost the child whom they had so fondly called Avadi. The old domestics had lost their Bayo, whom they had cared for with so much affection when she was growing up. Aai had freed herself from the web of life and gone to a place where she would be in the company of the great and the saintly.

Forty-first Night

And So to Ash

I was far away from Aai. I was not there to nurse her. I was studying. But I was studying to serve her. One night, I dreamt of her. She asked me, 'Why haven't you come to see me? You left in a huff. Are you still angry? Children forget their rages quickly. Why have you not forgotten yours? Come to see me.'

For days afterwards, I would get up in the morning, remember the dream and feel stabs of anxiety. *Is Aai ill?* I would wonder. I would have flown to see her had I the wings. The normal way, by train, boat and bullock cart, would have taken two days. I would still have gone, because I was really unhappy and very anxious. But where was the money?

I had made a new friend in Aundh. Namdeo. He loved me just as much as Sant Namdeo had loved Pandurang of Pandharpur. He and I were not separate individuals at all. We were one. He knew every thought in my mind without my saying a word. It was like those lines of Nanak's:

Anbolat meri birtha jani / apana naam japaaya' (God understands your pain without your speaking of it. All you need to do is take His name.) It was so with Namdeo. He understood all my joys and sorrows. He could read my heart, my life, the expressions on my face and in my eyes correctly. We were split images of each other. We were like twins, one mind, one heart, two bodies.

I said to Namdeo, 'I am yearning to go home. I have a feeling Aai is ill. I am very uneasy.'

'Why don't you go then?' Namdeo said.

'I just want to set eyes on her. But I don't have money.'

'Why, my money came yesterday by post, remember? Let's say it came for you. Ten rupees. Will that do? Please go and meet your mother. Give her my namaskar.'

I packed a few things and left. Namdeo came to the station to see me off. We were both tearful.

'Write as soon as you get there,' he said.

'I will.'

'I'd have come with you if I had more money.'

'You are always with me.'

The train moved. As it sped away, my face grew wet with tears. I went straight from Bori Bunder station to the dock to catch a boat. Had I stopped off to meet my brother, I would have missed it. The boat danced on the waves. I had Tagore's *Gitanjali* with me. I was reading the line, 'Mother, my tears will form a garland on your chest.' What else could I have given my poor mother except tears? I closed *Gitanjali* and looked out at the heaving sea. A myriad hues played on the surging waves. One wave gave birth to another. My heart too surged with memories, one giving way to another. All the memories of my mother, the events that brought back old emotions, unfurled before me. I was like a rishi lost in a trance, a dreamworld.

I caught sight of the lighthouse near Harnai harbour.

'Harnai! Harnai!' the sailors called. People who wanted to get off at Harnai began preparing to disembark. I made a bundle of my few belongings. I was impatient to see Aai's venerable feet, her love-filled eyes. The boat was now close to the harbour. Ferryboats came up to carry the passengers to the quay. As I got into a ferry, I sensed that somebody on the quay was looking at me. I couldn't make out the figure, but I knew its eyes were fixed on me. The ferry touched the quay. I hopped into the shallows and waded quickly to it. Then I saw her. The figure. It was my aunt Sakhu.

'What are you doing here, aunty?' I asked. 'Did you come to see Aai? Is she all right?' Aunty answered with tears. 'Shyam,' she said at last. 'Your mother, my Akka, has left us for God's home.'

I broke down. We went to the dharamshala. Neither of us could speak. Finally I said, 'Why didn't you tell me? I came because I had a dream. She was calling me. Now she's gone. Forever.' I broke down again.

'She was calling out for you on the last day, Shyam. She said she could see you. She said you were being as stubborn as you were when you were a child. We really didn't dream that Akka would go within two days of that. She died the very day I told her I'd write to you. We did our best for her. Made sure she didn't suffer. But she has left me her children. I'll make sure you don't miss her care. Hush. Stop crying now.'

'Sakhu aunty, I had built so many castles in the air. I had dreamt of making my mother happy. I told myself I'd tend to her like a flower. Why should I study now if I can't use my education to look after her? To make her happy?'

'Study for your brothers, for your father, for all of us and for the world. Give the world the love you had reserved for your mother. Give it to all the suffering mothers of the world.' Aunty had given me a new vision.

'Are you going back now?' I asked.

'Yes. I couldn't bear to stay on. Go home now. It's the third day tomorrow. You will immerse her ashes tomorrow. You were her favourite. That's why you came for the ashes. Bring back a fistful when you return. We'll immerse them in the Godavari.'

'How will I enter the darkness of that house?'

'Although the darkness will not be lit by your mother's face, your father is still there. He too loves you. Console him. Give him courage. You are wise. You have read the Gita and the *Gitanjali*. Go home now.'

'Who will say, "Shyam, have you come? Wait, I'll put some jaggery before God."?'

'There you are. What a lovely memory. You have so many such memories to treasure. Your mother has gone, but her love and her memories are with you, aren't they?' Aunty engaged a bullock cart for me. We could see her boat approaching in the distance. The ferries were ready to leave. My aunt, my mother's sister, was leaving.

During the cart ride home, I saw Aai everywhere. She rose from the depths of my heart. I saw her toil and her pain, her love and her care rise like a mountain before me. At long last, I was home. Once, I had arrived in the early morning and had heard Aai singing a sweet song about Krishna while she churned buttermilk. There was no song in the house today. There was sorrow, a tiny, flickering lamp and a terrifying silence. I pushed the door. It wasn't bolted from inside. It opened. Bhau was sitting on a piece of sacking.

'You are two days too late, Shyam,' he said. 'She has gone, my son.'

Purushottam woke up. He saw me and broke into tears. He clung to me. Nobody could speak.

Durva Aji said, 'She kept calling for you, Shyam. You were her favourite. It is good that you are here for her rituals. Don't cry. What's the use of tears now? I wish she had lived to see you grow up. But God did not will it.'

The next day, I went to the river to immerse Aai's ashes. The priest was with me. I went to the spot where she had been cremated. Her form in ash lay there, asleep. Not even the smallest part of it had been disturbed by the breeze. It was exactly as she had been. I bowed before that form that had lost all materiality but retained the shape of the material body. My mother's heart had already turned to ash. Now her body was ash. This ash was like the ash on Shankar's body—sacred. She had always been sacred.

I touched the ash. The form crumbled at my touch. I broke it because the form in my heart was unbroken and indestructible. I collected Aai's ashes. I found the beads from her mangalsutra. My uncle took them away as auspicious signs of her death as a married woman. He took them away to put around his wife's neck.

We completed the rituals and returned home. My days passed in the sacred joy of listening to Purushottam relating stories about the times I had not been present to experience. Radhatai and Indu also told me stories. I would break down when I heard about Aai's hardships.

Then came the day when a ball of rice had to be offered as a ritual to make sure that Aai's soul was at peace. A crow touching the ball would tell us that she was indeed at peace and on her way to her eternal home.

Had she gone with an unfulfilled desire? Would the ball of rice remain untouched? This was the fear that gnawed at me from within. We went to the river. We made the rice ball. We completed the rituals associated with it. We placed it on durva grass. The priest imitated a crow's call to invite the crows. My uncle said, 'There's one. And another.'

We were happy to see the crows gather. We moved away. They strutted around the rice ball but would not touch it. I felt dejected. I said, 'Aai, if it is your wish that I should marry, I will. I will not become an ascetic.' My uncle said, 'We will never forsake Bhau. We will always love him.' Even then the crows would not touch the *pind*. I shifted the rice ball to another place. The crows remained adamant in their rejection. If the rice ball is not touched, we are supposed to make a ball out of durva grass to see if that helps. But people gossip when that happens. 'Let us take the pind home. Perhaps a crow will touch it there. Let us not make a durva ball yet,' I suggested.

We came home with heavy hearts. We kept the pind in a corner of the garden near the banana plant. Several crows flew down, but none touched it. Finally, Durva Aji came out and said, 'Yashoda, don't worry. I'm there for Purushottam. I'll take care of him.' As soon as she said that, a crow flew down and quickly pecked at the pind.

My eyes filled with tears. Sakhu aunty had gone away by herself. Purushottam would now be in Aji's care. He was a naughty child. Aai must have been anxious for him, afraid that he would be scolded and beaten. Such was my mother's love! You couldn't put a value on it. It was as expansive as the sky and as deep as the ocean. When you think of how great the love of a mother can be, you realize how limitless God's love must be. God must have sent mothers down to earth only to show people what His love was like.

'Friends, my mother had died. But even when her life ended, her worries did not. A mother cannot be happy if her children are not. If even one of them has tears in his eyes, sighs sadly, has no food or clothes or knowledge, she will not find peace of mind. Until she is sure that brother will love brother, that each will help the other, encourage the other's growth, will not think of one as high and the other as low and will bring laughter rather than tears to each other, she will not be at peace. She will not be happy. She will not find salvation. She will continue to weep. And the anxiety in her heart will continue to burn like an undying funeral fire.'

Forty-second Night

A Ritual of Memories

'Friends . . . I cannot describe to you what these memories mean to me. They are like stars lighting up my heart. They will be with me forever, shining brightly on my path and showing me the way. I have chosen to tell you only those that I felt you might find interesting. I shall narrate the last of them today.'

My mother was loved not only by women but also by animals. I have already told you about the mutual love between her and our white-spotted cow. I will tell you today about her cat. I have mentioned this cat before. Her name was Mathi. Aai loved her. Mathi used to have her food sitting next to Aai. She would not touch rice served by anyone else. She would eat only when Aai ate. She was constantly with Aai wherever she went, whether it was to the well or for her bath. She would weave between Aai's legs, flicking her tail.

Then Aai fell ill. When her condition worsened, she could not mix Mathi's rice and milk for her. So Mathi would eat just a few grains of the rice that others gave her and go away. Even if Aai gave her plain rice, it was a feast for her. But she turned away from rice that others gave her even when it was mixed with milk or curd or ghee.

Mathi mewed plaintively the whole day that Aai died. She sensed that the river of love that had fed her had suddenly dried up. Mathi stopped eating and drinking. It is our custom to place milk and water in the room where a person has died for that person's soul. We had placed bowls of milk and water in Aai's room. Mathi spent all her time in that room, but not once did she touch the milk or water we'd kept there. Soon she stopped mewing. She seemed to have pledged herself to fasting and silence. On the third day after Aai died, Mathi breathed her last. She could not bear to live without my mother's love. She loved our mother more than we did. We were ashamed of ourselves. I muttered to myself, 'How can I say I loved you, Aai? My love is nothing beside Mathi's love.'

'That was my mother. In the marketplace of the world, it takes luck to find a mother like her. I owe everything to Aai. If there is any goodness in me at all, it comes from her. She died, but not before she had prepared me to serve my country. I have heard of a Japanese mother who plunged a dagger in her heart after she had written a note to her son, which read, "You have not gone to war because of me. Your attachment to me stands in the way. I shall remove it from your path." Perhaps my mother had a similar vision. Perhaps she felt her Shyam was enmeshed in the web of her love. Perhaps he would spend his entire life worshipping her puny body. This adoration will keep him from serving his brothers and sisters. It will prevent him from leaping into the battle for freedom. She might have wished for all the mothers in India to be my mothers. That is why she left. She has left me with her all-encompassing love for every creature that lives. Now I see a multitude of mothers around me. Govinda's mother is my mother. Vasantrao's mother is my mother. Krishna's mother is my mother. Subhan's mother is my mother. How can I even begin to describe the greatness of a mother who gave me such a vision of the world? Who ended the life of her own flimsy body to make me realize this vision?

'I can only pray that all my actions are inspired by the love, endurance and sweetness, the sense of gratitude and duty that prompted her own words and actions. Perhaps in the end, having served this great mother to the best of my small ability, I, too, will come to a blessed end as did my mother. And her cat Mathi.'

Translator's Note

Shyam's mother was a woman many of us grew up with in Maharashtra. We lived in cities like Bombay and Pune. Our mothers were often educated, even working women. Shyam's mother was neither. And yet her wisdom, spirit and humanity stood as a model for our mothers and for us. I read *Shyamchi Aai* when I was eight or nine years old. I remember weeping copious tears for a boy who had to struggle and suffer so much for an education that my friends and I had been given as a matter of right. Despite the great difference between Shyam's circumstances and mine, I related to many of the situations he described. I felt particularly sympathetic towards him in the story about his swimming lessons. Like him, I feared water. Like him, I stood at the edge of a swimming pool, counting up to three many times without finding the courage to jump in. Finally, an uncle pushed me in. Being underwater, unable to breathe till I came up gasping and spluttering, was the most frightening moment of my life. True, it helped me overcome my fear of water and I did learn to swim.

But, for many years after, I did not talk to the uncle who had pushed me in.

I must have been twelve or thirteen when I secretly decided to become a writer. The first book I was going to write was about my mother, about how she was taken out of school to look after her younger siblings, how she did her matriculation after she got married and got her BA degree after she had my sister and me. I would also write about the tiger cub her father brought home from the jungle as a pet for her and about how she taught herself to swim when an uncle dared her. That book, planned seventy years ago, remains unwritten. Shame on me for that. Mothers often put aside their own ambitions to help their husbands and children to achieve theirs. They work all day to keep us fed and clothed. But their work goes unnoticed, not only in the world but often even at home. So, although I haven't written the book, I have always acknowledged in my interviews how much I owe my mother for being able to do all the things I have done. In fact, it was my mother who told me that the greatest good I could do in life was to translate our best books into English. It is therefore with great happiness and pleasure that I share Shyam's memories of his mother with readers who cannot read them in Marathi, the language in which he wrote them.

It is always a great responsibility to translate from one language into another. It is one of the chief precepts of our art that we do not translate words, but worlds. I will explain the idea simply. Every word comes with a cluster of cultural associations attached. In the old days, it was the custom for boys to wear langots. These were home-made jockstraps. Shyam wears a langot. Suppose I were to translate the word as jockstrap, I would destroy his world. One, because the jockstrap was an American invention, which first came on the market in 1874, whereas langots had been worn in India for centuries. Two, because Shyam tells us even umbrellas were not sold in villages when he was a boy. Would jockstraps have been available? Even if they were, would a poor family that could not afford a proper meal of rice, dal and vegetables be able to afford them? So how does a translator render langot into English? Well, she either keeps the word langot in her translation, explaining the meaning in a footnote, or she translates the concerned sentence in a way that keeps its sense absolutely intact without mentioning the garment. Other than these exceptional cases, the translator must always stick to every single thing the writer has said.

However, there is one aspect of *Shyamchi Aai* that I have toned down. Doing this was a tightrope walk between being faithful to Sane Guruji and keeping today's readers in mind. You see, Sane Guruji was a very emotional man. Poverty is a terrible thing to have to live with. There is plenty of scope for tears there. The marvellous thing is that neither Shyam nor his mother weep because they are poor. They weep because our society humiliates poor people, holds them in contempt and makes it difficult for them to live with self-respect and dignity. They weep because of the death of loved ones. Shyam's mother died as much of a broken heart and malnutrition as the lack of proper medical care. It was not available in rural districts then, and despite the progress we are told we have made, it is still not available in many of our villages today.

If I were to reproduce all the tears in Shyam's stories in my translation, I might have put off today's readers. Today, young people play video games in which people are killed left, right and centre. Nobody sheds tears for them. They read stories of gruesome crimes in newspapers without weeping. They see class bullies torture weaker classmates without weeping. In short, today's young people are not, or cannot afford to be, as sensitive as Shyam was and might find his constant weeping a trifle unreal. With this in mind, I have underplayed his tears in my translation. Also, I have used language that is less sentimental than Sane Guruji's.

Although there are things in these stories that readers will find strange because, after all, Shyam's time and ours belong to different periods of history, there are many things they will relate to. We still believe in ideals like self-respect, independence of thinking and action, questioning customs that have lost their relevance, respecting every human being as a brother or sister and not hating people for their religion, caste or customs. If proof is required that Shyam's stories are still relevant to our times, check out these facts.

Shyamchi Aai was first published in 1935. Its last edition came out in 2016. So the stories have been read consistently over eighty years from Sane Guruji's times into our times. In this context, it is amusing to read how his preface to the first edition of the book ends: '*Shyamchi Aai* is leaving my home to meet her readers outside. She will enter houses where the doors are open. If she comes upon a closed door she will knock. If all doors remain closed to her, what then? Why, then she will return home to live with me.' Today we know what he did not. The doors are still wide open to *Shyamchi Aai*. With this translation, she enters an altogether new world, the world of readers who want to read Sane Guruji's stories but do not know Marathi, the language in which he wrote them. I feel very important to be the bridge between him and you.

Shanta Gokhale is a novelist, translator, columnist and performing arts critic. Her Marathi novel Rita Welinkar *was published in 1992 and won the Maharashtra State Award for the best novel of the year. In 2009, her novel* Tya Varshi *also won the Maharashtra State Award for the best novel of the year, which was later translated into* Crowfall. *Shanta Gokhale was honoured with the Sangeet Natak Akademi Award in 2015 and the Lifetime Achievement Award for her exceptional body of work and impact in the Indian literary field at the Tata Literature Live! festival in 2019.*

PUFFIN CLASSICS

Shyamchi Aai

With Puffin Classics, the story isn't over
when you reach the final page.
Want to discover more about
the author and his world?
Read on . . .

CONTENTS

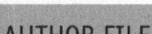

AUTHOR FILE

NAME: Sadashiv Pandurang Sane (pronounced Saanay)

BORN: 24 December 1899, in a Brahmin family in Palgad, a village in the Konkan on Maharashtra's western coast

FATHER: Pandurang Sane

MOTHER: Yashoda Sane

QUALIFICATIONS: BA in Marathi and Sanskrit Literature and MA in Philosophy, both from New Poona College (now known as Sir Parashurambhau College)

PROFESSIONAL LIFE: He chose to teach in Pratap High School, Amalner, a small town in Jalgaon district, although he could have taught wealthier students in the city and made more money.

MARITAL STATUS: He remained single all his life.

FAMOUS FOR: He was such a fine teacher that he was given the title of National Teacher and came to be known as Sane Guruji. He was a writer and a poet. The first line of his most famous poem, which every schoolchild can recite, is: *There is but one true religion / To offer love to the world.* He wrote seventy-three books in all, mostly for children, of which the most famous and loved is *Shyamchi Aai.* Editor, playwright, orator, film-maker Acharya Atre made a film on the book, which won the President's Gold Medal for Cinema in 1954 at the first edition of the National Film Awards.

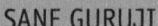

SANE GURUJI

As we can see from the autobiographical stories in *Shyamchi Aai*, Sane Guruji was a sensitive human being. His actions were driven by two loves: his love for all human beings, particularly the disadvantaged and the socially downtrodden and his love for India. For him, India was not a piece of land, territory or property. India was its people. They made the country. Freedom had no meaning for him unless every last Indian was free and happy in the country. It is easy then to see why he was influenced by Mahatma Gandhi.

Sane Guruji began wearing khadi in 1921. He threw up his teaching job in 1930 to join the civil disobedience movement, which aimed for complete self-rule for India. He was an excellent orator, able to win over the hearts and minds of people. He toured the rural districts of Khandesh for four months, spreading the idea of independence. The British rulers imprisoned him for this. He participated in various agitations for independence between 1930 and 1947 and was imprisoned eight times in all, spending a total of six years and seven months in Dhule, Trichinapally, Nashik, Yerawada and Jalgaon jails. He wrote *Shyamchi Aai* during his jail term in Nashik and learnt Bengali and Tamil during the time he spent in Trichinapally jail.

Mahatma Gandhi had promised Dr Babasaheb Ambedkar that he would spend the rest of his life fighting for the abolition of untouchability. Sane Guruji, who also believed it to be a blot on our culture, travelled through the length and breadth of Maharashtra to make people aware of the inhumanity of the practice. He fasted at Pandharpur for eleven days to put pressure on the priests to open the doors of the famous Vitthal temple to Harijans, the name Gandhiji had given the erstwhile

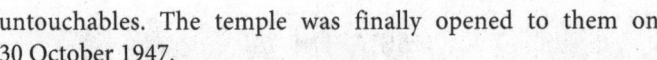

untouchables. The temple was finally opened to them on 30 October 1947.

Sane Guruji was a fervent Hindu, but he saw the religion very differently from those who made it a political instrument. He vehemently opposed Hindu nationalism championed by certain right-wing organizations. Mahatma Gandhi's assassination soon after Independence by one of their number grieved Sane Guruji profoundly. He fasted for twenty-one days as penance for the fact that a Maharashtrian had committed the ghastly crime. Gandhiji's assassination, the bloodshed after Partition and the continuing inequalities and divisions in Indian society depressed him greatly. As a result, he ended his life on 11 May 1950.

Three of Sane Guruji's cherished loves have been kept alive by his followers. Prakash Mohadikar started the Sane Guruji Vidyalaya in Shivaji Park, Mumbai for children from poor families. *Sadhana*, the magazine he founded and edited, continues to be published regularly. A group of prominent like-minded people have given shape to Antar Bharati, Sane Guruji's dream project aimed at integrating the country through a mutual understanding of its diverse cultures and languages.

The Indian Postal Service issued a postage stamp in his honour in 2001.

SHYAMCHI AAI

The stories in *Shyamchi Aai* are autobiographical. Although they happened the way the author describes them, he admits in his preface that it is possible he added 'a person, a situation or a remark here and there that is imaginary'. Remember, the stories about his mother's illness, his aunt's arrival to nurse her and her eventual death happened during his absence, when he was away at school. The events were reported to him by his younger brother. There could have been gaps in those accounts that he would have had to fill up using his imagination.

Sane Guruji wrote *Shyamchi Aai* when he was imprisoned in Nashik jail between 1932 and 1934. He says in his preface, 'I wrote thirty-six nights in the jail and nine after I was released. So there should have been forty-five nights in all. But I held back three for a variety of reasons. I started writing the stories on the night of Thursday, 9 February 1933 and finished them on the morning of Monday, 13 February 1933. In these five days, I would work during the day and spend the late night and early morning writing.' He must have written at a furious speed to finish the stories in five days.

Storytellers use a device called 'cover story' when they want to link chapters of a book together. In *Shyamchi Aai*, Sane Guruji imagined a cover story that matched the actual location and narration of his stories. The location was the prison and the narration was to his fellow inmates. In the cover story, he narrates them in an ashram to fellow residents. The routine in both places is the same—work through the day and listen to stories at night. All he needed to do was imagine the ashram. That was easily done. He located it in a small village with a temple, a river and a hill, very much like Palgad, his childhood village. The only difference was that Palgad was on the coast while the ashram was in the interiors of the country. This was a necessary difference because his stories were full of descriptions of Konkan's unique culture. If the ashram had been located in the Konkan, his listeners would have known and experienced these things themselves.

Some of the stories in *Shyamchi Aai* were published in a children's magazine called *Shalapatrak*. The editor of the magazine received many letters asking him to publish more stories about Shyam and his mother. This convinced Sane Guruji that a book containing all the stories might find an appreciative readership. That is how *Shyamchi Aai* was published two years after the stories were written.

a) **The plight of women in India**, particularly in villages during Yashoda Pandurang Sane's life was incredibly pathetic. Girls did not have an automatic right to education. Yashoda often calls herself illiterate because she had not been to school. Girls were married young as Yashoda was. They were pushed from skirts into billowing saris before they knew how to take care of themselves. Yashoda was fortunate not to be ill-treated by her in-laws. Her daughter was not so lucky.

Women in villages were worse off than their counterparts in cities. Yashoda's sister lives in Bombay and earns an independent living. The only time we hear of Yashoda earning some money is when a neighbour asks her to bathe her baby grandson. Otherwise Yashoda is financially dependent on her husband although she works as hard as him, perhaps harder, cooking over a smoky chulah, cleaning and washing, grinding and fetching water in heavy pots from the well. Her hardships wear her down. Like many women of her time, she dies young for lack of nutrition and healthcare.

b) **Corporal punishment**, which is a strict no-no in schools today was once accepted not only as normal but as good. Shyam's father says to him in one of the stories, 'A teacher is supposed to beat children. What sort of a teacher would he be if he didn't?' The short answer to that question today would be, 'A good teacher.' Studies by child psychologists have shown that beating children does not necessarily make them improve either in schoolwork or behaviour. However, a large majority of parents still believe it is the right thing to do. Psychologists say the danger of such a belief is that, if a one-time beating is found not to have the desired effect, more beatings follow. This makes children defiant rather than compliant. The debate has not ended. One group of parents and teachers believes that explaining why a child's action is wrong is a better, more humane and effective way of bringing about change; the other group thinks a good spanking is the best cure. The first group is rewarded with the child's trust. The second group is rewarded with fear. Sane Guruji makes it clear that he does not believe in corporal punishment.

c) **Konkan** is a 700 km strip of land that runs between the Arabian Sea and the Western Ghats along the western coast of the country. Dotted with pristine beaches, it is bounded on the north by the Daman Ganga River and to the south by the Gangavalli River. Farming is difficult in this rugged terrain, the main produce being rice, cashew, coconut and mangoes. The coastal people are poor, depending for their livelihoods on industry in and around Mumbai. However, the Western Ghats are rich in biodiversity. Stretching from Gujarat to Kanyakumari, they host hundreds of species of flowering and non-flowering plants, mammals, birds, amphibians, insects and freshwater fish. At least 325 of these species are globally threatened. As recently as September 2019, a new species of cat snake was discovered in the Maharashtra stretch of the Ghats. On 1 July 2015, UNESCO named the Western Ghats a World Heritage Site.

The Ghats descend in steps to the Deccan plateau that forms the Indian peninsula. They block the south-west monsoon winds, resulting in torrential rains in Konkan and scanty rains on the plateau. Climate and agricultural produce influence people's food habits. The staple on the coast is rice with a liberal use of fresh coconut in dishes. On the plateau, it is millets like bajra and jowar.

d) **Famous people** born in Ratnagari district, in which Sane Guruji's Palgad and Dapoli are located, are mentioned in the twentieth story. Three of the most prominent were Bal Gangadhar Tilak, Dhondo Keshav Karve and R.P. Paranjpye.

Bal (real name Keshav) Gangadhar Tilak was born on 23 July 1856 and died on 1 August 1920. He had a degree in mathematics and another in law. He became a journalist, founded a newspaper called *Kesari* and fought fiercely for independence. His most frequently quoted line is, 'Swarajya is my birthright and I shall have it'. The British called him 'the Father of Indian Unrest', Mahatma Gandhi called him 'the Maker of Modern India' and the general public gave him the title of 'Lokmanya', people's choice.

Dhondo Keshav Karve was born on 18 April 1858 and died on 9 November 1962. He was a social reformer who fought for women's education and widow remarriage. He established the Widow Marriage Association in 1893 and himself married a widow after his first wife died, shocking orthodox Hindus. He also founded the Shreemati Nathibai Damodar Thackersey Women's University. He was awarded India's highest honour, the Bharat Ratna on his 100th birth anniversary.

Raghunath Purushottam Paranjpye was born on 16 February 1876 and died on 6 May 1966. He was the first Indian student to acquire the prestigious title of Senior Wrangler at the University of Cambridge. This title is awarded to the undergraduate who tops the first class honours list of his year at the university. The position of Senior Wrangler has been described as 'the greatest intellectual achievement attainable in Britain'. Wrangler Paranjpye was ultimately appointed vice chancellor of Bombay University and then Lucknow University. He founded the Indian Rationalist Association in Madras (later Chennai) and remained its president for several years. Sai Paranjpye, the film-maker, is his granddaughter.

e) **Shyamchi Aai, the film**: It is well known that the film *Shyamchi Aai*, written and directed by Acharya P.K. Atre, won the Golden Lotus for Best Film in 1954. Vanamala, who had acted in a few Hindi and Marathi films, made her name with this film. Shyam was played by a twelve-year-old child actor from Pune called Madhav Vaze. He published a book in 2017 at the age of seventy-eight, titled *Shyamachi Aai, Acharya Atre Ani Mi*, a no-holds-barred account of working in the film. Away from home, living in Atre's flat in Shivaji Park with no friends to talk to or play with, he was very lonely. The experience was not a happy one. Most surprisingly, Vanamala, who played his mother in the film with much love and affection, showed him no warmth off-screen. However, Vaze confesses that the film brought him unending love and goodwill from viewers both here and abroad. He narrates one incident when a Gujarati official at the Indian High Commission office in London helped him get a French visa because Vaze as Shyam had made him weep.

LESSONS FROM AAI

Shyam's mother gave him many important lessons. Perhaps we might find them useful guides in our confused age when we face many more temptations of different kinds than Shyam did.

* **Self-respect**: Yashoda talks again and again of the importance of self-respect. She believes a man who works hard for his living is to be respected more than a man who lives off somebody else's work without doing any himself. She also believes that to live in a hut and be independent shows greater self-respect than living in somebody else's house and being obliged to them.

* **Pulling your weight**: Yashoda believes that where a common cause is involved, everybody must contribute their mite, whether your village, your country or even the world at large needs you. You must always believe that your contribution, however small, will make a difference by adding that much to the common cause.

* **Being human**: Yashoda believes that greatness is not about having money or power. It is about being a good human being, that is, one who is honest and generous, does not exploit anybody and loves plants, animals and people equally.

* **Gender and work**: Yashoda questions why men cannot do women's work since women do men's work when required. She tells her neighbour Janakibai indirectly that Shyam is right in helping her with her chores although he is a boy. A majority of people in our country are Janakibais who believe that girls are duty-bound to do housework while boys are allowed to roam free.

* **Honesty**: Anybody can make a mistake or sometimes even do wrong knowingly. The important thing is to be honest with yourself and admit you were wrong. If you try to wriggle out of a mess you have created by lying, you will have to follow one lie with another till you are inevitably found out.

* **Why read books**: Reading stories about great human beings and their deeds serves no purpose unless you try to learn something from them. Reading good books should make some difference to how you think and act. Otherwise it is a waste of time.